MONKEY-SHINES

MONKEY-SHINES

by

Michael Stewart

MACMILLAN LONDON

ISBN 0 333 34729 3

First published 1983 by
Macmillan London Limited
London and Basingstoke

Associated companies in Auckland, Dallas,
Delhi, Dublin, Hong Kong, Johannesburg,
Lagos, Manzini, Melbourne, Nairobi,
New York, Singapore, Tokyo, Washington
and Zaria

Printed and bound in Great Britain
at The Pitman Press, Bath

this is for Maggie

Monkey-shines, *pl.*, *U.S. slang*: monkey-like tricks or antics.

Shorter Oxford English Dictionary.

Acknowledgements

Special thanks and acknowledgements are due to the following:

Dr Gordon Mangan, Department of Experimental Psychology, University of Oxford; Niam McAleer, Disabled Living Foundation; Dr Nicholas Rawlings, Department of Psychology, University of Oxford; Ellen Ryan, Department of Biology, University of Oxford; the Brain Research Trust; the Institute of Neurology; the Institute for Psychical Research; and John Mole, *sine quo non*.

The man in the wheelchair slept. Afternoon sunlight filtered through the windows. From the distance a college clock struck five. The curtains moved lightly in the wind, then settled.

In a corner of the room the monkey stirred. She stretched, rose to her hind legs and moved hesitantly towards the still figure. She paused by the chair, one paw on the wheel, the other uncertainly scratching her head. For a moment she studied the man's face, then scampered away and swarmed up onto the window-sill. There she sat, hunched up into herself, alternately staring out at the hazy afternoon and swinging round to peer at the man's unmoving face. She must have stayed like that for twenty minutes, watching, puzzling. The man's breathing was shallow and uneven.

As the wind rose again in the trees outside, the monkey seemed to reach a decision. She came down off the sill and approached the chair again. Quietly but with deliberation she pulled herself onto the arm and then folded herself on the man's lap. Still he did not stir. At last, from the furry heap a long, thin arm stretched hesitantly towards his face. With the back of her paw the monkey began stroking his cheek, softly, gently, until he woke.

One

Few people noticed the man out running at five in the morning: a solitary figure who wore a tracksuit and a mask.

As he ran, the man left eddies in the sheet of mist lying at knee-height over the plain. For a mile in any direction there was not another person about, just a group of half-wild horses and a single holm-oak torn by the wind. In the distance the city skyline, a thin ribbon of chimneys and spires, floated on the low white marsh mist which the dawn sun was too weak to shake away. The plain was known as Port Meadow.

The runner wore a wartime gas-mark. The round goggles steamed up and gave him the sensation of tunnel vision. He set his sights on the solitary tree. A hundred paces away, he doubled his speed. He pumped his knees higher and higher until they pounded against his chest. Eighty. Ninety. Ninety-five. One hundred. The man threw himself round the coarse bark of the tree and sank to his knees. He kept his arms up, clutching at the lower branches so that he wouldn't be able to rip off the mask.

Psssss-in. Pfooof-out.

He forced himself to breathe rhythmically. Control was everything. The mask stank of perished rubber and the sound of his breathing was deafening. Suck-hard-in. Force-hard-out. On every intake of breath the carbon filter flapped and allowed him to drag a little air in through its tight granules. On the out-breaths, the sides of the mask shuddered against his cheeks. The lungs, forced to work for their oxygen, made the body use its

11

life-air efficiently. That was the whole point. He rose to his feet, adjusted his blue tracksuit, looked at his watch, clenched his teeth and began another cycle. Walk for a hundred. Jog for a hundred. Run for a hundred. Sprint for a hundred. Then over again, until the hour was up.

Yesterday it had been the haversack filled with bricks. The day before, lead ankle-weights borrowed from a friend in the diving club. Tomorrow it would be nothing, for tomorrow was the race.

Walk. Jog. Run. Sprint. Walk. Jog. Run. Sprint. Breathe like an asthmatic. The lungs tugging for air. Throat and windpipe scorched. Somebody working a blowtorch over the inside of the lungs.

In-two-three-four!   Out-two-three-four!   *Win*-two-three-four . . .

Why am I doing this? My lungs are scalding. I'm slashing my stomach open. My insteps are shrieking in pain. What am I doing it for? No sex for days. Given Linda up. Get up at five every morning out of my warm sweet bed. Given up booze. Given up parties. Whip-two-three-four!

Allan Mann looked at his watch; it was almost six. He could go back to his flat, have a cup of tea, then cycle over to the Sports Ground and join the other members of the Oxford team who would be rubbing the sleep out of their eyes and sounding off their ritual complaints and hauling on their tracksuits and spikes to begin the early training session. After that, Allan would go off to some lectures, perhaps to the library too, and try, like all the other students facing their Finals, to do in three weeks what he should have done in three years.

As he turned out of the plain and through into Walton Street, he put on a sprint. This was the homeward run and he *caned* it. There were already people about: the newspaper boys, the dustmen, people coming off night-shift. Allan dodged them in his blinkered, be-goggled dash for home and arrived on his doorstep howling with pain but knowing he'd feel the better for it later.

Two

For a large man, Geoffrey Fish moved fast. He left the doors of the operating theatre swinging behind him. Not waiting for the lift, he took the stairs two at a time. He strode through the main doors of the Radcliffe Infirmary and headed for the street. The night sky was pale. He took a short-cut through his old college and down a back alleyway, aiming for the bleak building ahead that housed the Department of Medicine and, within it, his own laboratory. Tight against his chest he held a metal container resembling a Thermos flask. Inside the flask was a piece of brain tissue. Human brain tissue.

Geoffrey rubbed his face. The skin felt looser than he'd imagined. This was going to be another all-night session. His shoulders weighed heavy and fleshy. His eyes kept watering as they did from the years of too little sleep and when he ran his hand through his wiry red hair he was all too conscious of how it was retreating. A case of human entropy, he thought. But he kept up his pace.

'An amazing piece of luck,' he muttered to himself.

A neurosurgeon, Dr Samuels, had invited him to attend a brain operation. The patient was an epileptic girl of no more than fourteen. The operation was to find and ablate the epileptic *focus*. He shuddered to recall the operation. The girl had been fully conscious throughout, with the surgeon on tip-toes over her open head, passing thin electrode wires through the pink-grey folds of her brain. At one point the girl made a soft sound, between a giggle and a purr. The surgeon then pushed the electrode a millimetre further in, and she screamed. He had nearly vomited.

'We're getting warmer,' the surgeon said and probed the spot again. The girl screamed. He said, 'Very warm now.'

It was not a scream of pain. The brain is an organ quite without feeling. Samuels had passed the electrode through a region of the temporal cortex and hit a bank of memory cells. Memory was Geoffrey's field, although monkeys and not humans were his subjects. The wire had triggered off memories, images, some pleasurable, others terrible, which went flashing across the girl's mind. He was on the point of asking Samuels to cross-reference the cell-bank when something went wrong, something to do with the girl's breathing, he couldn't be sure. All hell broke loose. Samuels moved to the other side, withdrew the electrodes, snapped orders to the assistants, grabbed the defibrillator and within a matter of seconds was battling for the girl's life. They tried everything, but it was no good. Geoffrey stood in the wings, feeling redundant and guilty. After an hour the girl was pronounced clinically dead. It was then that Samuels took him on one side and said the girl's parents had signed the necessary consents "in the event" and that he was welcome to a section of the brain tissue for his research. Geoffrey was now taking off to his laboratory a small cube cut from the main association areas in the frontal cerebral lobe, suspended in a tepid glucose medium to keep it alive.

The night porter at the labs signed him in and said, 'Working late again, sir?'

'All night,' he answered with a sympathetic grin and punched the lift button. 'You too, eh?'

The corridors were low-lit and empty. He unlocked the three security bolts on his lab door and went in. Instinctively he looked around the large wire cages on each side to check that the monkeys were all right. The low blue safety light was on, but the animals stirred at his presence. Pairs of large, brown eyes appeared at the bars, quick-blinking and inquisitive, following him as he went to the small office at the end of the lab. There he took off his jacket, put on a white coat and picked up a pen and clip-board. Then he walked back through the lab to another small room which housed the main equipment. He turned on the

power and took out a series of Petrie dishes and culture g
Into the largest of these he carefully poured out the cont
the Thermos flask. With a pair of sterilised forceps he tran
the cube of brain tissue to another dish into which he poured a
specially-prepared sterile liquid designed to simulate the brain's
own cerebro-spinal fluid. He went out into the corridor and
brought back three plastic cups of black coffee which he set down
in a line on the table. He was ready.

From the lab he could hear a chattering. It grew more insistent.
He ran a pinkish hand through his hair and thought, Oh, very
well then. He went into the lab and slipped the catch off one of
the cages.

'Come along then, beauty, if you must.'

She reached out a long, slender arm and swung herself down
onto the lab floor in a single, graceful movement. She followed
Geoffrey into the smaller room and climbed up on top of a bank of
oscilloscopes. This was her place. From here she fixed him with
bright, black, deepset eyes which constantly flickered from his
hands to his face and to whatever he was doing. The hair on her
face was shorter than over the rest of her lithe little body and
grew dark over her crown and down her spine. She had the habit
of cocking her head from side to side and parting her pink lips in a
smile that he found almost cheeky. This was his favourite
monkey and the only one he liked to keep him company. She was
no more intelligent than the other Capuchins, but there was
something *special* about her. All the others had names, except
her.

'Now, if you're going to stay here, you've got to be still. This is
going to be very tricky. None of your pranks, like last night.'

The monkey puts her paws to her mouth and sat quietly on her
haunches, watching. Geoffrey placed the section of brain tissue
in the cryostat for freezing so that he could more easily cut it into
the 20-micron-thin slices. Half of these slices he planned to
scintillate and then develop up in an incubator, while the other
half he'd mark with a radio isotope and then subject to the
standard histological tests. The end product would be a series of
solutions which, when combined with various drugs, would be
injected into his monkeys. He wasn't sure what would come out:
perhaps something of significance, perhaps nothing.

From her perch, the monkey kept still and watched.

15

The coffee bar where he met Melanie the following afternoon was stuffy, cramped and smelled of cheap cigarettes and frying bacon. It was Oxford's bohemia. Geoffrey was uncomfortable: the hard stools were only big enough for one buttock at a time and his knees got squashed under the Formica-topped table. Twice he'd slopped Melanie's Russian tea as he tried to ease himself free. Outside the day was adolescent and bright. Inside it was sweltering. He loosened his knit tie and ran his hand round the damp rim of his collar. The hand was shaking. I'm getting unfit, he told himself. Unfit and unslept.

'You'll never guess what I saw him doing the other morning,' he heard himself saying. 'I was going home from the labs – it must have been six in the morning – and just as I turned into Walton Street I saw this apparition: Allan in a gas-mask, running for his life as if they'd dropped the bomb on Cowley. He scared the Holy Roman daylights out of me, I can tell you. Even my landlady's dog took one look and ran for it.'

'But Allan seems so relaxed and easy-going on the surface,' said Melanie. She spoke in a soft American lilt. To Geoffrey it had the texture of a rich, rounded bourbon.

'On the surface,' he agreed.

'But it's the *way* he runs. It's fantastic.'

'It's masochistic,' he said. 'He's wilful and, if you ask me, there's a bit of self-hate here too. You like to call it will-power and determination, I know.'

He looked at Melanie, then dropped his eyes to his tepid coffee. This woman caused a major neuro-chemical disturbance in his hypothalamus. Why did she do this to him, even now? Allan had put it more simply: Geoffrey was love-sick. He shot a glance at her. Her face was pale and oval, curtained by long, dark hair. Her legs were too slim, he knew, and her breasts too lovely for an academic. It was the wrong time to think about such things: Melanie's mind, he was sure, was on other things, perhaps on her article for the *Zoological Review*, perhaps on the sports match they were on their way to. The wrong times were getting more frequent, Geoffrey thought. Or maybe it was just the right times were getting more seldom.

'You look ghastly,' said Melanie, not unkindly.

Geoffrey touched his face. It felt like someone else's he'd

borrowed. 'I had work to do. An idea I wanted to investigate. Samuels – you know, the neurosurgeon at the Radcliffe – gave me a sample to work on.'

'If you're going to tell me about cutting up brains, don't.'

'Not a monkey's this time,' he said and toyed with the hardening rim of froth round the cup edge. 'A young girl's.'

Melanie shuddered, as Geoffrey knew she would. She was an ethologist, aged twenty-eight, a graduate of Berkeley working on a second Doctorate in Oxford. Her work was with gorillas and she studied them in the wild. Geoffrey worked with monkeys and studied them in cages. That formed an automatic chasm between them and from the beginning of their affair they'd avoided the whole topic. Melanie got up.

'We'd better be going,' she said, looking at her watch.

She led the way into the street. She had a slightly awkward way of walking, the legacy of polio as a child. They sauntered with the tide towards Magdalen Bridge, in the direction of the Sports Ground. The sun was dazzling and the college lawns as green as in a childhood memory. The river was full of rowdy laughter and old customised cars roared down the High. The more bookish students, pale as slugs from under stones, left the libraries and crept on the shaded side of the street into the Botanical Gardens. Between the chimes of the tower clock striking three, Geoffrey could hear the *toc* of croquet being played in the Dean's garden and, in the distance, the muffled cheering from the sports grandstand. The street was awash with blazers and boaters, sandals and sun-umbrellas. The old city had been turned inside-out like a sock.

Melanie said suddenly, 'But why a human brain?'

This was some kind of test, he thought. 'Because I've never made up a formulation based on human tissue. I happened to be there at the operation. It went wrong and the girl died. Samuels had got consent and offered me a slice of the action, so to speak.'

'I see,' said Melanie shortly. Geoffrey had failed.

'You don't see. But it doesn't matter.'

He looked above him at the rough stone gargoyles, ready to spit down on everyone when it rained. Their expression seemed meant for him. For all the heat, he felt cold. He remembered he hadn't eaten anything since supper the previous night. The crowds began to oppress him. It was, he knew, the chlordiazepoxide he'd taken that morning now wearing off. It always led to a mild paranoia. One of his former pupils cycled past with a girlfriend side-saddle on the cross-bar. The bicycle wobbled and the girl screamed in joy and terror. This boy has chosen hedonism, thought Geoffrey; he'll get a lousy degree but make a great success in life. He looked down at the pavement. It seemed infinitely far away.

'I was talking to Allan's trainer,' Melanie was saying. She put an arm on his sleeve, but it was only to steer him out of the way of a large woman with panniers loaded with shopping. 'You know what Charlie thinks of Allan. Allan's Olympic material. I think he should go all out for that. He can always go back to Law later.'

'Allan would self-destruct first,' said Geoffrey. He knocked into the woman's pannier and she scowled. He shrank back as if she'd bit him. What were they talking about? He mustered his concentration and went on, 'Look at the way he trains. He can't accept failure. That's a failing, Melanie. If he didn't make the Olympics . . .'

'Allan fail?'

'Christ, Melanie, he's only human.'

He shook his head. He didn't want to get into an argument. They fell silent and she began talking Departmental gossip about who was angling for what posts and grants in the coming year.

They had reached the Sports Ground. A narrow driveway led to the vast open field in which the Oxford-Cambridge athletics match was being waged. It was a radiant day, Geoffrey suddenly noticed, typical of the best of May. The darling buds were out in force. Budding chestnuts rimmed the Ground. Budding Ministers and musicians, dons and drop-outs clustered on the grandstand. Budding alcoholics stood in the bar with their backs turned on the events of the field. It was one of those sunny, cloudless days when the University simply reeled under the headiness of its own potential.

'There's Linda,' said Melanie and pointed.

Geoffrey looked across the field. Linda was standing on a knot of friends by the entrance to the grandstand. She always had stood out in a crowd.

'Let's join them,' said Melanie and put her arm through Geoffrey's.

He caught a moment of her scent on the hot summer air and let her lead him over to their friends, all the time wondering if Samuels could dig around inside *his* brain and whip out the *locus amoris*. The clock over the grandstand stood at three-fifteen. Perfect timing for Allan's race, he thought. And then afterwards he'd get back to the lab. There was nothing he could do until then.

A wave of tiredness swept over him with such force that he clung to Melanie's arm. 'I'm going to grab a drink,' he croaked drily. 'How about you?'

'It's the middle of the afternoon,' said Melanie, freeing her arm.

'Not by my body-time.' He left her with Linda and the others and went to get a very large brandy. It was also something by way of a celebration, too. He didn't know what for, but he sensed it wouldn't be long before he found out.

Three

Allan Mann had taken up his position in a far corner of the ground, behind a spreading beech-tree. He sat cross-legged, in the lotus position. On the grass in front of him lay his watch and a yellow rose Linda had given him for luck.

His breathing was slow and measured. The muscles of his lean, sculpted face were in repose. His hands rested on his knees with their palms upturned. Allan was out of his body. He was concentrating on a point deep within himself and following it through and out the other side. But a money-spider would land on his palm or a cheer would rise from the grandstand or the starting-pistol would crack and he'd be jerked involuntarily back. Then he'd roll his eyeballs back again and wait until he could feel his eyelids fluttering. He'd focus his mind closely on the rhythm of his breathing: three heart-beats to breathe in, two to hold, three to breathe out again. And, once again, he'd feel his mind rising free of his body and floating upwards, upwards.

This was the way he prepared for an important race.

His watch buzzed. It was time. Slowly he let himself come down. He opened his eyes. The other milers were forming up around the starting-line. He got up and stretched, pulling the coaxial muscles along his spine in turn. Then he bent down and worked over his right calf. He'd gone on after Charlie had told him to stop the evening before and he'd overstrained a muscle. But Charlie wasn't going to see that.

Allan broke into a gentle run. His pace was measured and his step high. All the training with weights and packs had helped.

He listened to the tune of his body. Pretty rough; could be better. He ran past groups of friends and supporters but didn't see them or hear their calls. He looked neither to the ground nor to the side. His gaze was fixed on a point ahead, a point that lay in his mind, a point exactly one mile ahead down four circuits of the track: the finishing-line.

They took their positions on the starting line. But before the pistol cracked, the Cambridge number three broke away in a false start. The others followed for several paces. Only Allan remained where he was. The starter called the field back and started his three-part ritual again. Ready . . . get set . . .

From the moment the gun went, it was Cambridge in the lead in the first three places. The third was holding back, to give the front pair as much lead as possible. Allan led Oxford in fourth. The six runners held these positions until half-way. Then, in a well-rehearsed manoeuvre, the front pair changed places and their number one settled back alongside the number three to form a wall against Allan.

They're boxing me in, he thought.

He waited. The leader widened the gap with every stride. Still Allan hung back. It had to go to the impossible, and then beyond. The leader turned into the final lap. Allan dug his toes in. A surge of new thrust powered his legs. His knees rose higher, higher and faster-pumping.

Then it happened. A sharp, snapping twang in his right calf. A blaze of pain streaked up his leg. He stumbled. He lost his stride. He swerved. The spectators caught their breath.

Control it! his mind hissed. *Externalise the pain. Put it beyond the finishing-line. Now run towards it. Run to greet it. Toes in! Stretch the stride! Pump the knees! Faster! Go, GO!*

He pulled out wide and clear of the two runners ahead of him. The crowd's cheering rose to a scream. He was running too wide, far too wide.

At the two hundred and fifty yard mark, he cleared the two Cambridge runners. He began closing fast on the leader. To the spectators it seemed as if his legs actually grew longer. Allan felt exultant: he was flying, not running. His feet skimmed the track without actually touching it at all. The finishing-line was in sight. He was already there in his mind, running simply in a kind of stretched present.

With fifty yards to go, he pulled alongside the leader. The rest of the pack lay far behind. His stride became even longer, smoother. He seemed to devour the other man's pace. And it was Allan Mann for Oxford who breasted the tape. His lead was ten feet. He had taken a quarter of a second off the Varsity record.

Three paces beyond the line, he swerved off onto the grass and keeled over. Four hundred yards of suppressed agony sprang up on him like a thick elastic band and smacked him in the pit of the stomach. He wanted to throw up. A thick welt of pain enveloped him and he slumped over.

But he forced his body back under control. He took the pain out of his leg and willed it into a small imaginary box that he laid apart on the track. With all the violence he possessed, he kept the box tight shut. Only when he knew the thrashings had subsided did he let up. He got slowly to his feet.

Then he heard the applause. It flooded over him. A roar went up when the new record was announced over the speakers. Charlie the trainer was beside him, his shoulder under Allan's arm. Linda was there too, rubbing her scented hand through his soaking hair. Others crowded round him, others he knew but couldn't see.

Slowly and carefully, he bent down to pick up his tracksuit. He shook hands with the other runners. Without limping, he walked over to the grandstand and the changing-rooms beneath it. He paused for a moment and raised his hand. He stood there as the cheering washed over him.

Then he walked down the tunnel leading to the changing-rooms. When he was completely alone, behind the locked door of a lavatory, he let go and the little box flew open. The pain assaulted him with such a wave of violence that he lurched backwards against the door, and then slipped to his knees on the cold ceramic tiles of the lavatory floor, racked with silent sobs. But he had won.

'Christ, that was close! For a moment I thought he'd blown it. Why did he leave it so late to break? I nearly died.' ·

Linda Aikman lit a cigarette as she spoke. She pulled deeply on it, held the smoke for a moment and exhaled with a sigh. She shook her fair, shoulder-length hair impatiently.

'That's Allan for you,' said Geoffrey. He mopped his forehead with the back of his hand. 'Allan has to work himself up into a rage in order to win. All that business of meditating before the race: that's part of it. He has to hype himself up. It's a kind of mania.'

Geoffrey could hear announcements of other races in different parts of the Ground: the 400 metres hurdles, the women's relay, the 100 metres sprint. He looked at Linda. She was craning her head to see down the tunnel into the changing-rooms. She was constantly moving, fiddling, toying with things. She played with the Victorian rings on her fingers, she swept a hand through her hair, she rolled her lighter around her palm, she flicked the ash off her cigarette before it had hardly formed.

'So he hypes himself up,' said Linda. 'So do we all. I do in the dressing-room before a performance. But that doesn't explain why he has to play games like that. It's bad for my nerves.'

'You don't get what I'm saying,' persisted Geoffrey. 'I'm saying Allan has to pile the odds against himself until they're almost impossible. It's quite deliberate. Then he gets so mad he's about to lose the race that he forces himself to do the impossible and win. But he has to madden himself first.'

'Q.E.D.,' said Linda in the same tone. She shook her charm bracelet and turned to Melanie. 'I think that's rubbish. Your Geoffrey is the mad one.'

Your Geoffrey. He was tired. He could hear himself bludgeoning the point to death. The green of the grass was dazzling him. He felt himself breaking out in sweat. He wanted to take his jacket off but he knew there would be a large damp patch on his back. He caught Melanie's eye as she looked up from a score-card. She was quite unlike Linda. Her features were neat and precise, her movements were economical and she spoke only after reflection. She moved through life at a calm and steady pace. Geoffrey remembered a child's party game in which you gave people colours. Linda was buttercup-yellow, or maybe vermillion. Melanie was a violet, something with a kind of low-frequency hum about it. Geoffrey blinked. It was the lack of sleep.

'So how are Finals?' he asked.

'Screw Finals,' said Linda gaily. 'I mean, who needs all that in the *real* world? It's just not relevant.'

Linda was doing her English Finals that term, just as Allan was

23

doing his Law. She was one of the lucky few coming off the university production-line who knew what she wanted to do: to act on the stage. She was already well on her way. Geoffrey couldn't forget her part as Clytemnestra in the *Oresteia*; a stunning and lascivious performance. She'd got a contract to do a television drama series in the coming year. She was right for Allan; they made a good pair.

Linda went on, 'In all the auditions I've been to, no one's asked me about work, what degree I'll get, all that. It simply doesn't matter out there. I keep telling Allan that. He'll make far more money carrying on with athletics than swotting for a good degree and ending up as some dreary little clerk in Chambers. A degree's only worth it if you're going to spend the rest of your natural in the groves of Academe. Like you, Geoffrey.'

'True.'

Linda made his life-choice really sound like the last scrapings of the barrel. Why was he there, at thirty-eight, still in a tweed sports-jacket, still going to Sports Days? Linda was talking again, this time more impatiently.

'What's Allan up to in there anyway? He's been ages. I'm going in to dig him out.'

'Give him a chance,' said Geoffrey quickly, instinctively defending male privacy.

But at that moment Allan came out of the changing-rooms into the dazzling sunshine. In the buttonhole of his dark blue Athletics Club blazer he wore the yellow rose Linda had given him. His flannels and white open shirt accentuated his slight tan and the whole gaunt fitness of his body. His face broke into a smile when he saw his friends.

'A reception committee!' he exclaimed. He kissed Linda on the lips and Melanie on the cheek. He clapped Geoffrey on the arm. His dark hair was sleeked back and still wet from the shower. He was as tall as Geoffrey but seemed to have grown in height. The lines streamed out from the sides of his eyes as he laughed and, under the thick dark line of his brows, the deep blue eyes sparkled. His walk betrayed the traces of a limp.

'Are you okay?' asked Linda quickly, concerned. She ground out her cigarette in the turf and reached out to touch Allan's sleeve.

'Fine, fine,' said Allan. He squeezed her hand. Geoffrey could see the knot clenching in his jaw. 'Just a bit stiff. How are we doing in the hurdles?'

Melanie knew, of course. 'We lost the 400 metres, I'm afraid.'

'Linda, you should have doled out your roses to everyone, darling,' said Allan. 'Where's the dog?'

'Oh, I left her in the car.' Suddenly Linda looked grave. 'Don't do that again, Allan. You took years off our lives.'

Allan laughed. 'Got to give 'em a run for their money. That's what it's all about, isn't it?'

The group walked over to the car park. A small boy ran up for Allan's autograph. He signed with a flourish saying, 'Ah, recognition at last.' He asked the small boy which sport he liked best. 'The sack race, sir,' replied the boy and ran off.

'Well, see you all at Jeremy Marsh's tonight, everyone. Geoffrey, I've got to drop off some books at the library after dinner. Will you be around in your lab then?'

'Sure. Come up and see me,' said Geoffrey warmly.

Linda had a rehearsal to go to. She climbed into her red mini estate, brushed the small yapping dog off her, lit a cigarette and started the engine, all at the same time. It made Geoffrey dizzy just to watch. She revved the car to a roar.

''Bye, darling. And well done.'

Linda let the clutch out with a jerk and the gravel spattered up behind the car. It hiccoughed down the driveway into the street and growled through a rust-holed exhaust all the way over the Plain and Magdalen Bridge and up the High until it was out of earshot.

Melanie laid a hand on Allan's sleeve and let it linger there. Her pale, ivory face was moist; she seemed illuminated from within. In her serious, American tone, she said, 'You were great, Allan. Really great.'

'Really great, Allan,' echoed Geoffrey beside her. 'A really first-rate piece of running.'

Geoffrey got into Melanie's car, a rustfree orange Volkswagen. She'd offered him a lift back to the labs: she worked just around the corner, in the Department of Zoology and Psychology. She put on her glasses to drive and let out the clutch carefully, leaning forward as she drove.

Geoffrey turned as they went down the driveway out of the ground, to catch a last glimpse of Allan. He was walking back to the changing-rooms. The limp in his right leg was now marked. He was having to stop and hold onto the railings. Should he go back? Geoffrey wondered. No, the trainer was there and he'd look after Allan. Besides, he couldn't wait to get back to his laboratory and to the tissue cultures waiting for him there.

Four

Allan walked back to college alone after the brief presentation ceremony of the cups and trophies. He took the short cut over the half-sunken ferry barge that led to Christ Church meadows. From behind the elms on the west side, the sun was lengthening the violet shadows across the bridle path. Through the heavy young foliage streamed orange beams of sunlight. Despite his leg, he felt fit and taut with energy.

He'd drunk his champagne from his silver cup, according to tradition, and he was already feeling light in the head. Light-footed, too, as if treading air just an inch above the ground. He was as tall as the chestnuts and elms.

And yet he felt disappointed. *Post cursum triste:* he knew it was that. He'd striven for it, made agonising efforts for it; now he'd got it, was it worth it? Always, after a race or an exam, he had to be alone. Alone, to remind himself just why he was doing it. He stopped on the hard earth pathway with its lattice-work of tree roots and rubbed a hand over his face. Lean, bony eyes set deep under overhanging brows, dark hair already a little too long. A body that was muscular and very fit. Fit. Was that what all the agony was for? No. It had to be more than that.

Allan had come a long way from Manchester and his parents' Edwardian house in the suburbs. It had been sheer hard graft all the way. He'd got to top of the school: top of form, captain of games, head of school. He *had* to be top. What was it that drove him there? What made him feel that mediocrity was a kind of deformity, a disease, to be fought and fought against? He'd fought, he'd won, he'd broken a Varsity record. Was that the triumph?

These were what his father called the best years of a man's life. True, everything was good to him. He loved Linda. He loved the challenge of running. He was even looking forward to his Law Finals as a chance to compete again. He remembered how, as a boy, his father had come into his room late one night when he was swotting for exams. His father had said, 'Life's not about being top of the class, lad. Life's the art of compromise. There's plenty of second-bests in life.' That night Allan hated his father. No, no, no! Jock, his father, was second-best: worthy, unambitious, cowed by authority, Jock worked as an area manager in insurance, without questions, without ideals. He'd given up. He'd resigned himself to life's second-best. *Children first love their parents; then they hate them. Sometimes they forgive them.* Who'd written that? That night the young Allan hated his father and the world. Now he felt differently. He forgave them, but he would not forgive himself if he became like them.

A lecturer he knew slightly stopped Allan on the path and congratulated him. A punt sidled past in the shallow water, carrying a girl he'd seen before in the library staring at him over her books. She blushed and gave him a small wave. Everybody else is happy for me, he thought. They think I've triumphed. Why do I doubt it myself?

Allan found his mind turning to the day his father's brother had bought him lunch in London to celebrate his scholarship to University. He couldn't forget the man's bleak little cell behind the Pensions Office in Whitehall. The old fellow was going blind but he refused to let anyone see it. He'd memorised the menu at the lunch place. But that day they'd changed the menu. Allan remembered being appalled by his efforts to pretend that he could still read it. But, although he fooled nobody, he managed to get by on his own. Now, looking back, Allan asked himself: wasn't *that* a real triumph?

He took a deep breath and sucked in the scents of the evening. The air was heavy with Spring passion, sharp with the uncertainties of the life ahead. It carried faint whiffs of Gauloises and mown grass lying in the sun and food cooking in distant college refectories. Above all, it had the indefinable smell of hope and youth and excitement: the world flowering all around, bursting with promise like a seed-pod, and in all directions horizons without limit. The trees whispered: *Everything is possible. Stretch out your hand and it's yours for the taking.* How deceptive. The real winning was in the struggle against yourself, getting up at five and running till it hurt, and then more.

Allan had turned into the wide avenue of trees leading to the college when a streak of pain tore up his right leg. He grabbed a bench and bit hard on his lip. Gradually he mastered it. It was like taking on the Devil in a contest of forearm strength on a table-top. He hobbled the next few steps. But as he came through the Gothic wicket-gate into his college, his step was more decisive. He'd had his time alone with himself and how he felt clearer and stronger. Through the cloisters and quadrangles black-gowned figures strolled and debated and joked. Allan met his old scout Arthur coming out of a staircase. Arthur's hand, when he held it out, trembled with age. He was better known in the college as Rigor Mortis.

'Congratulations, sir. There's some gentlemen asking for you in the Buttery.' Rigor Mortis' sunken eyes gleamed waterily. He added, 'They're saying it was a record, sir.'

'Thanks, Arthur. Yes, I just scraped home.'

He slowly made his way up the stone steps to join his friends. Damn it, he smiled to himself. This *is* a man's Golden Age.

Five

Love is a bunch of macromolecules. That's all there is to it. That puts it into perspective. What did the poets ever know about love?

Geoffrey concentrated as he fed the needle into his bulging vein and tried to think of it as someone else's. This was an anti-depressant — tranylcypromine, trade-name Parnate. He knew precisely how it worked on the brain, how it inhibited transmitter substances across the synapses and how that affected the nervous system to induce a general feeling of euphoria. Given time, Geoffrey could tell the poets how love itself worked — what cells were firing when and where in the hypothalamus and the cortex, what new synapses were being formed, what extra proteins manufactured. *Love is protein.*

He eased himself back in the sponge-seated swivel chair until it creaked. The fluorescent tube in the ceiling of his small office was malfunctioning and Geoffrey sensed a migraine coming on. Dimly he wondered what wave-length the flicker was affecting in the retinal system . . . but his mind wandered. The Parnate was beginning to do its work. He stretched, feeling a huge gentle smile coming over him. He knocked an empty coffee mug over. He rubbed his face: he'd forgotten to shave.

Geoffrey's office was whitewashed and windowless. Its furniture came from ex-War Department stocks, or so it seemed. The filing cabinet, in Admiralty grey, bulged with computer print-outs, old copies of the *Lancet* and the *Journal of Physiology* and an assortment of surgical gloves and masks. Caught in the door was the sleeve of a wide-lapelled dinner jacket, for use when visiting notables dined on High Table. Against one wall stood a series of glazed locking cabinets in which he stored his drugs. Each bottle was carefully labelled and every single tablet or gram removed was strictly recorded on a card. The surface of the desk was hidden under box-files, theses, drug companies' prospectuses, books and bits of apparatus he hadn't got round to mending. To the right sat the computer terminal and printer. The main instruments were next door, in the laboratory with the monkeys. Geoffrey shut his eyes and waited for the anti-depressant to work through. The room was quiet except for the whirr of the electric clock on the wall and the chattering from the monkeys in their cages.

Now, suppose love is protein. It follows that a protein inhibitor will inhibit love. Let's make up a *dis*-love potion, an antidote. Puromycin, for example. Injected into the brain, puromycin can prevent all protein synthesis for a matter of hours. Half-seriously, he toyed with the idea of an experiment . . .

A timing-clock buzzed from the lab. Slowly, feeling light and balletic, he got up. The incubator light was on; it stored the tissue culture he was developing from Samuels' little gift. Some was still on ice in the cryostat, but he had placed this section in a dish to allow the natural enzymes and amino-acids to propagate. It was a shot in the dark. He wasn't testing any theory, just having a go at a hunch. After all there weren't any theories to test about the results of using human brain extract in animals.

Geoffrey was a Senior Reader at the Department of Experimental Medicine, a branch of the Department of Medicine proper. His area was psycho-pharmacology. Mind drugs. Specifically, drugs in the learning process. He used monkeys, a status step up from the rats on which he'd done his Doctorate in Cambridge. (Did Melanie think her gorillas made her superior?) His research was slow work. This was partly because there appeared to be something fundamentally self-contradictory about using a brain to understand brains, using a thing to describe itself. But it was also because the field was full of charlatans who made sensationalist claims which had to be painstakingly checked out. Geoffrey remembered wasting almost six months on scotophobin, an enzyme fabricated in

31

Houston, Texas, from mushed-up rat brains. The rats had been conditioned to fear the dark. The enzyme said to be responsible for this was extracted and injected into the guts of normal rats. Then they turned out the lights. Did the rats get terrified? Had a specific memory peptide been isolated? Was this, at last, memory transfer? No, Geoffrey finally reported.

He chuckled to himself. It had infuriated him at the time. But now Parnate was making it seem mildly funny. Parnate incarnate. It would set him up for the party. He'd be able to go another night without sleep. And he'd have it out with Melanie, once and for all. Sure as EEGs were EEGs.

'Geoffrey? You there?'

It was Allan. He put his head round the outer door of the lab. Geoffrey had left it open: not a common practice with all the anti-vivisection feeling about. As it was, the door had a spy-hole and three separate locks. Geoffrey closed the incubator and advanced towards his friend. He gripped him firmly by the hand.

'Hero of the day,' he called. Turning to his monkeys, he bawled, 'Silence!'

Allan put his motorcycle helmet down on the lab bench and looked around. He'd been there a few times before, but visitors were generally discouraged. He'd never been to the main animal house, though, a separate fortress on the roof with cats, dogs, rats, tortoises, monkeys and a couple of goats. (Goats, Geoffrey had once explained, were very useful for experiments on vision because they had forward-pointing eyes.) The lab they were now in held only the monkeys being specifically used at the time. They were divided into two separate cages, each the height of the room and about six feet wide. At the far end a plywood partition separated off another room where the individual experiments took place. It was not diplomatic to perform tests on one monkey in the sight of the others; it tended to create abreactions. At that time Geoffrey had ten monkeys in the lab, five on each side. They were constantly moving, leaping and swinging and throwing themselves around the cages. They were fair-haired, wiry and quite small. All except one wore a curious belt with a hook on the back, for catching.

'God, I always forget what a grim place this is,' said Allan. Under the harsh overhead lighting he looked quite cadaverous to Geoffrey.

'Grim? Nothing could be grimmer than your Law Schools.' He followed Allan's eye to a poster on the lab wall. It advertised a new model of recording electrode. There was a picture of a small ginger cat with thin wires feeding out of a patch in its head and leading to a bank of instruments like those in Geoffrey's office. The cat had a chubby, friendly face. Once, under LSD, Geoffrey had recognised the face. It was the face that stared at him every day from the shaving-mirror.

'Iontophoresis,' said Geoffrey.

'I'd rather not know,' said Allan.

'Come on, that's nothing,' insisted Geoffrey. He ran a hand through his hair. 'We've been through this before. The animals don't feel anything. There's no sensation in the brain. Okay, they get a headache from time to time, but don't we all? Anyway, they're better off here than in a bloody jungle, even if they never came from a jungle in the first place.' He paused. 'In any case, you know I only use drugs. I don't cut them up as some people do. Roach, for example.'

'Roach?'

'The guy who has the lab next door. My dear colleague and friend. I'll introduce you next time you come.' Geoffrey's voice was laced with venom. What he meant was: Roach is a dirty, ambitious, sneaky little bastard. He perched on the bench in the same attitude as Allan, one leg up and his hands in his pockets. A coin rolled across the floor from a hole in the lab coat. He followed it with a fixed stare. I've overdone the Parnate, he thought. I should have allowed for an empty stomach. He went on, 'Roach and I work in roughly the same area.'

'Vivisection? That's what they're calling it these days.' There was a hard inflexion in Allan's voice.

'Oh, you saw all that too. Christ knows why they can't stop them doing it.' Geoffrey settled himself on the bench and sat on his hands.

'Well, they've got a point, haven't they?'

All over the country a fierce campaign was being waged against the use of animals in scientific and medical research. The Department of Medicine at Oxford was an obvious target. One night the previous week, someone had sprayed slogans all over the walls: STOP LIVE EXPERIMENTS! NAZI TORTURERS! ABOLISH VIVISECTION! The Department had tried all known solvents to get the stuff off. Professor Burbage, the Departmental head, had quite seriously suggested at a Faculty Board meeting that they set up a project with a brief to bio-engineer an enzyme capable of gobbling the offensive lettering off the walls.

'We're getting a lot of flak. We've got to face the Grants Committee in a few weeks to talk about next year's money. We need better P.R. than that.' Geoffrey frowned and met Allan's eye. It was all Roach's fault. But Roach was Professor Burbage's blue-eyed boy. The flak seemed somehow to bypass Roach. 'Don't look like that at me, Allan. I'm not responsible for any of the vivisection around here. It's Roach and his team who are getting the Wing a bad name.'

The Wing was short for the East Wing, where Experimental Medicine was housed. The word was misleading, since the building was an almost perfect cube, and a very ugly one at that.

'Try telling the world that. You're tarred with the same brush, the way they see it,' said Allan with a smile.

'Well, anyway.' Geoffrey got to his feet. 'I'd better check the cages and shut up shop. Are you sure I can't give you a lift?'

'I've got my bike, thanks,' said Allan. 'Take your time. Jeremy's parties always start late.'

Geoffrey nodded. He went over to one of the cages and opened the door. He reached inside and pulled out a monkey. It was the one without a belt and hook for catching. He cradled the small creature in one arm while he parted its eyelids wide and peered with an ophthalmoscope into its retinas. Satisfied, he slipped it gently back into the cage. He caught the look of curiosity on Allan's face.

'She's different from the rest, that one. She's special. I'm trying out something new on her.'

He checked the cages were properly locked and went on, 'These are all of the species *cebus apella*. They're Capuchins from the New World. Friendly little buggers, too. Christ!' He had put a finger between the bars to fondle a monkey and got sharply bitten. 'Only they have a nasty habit of munching. No, you see, Roach and I have fundamentally different ways of going about our work. We're both working on the mammalian brain. But Roach is a *reductionist*. That's the Oxford way. He looks at the brain from its smallest molecule and tries to build up an understanding of how it works, cell by cell. That involves a lot of

34

lesion and ablation. Knife-work. Vivisection, if you must.'

'And your approach, Geoffrey?'

'I'm what you might call a *holist*, I suppose. I think of the brain as a whole system, a totality made up of subordinate systems. I work downwards, if you like, while Roach works upwards. I use drugs, not knives. There's a world of difference.'

'If you say so,' said Allan, unconvinced. 'That's not what Melanie thinks.'

The name made Geoffrey start. 'Let's just say Melanie and I don't see eye to eye on certain things. It doesn't make things easier between us, I can tell you.' He took off his lab coat. 'Anyway, enough of all that. The night is young and full of fancy and we've got your record to celebrate. Are you ready?'

He dimmed the lab lights. The chatter died down almost at once. Night had fallen in the jungle. He triple-locked the door and peeped through the spy-hole a final time. As he led Allan down the corridor, he stopped outside the next-door lab. The door bore the name of Dr George Roach. Geoffrey fiddled with his key-chain and opened the locks.

'Take a look in here,' he whispered. 'You'll see what I mean.'

The room was in darkness except for a low blue safety light. Geoffrey fumbled for the light switch. Something, maybe a calendar, fell to the floor and he swore. The lab was similar in layout to his own; only the partitioned section at the back was much larger. The smell of formaldehyde was overpowering and mingled with the stench of urine on wood-chips. He beckoned Allan behind the partition. In the centre stood a bench, on a slope. All round the bench ran a shallow gulley and two opaque polythene bags dangled at the lower corners like sacks on a billiards table. The board was drilled with peg-holes. Its purpose was abundantly clear.

'Christ, Geoffrey, what the hell's this?'

Allan had gone over to the corner and was examining a large perspex box. From the faint, regular plashing sound, Geoffrey knew that Roach had a rat inside. It was paddling away just below the surface, swimming endlessly for its life.

He laughed tersely. 'That's called aversive conditioning. You condition by the stick or by the carrot. I favour the carrot, Roach favours the stick. He gets results, though. Drowning concentrates the rodent mind wonderfully.' He swallowed. 'Okay, let's go. Allan, are you all right?'

Allan was in the corridor, green-faced. 'Nothing. Just my stomach. It's often like this after a race. Couldn't hold a thing down at dinner. Threw the lot up.'

'You need some air. Come on.'

In the car park Allan remembered he'd left his motorcycle helmet in the labs. Geoffrey offered again to take him in his car: Allan could pick up his helmet the next day.

'Thanks, but I'd rather have my own wheels,' said Allan. 'Give me the keys and I'll get it myself.'

'No. Security,' said Geoffrey. To emphasise his point, he pointed to one of the Department vans in the car park. A red swastika had been sprayed on its side. It was a vicious sight.

It was only later that he realised what a close thing it had been. If only he'd insisted on giving Allan a lift. If only . . . Historical hypotheticals. How could one tell that this point, rather than any other point in the whole chain of random, contingent events making up life, that *this* was the one on which history turned, that *this* was the tiny lever that formed a fulcrum and moved a world? Wasn't there once a king who, for the sake of a shoe lost a horse, and for the sake of a horse lost a kingdom?

The trouble was, you could only separate the pivotal events from the merely irrelevant when it was too late.

Six

By the third tumbler of whisky, Geoffrey was lifting off. He stood stooping under the low beams of Jeremy Marsh's little cottage in Nettlebed. Through the base of the tumbler his feet looked a mile away. Then it occurred to him he was a kind of Samson, holding the cottage up like a pillar. If he moved from the spot the whole thing would come tumbling down, lath, plaster, beams and all.

The party was horribly noisy. Geoffrey looked across the smoke-blue room to where Melanie was talking to another student in Zoology. She seemed to have no difficulty in making herself understood. Maybe she was using gorilla-speak.

'Cheer up, Geoffrey. It may never happen.'

'Oh, Linda, it's you. Who's to say it hasn't happened already?' The drink was making him gloomy.

He emptied his glass and raised his hand to catch their host's arm. He knocked Linda's glass and spilled her vodka-tonic over her black tight-fitting dress. He pulled out a handkerchief and wiped her down, trying not to touch her breasts too much. Linda threw back her fair hair and seized the handkerchief with a laugh. Geoffrey looked at her face, animated, wide-featured, her lips exaggeratedly painted in a Cupid's bow. I'm almost twice her age, he thought.

'Black suits you,' he said.

'You mean white doesn't,' said Linda quickly. She offered him a Balkan Sobranie. Black. 'Oh, I forgot, you don't. No vices?'

Geoffrey winked. 'How's your glass? Let me freshen it up, as

Melanie would say. Wait, I won't be a second.'

'No, I'll come with you. Actually, I want to ask your advice about something. It's about Allan.'

'Follow me,' he said and led the way through to the kitchen. The cottage didn't come tumbling down when he moved, although he nearly knocked himself out cold on the low door-frame.

The music was now at the far end of the cottage, a mindless, muffled thump coming from an old Dansette record-player that served as the disco. In the middle of the room someone dropped a glass and for a moment the academic laughter and banter stopped. From the garden and shrubbery, through the open windows, Geoffrey caught the whoops and bugle-calls of the young bloods. A typical Oxford party, he thought with rising despair. But there was plenty to drink. Untypical, that.

The kitchen was packed and there was no room to move. No room, in a favourite Department phrase, to castrate a cat. He took Linda's shoulder and steered her back through the corridor. There she stopped, turned and looked him full in the face.

'I had an abortion yesterday, Geoffrey. I went up to London to have it. Don't look so shocked. I'm perfectly all right. I caught it early enough. Look, you know Allan. Well, I'm wondering . . .'

'It is *his*, I suppose. I mean, it was his. I mean, Allan was the father, right?' Geoffrey looked into his glass for some Delphic clue. Then he took a large gulp. God, he was going to be asked to *cope* again.

'Of course, stupid.' She rattled her bracelets impatiently, and began picking at the rim of her glass with a brightly-painted nail. 'What I'm wondering is, should I tell him? I mean, he's quite old-fashioned at times. I don't want to upset him, especially now he's on top of the world. But I just feel he has a right to know.'

Geoffrey nodded, swilling the whisky round the tumbler. He waited for something to come to him, some idea, some line of thought. Nothing came. Out of a million billion neurones under his skull, not so much as the slightest spark. Then one of Linda's phrases recurred. *Right to know.*

'Well?' she asked.

'Allan has a right to know,' he said. He paused, aware that this wasn't enough. 'Allan's a perfectly reasonable, balanced chap. No harm in telling him. It's only the truth, after all. One mustn't

38

be afraid of the truth. One has a right to know.'

Linda took out another cigarette and again absent-mindedly offered him one. She lit hers and said decisively, 'You're right, Geoffrey. Thanks.'

'I think so. After all, Allan's a level-headed sort of bloke,' Geoffrey found himself repeating. It only occured to him later that he'd called Allan *mad* that very afternoon. Linda reached up and gave him a kiss on the cheek, a sticky red kiss that he could feel there long after she had disappeared into the party in her tight black dress.

Suddenly he felt ragingly, massively hungry. He went back into the kitchen and fought his way to the food table. After that, the Parnate seemed to ebb and he remembered little afterwards. He felt it was all taking ages to filter through to him. At some point he retreated to Jeremy Marsh's study, to sober up. He had probably spent fifteen minutes there when the sound of quarrelling voices from the garden made him look up and through the leaded windows.

The garden was really an orchard. The pathways between clumps of trees were lit by garden flares. Occasional couples strolled among the shadows or stood under the apple-trees with only the glowing tips of cigarettes to mark their position. Coming onto full stage in the centre of the garden were Linda and Allan. They'd been having a terrible row. Linda was hanging onto Allan's jerkin, but he brushed her off, walked briefly into the floodlight over the gravel path that ringed the cottage and then went inside. Linda, visible only as a fair head and white hands, stayed behind. She struck her lighter and lit a cigarette. From its bright-burning glow Geoffrey knew she was pulling hard on it and that she was hurt and angry too. *One has a right to know*, Geoffrey found himself mumbling, partly in self-justification, partly in apology.

A moment later, he heard a motorbike being gunned into life. It revved up to a scream. The rider engaged the clutch and, with a squeal of tyres, the bike roared off into the night. For a good mile Geoffrey could hear its angry, high-pitched howl as it tore through the dark and winding lanes of the Oxfordshire countryside.

The bike was Allan's joy; it was mechanised sprinting. A twist of

39

the throttle, a kick of the pedal and the machine bucked and roared ahead. He respected his motorbike, as one professional respects another.

Black outlines of trees flashed above his head. The night air, sluggish with heavy scents of flowers, tugged and clawed at his leather jerkin like sirens set to seduce him. Allan gave the bike its head. After a while he began to grow calmer. His breathing grew deeper, more measured. *In-two-three-four, hold. Out-two-three-four, hold.* Gradually all his anger flowed away. In its place came exhilaration. He was flying, not riding. Flying through the dark night air, a mechanical Pegasus. Running as he'd run that afternoon. Running but not touching the ground. Flying above it, above it all.

A mile down the lane, he slowed. Carefully and correctly he pulled out onto the bypass and headed for the sodium bruise in the sky that was Oxford. He kicked the bike into a lower gear. Ahead, a lorry forged its way through the night. Allan made after it. He closed the gap effortlessly, just as he'd dealt with the Cambridge number two that afternoon.

He drew level with the lorry and twisted the throttle hard towards his body. The bike dug into the tarmac and gave a thrust of power and savage joy. He'd almost overtaken the lorry when it happened.

The bike engine choked. It simply choked. Allan urgently played the throttle back and forth, but there was no power, nothing at all but a terrible gasping from the engine, a suffocating, spluttering series of coughs. Pegasus pegging out at full gallop.

Later Allan recalled the oncoming headlights. How they flashed once, twice, then repeatedly. How he stamped the foot-brake. How the pain knifed through his right leg. And how, this time, this one time of all times, his leg disobeyed his will and mutinied. It was powerless.

The bike lurched. It caught the side of the lorry and sheered off towards the headlights. One moment he was under the headlights, the next flying above them. Pegasus had taken wing. It was ecstatic and awesome. It was life, yet it was death. And it took place in its own time, at its own ineluctible slow pace.

Seven

From his knowledge of the anatomy of monkeys, Geoffrey knew what to expect. Allan had suffered a fracture at C-1, the topmost spinal vertebra, an injury second only to the terminal hangman's fracture. From Dr Wiseman, the senior consultant surgeon in the Buckinghamshire hospital to which Allan had been moved, Geoffrey learned exactly what it was. It was a rupture of the transverse ligament of the atlas, with anterior atlanto-axial subluxation. It caused loss of all muscle control below the neck. From there down there was reaction degeneration to electrical excitation and an absence of tendon reflexes. Wiseman performed an operation in a bid to rescue some movement in the limbs, but the operation failed. Allan could move nothing from his neck down: he could speak but not shrug, he could swallow but not feed himself. In a word, he was paralysed.

Apart from a month's trip to Canada in the long vacation, Geoffrey remained in Oxford during the summer and paid frequent visits to his friend in hospital. The other university alumni had gone their separate ways. Linda went down and spent the summer on the island of Mustique. Her cards to Geoffrey became fewer and fewer. The Oxford academic calendar marked the passing of time the way it had every year since the twelfth century. In the autumn the university re-convened for the Michelmas Term. Melanie came back from the States and continued with her second Doctorate. She spent a full day with Allan in hospital over Christmas. It was now well into the cold, dark Hilary Term.

Allan, of course, hadn't been able to take his Finals. Horizontal and immobile in the traction equipment, he told Geoffrey quite calmly that he was going back to sit them again. If Geoffrey took him seriously, his parents just nodded indulgently. But in time they realised that their son was adamant, quite immovable on the subject, and that they had to start making arrangements for a very new kind of life for their boy.

Visiting Allan took Geoffrey's mind off his work and his feelings about Melanie. He'd been hurt she had turned down his idea of a summer holiday together and instead returned to her family in Minnesota. They still went around Oxford as a couple, seeing films and going to dinner parties together, but Geoffrey knew it was slipping into a different focus. She'd grown easier to handle, less antagonistic and abrasive.

Faced with Allan, his own hurt diminished in perspective. Allan's moods fluctuated violently, however. Some days he was cheerful, ribald, playful. Other days he was consumed with impotent rage, sometimes he became almost catatonic. But underneath there was an astonishing will to recover, the kind of obstinate force to win through that Geoffrey had recognised so well in Allan's running. It was as if, at times, Allan relished his condition as the ultimate and complete test of his will. Geoffrey thought he understood and forgave him for all the times he was bitterly aggressive and harsh, for he knew that Allan was ten times more harsh with himself. In this way Geoffrey came to find these visits worrying but also uplifting. Through Allan he felt a new kind of access to the human condition.

All the same he couldn't forgive the consultants for not being able to heal Allan's body. At the micro-biological level at which he worked, Geoffrey believed that anything was possible, given time and application and precision. But the doctors and surgeons dealing with the whole body were no better than clumsy gardeners, pruning a twig here and training a branch there. Their science was so imprecise, so much trial and error. After all the talk of lesions and lumbar sections, all Dr Wiseman could really say was, 'Only time will tell.' That's not good enough for my friend! Geoffrey cried to himself. But time was to tell and, nine months after the accident, Allan was coming home.

It was not a kindly day for a homecoming. Dirty snow, melted and re-frozen, rimmed the city streets. The sky hadn't moved for days. It lay on the roofs and the gardens like a leaden lid. It gave no shape to the days, no beginnings nor ends. It offered no promise of a break to the interminable grip of winter. Eliot was wrong, thought Geoffrey: February is the cruellest month.

Allan's parents, Jock and Dorothy, had been working for half a year for this moment. They had prepared a small surprise party to welcome Allan home, though *home* was not a word Dorothy easily used of this hare-brained idea of a flat in Oxford all on the boy's own. She was short and grey-haired, and the worry of the past nine months had deepened the lines in her round, kindly face.

'I still don't think it's *right*,' she said. 'Allan just won't get the care.'

'It's what the lad wants,' said Jock with rehearsed patience.

Jock took Geoffrey's duffle coat and winked. Geoffrey had witnessed this conversation time and again. He'd helped them choose the flat, a ground floor apartment in a Victorian red-brick house close to the Parks. Allan had to have a ground floor flat, of course. And to have it heated, as it was now, to a subtropical temperature. The heat and the smell of fresh paint and disinfectant made Geoffrey feel slightly nauseous and he followed the couple to the kitchen and poured himself a glass of water. He looked around the room, noting the improvements. He knew what sacrifices they'd made: Jock giving up his pipe, Dorothy shopping in the sales, the reduced housekeeping and the second mortgage. Jock looked older than his years. He was tall and lean, like Allan, but stooped and the bright Canadian check shirts he wore showed up the pallor of his face. He only looked really well when enthusiasm for this flat flushed his face.

'It's so much better for Allan's morale to be here,' said Geoffrey.

Dorothy was about to say her piece (this was a ritual argument) when the front door-bell rang and Jock said quickly, 'Ah, people are arriving.'

It was Charlie Cunningham, Allan's old trainer, and Rigor Mortis his scout, followed by the District Nurse and a nurse under contract called Maryanne and two of Allan's friends who had stayed on to do postgraduate work. Jock marshalled them in and took them on a conducted tour. Geoffrey tagged along, to be polite. Jock's eyes, he could see, glistened as he retailed his achievements.

'It was quite a job, let me tell you. I had to widen all the door-frames and fix that ramp up the front path. Dorothy, bless her, says I'm a fully qualified electrician *and* plumber *and* decorator. Here we have the bedroom, Allan's room. Self-explanatory.' Jock pointed to the thick steel girder above the bed and the straps which hung down from it. Geoffrey had helped them select it through the Disabled Living people. Jock went on, excitedly, 'Vinyl flooring throughout. Special light switches. I re-wired the place for the Possum. Electric curtains. You can't imagine how often I fused the lights! Here's the kitchen, the galley, where young Maryanne will get the lad his food. There's an intercom connecting all the rooms. Listen, I'll show you. *One, two, three, testing, testing.* Now we come to the main room, the living room. Ah, you've put up Charlie's present, dear. Doesn't it look splendid there!' Jock pointed to a liquid-crystal thermometer of the kind executives have on their desks which Dorothy had put on the mantlepiece. 'The lad'll be able to read it from his wheelchair. Well done, Charlie!'

To Geoffrey the mantlepiece looked like an altar. On the first layer stood a line of Allan's athletic cups, each on a black plinth. Above these Jock had hung a panoply of photographs, all framed in what struck Geoffrey as rather funereal black beading. The centre photo was the one of Allan breasting the tape on the day he broke the mile record. Higher still, in an artful curve, were pinned the shields and plaques Allan had won at various times during his schooldays. It was a shrine.

'Dorothy spent hours cleaning the cups,' said Jock proudly.

At that moment Melanie arrived. She took one look at the mantlepiece and turned away. She said nothing.

Dorothy came up to Jock and took him by the sleeve. She held the gift that Rigor Mortis had brought for Allan. By the way she held it, it seemed to Geoffrey she thought it was infectious.

'Look what Arthur's brought,' she said in a whisper that could be clearly heard. The scout was next door. 'We *can't* give Allan that!'

It was a mouth-organ. Jock looked at Dorothy and Dorothy looked at Jock.

'Oh dear, a *mouth*-organ,' said Jock.

'*Do* something!' hissed Dorothy. "Quickly!"

Melanie stepped forward and took the instrument. 'I have an idea,' she said. 'I'll be back in a minute.' She left the room and Geoffrey heard the front door closing. He could see the immense look of relief on Jock's face as he went back to playing the host.

A car door slammed. Jock, who had been fiddling with the bottles of sherry, went to the window. Geoffrey followed. Everyone's eyes went with them. Was it Allan? It was Linda. She paid off a taxi and swept up the path and burst into the flat wearing a shaggy Afghan coat and a thick knitted hat.

'Oh good. I'm not late. Blasted trains, they're never on time.'

Geoffrey was taken aback by Linda's appearance. Her face was red from the cold and she wore no make-up. Beneath a simple green knitted dress she wore leg-warmers and sensible shoes. She looked lined, worn and tired. Obviously the outside world was tougher than it had looked from inside the ivory tower. But she'd lost none of her vitality. She radiated smiles and greetings to everyone and gave Geoffrey a kiss. Her skin was cold and dry and smelled faintly of make-up sticks and dressing-rooms. She'd left her dog behind.

Jock was behind her saying, 'You know everyone, Linda?' With Jock and Dorothy, they were twelve. The twelve apostles, thought Geoffrey. There was only one person Linda didn't know: Dr Wiseman. Wiseman was looking out of the back window into the garden, his hands in his pockets and his back to the room. Geoffrey overheard Jock saying in a low voice, 'That's John Wiseman, the neuro-chappie who did Allan's op. I thought it right he should come along too. He did his best for the lad, I suppose.'

Dorothy came in with a cut-glass bowl of avocado dip. She caught Jock's last remark and shot him a hard glance. Geoffrey suspected that, for some good reason, Doctor Wiseman was a subject on which Jock and Dorothy deeply disagreed.

'Can I get you a drink, Linda?' asked Jock.

'I'd love a Bloody Mary,' she said and shook her long fair hair.

'Well, actually, I thought sherry . . .'

'Sherry would be wonderful, Jock,' said Linda at once. She ran a bangled hand through her hair which Geoffrey noticed she'd streaked red. She took out a cigarette but then asked quickly, 'Is it okay to smoke in here?' Jock nodded, but she hesitated and put the cigarette back in its pack. No one was smoking.

Jock looked at his watch. 'He shouldn't be long now. It's just an hour's run from Stoke Mandeville, though I expect the ambulance will take it slowly.' He looked around the room, flushed with pride and excitement as Geoffrey could clearly see. He said, 'Just wait and see his face when he finds all of you here!'

'He's here!'

Dorothy let out the cry from the window. Jock quickly straightened the sherry glasses and everyone went to the window. An ambulance had drawn up at the kerb. Geoffrey could sense the suspense and uncertainty in the room. What was Allan going to be like? Most of them had visited him in hospital. He fitted into that special context, but would he fit *here* again?

The ambulance driver opened a flap at the back into a platform and went inside. A moment later he wheeled out a chair onto the platform, jumped down and lowered it to the street. Over the back of the wheelchair Geoffrey could see the top of Allan's dark hair. He could hear the driver's boots scrunching on the grimy frozen snow as he closed the ambulance door. The wheelchair hadn't moved.

Then, quite suddenly, it turned by itself. Allan sat facing the house. Someone next to Geoffrey dropped the net curtain, ashamed or afraid. Jock and Dorothy were out on the porch and Jock was already walking down the concrete ramp towards the gate. But the sight of Allan's face shook even Geoffrey. It was the face of a man aged by suffering. His dark eyes were sunk further than ever in their greyish hollows beneath his brows. His head, lean and angular, seemed to have grown too large for his body. It was the body of a wraith, a husk with all the juices sucked out. His face was neither young nor old, neither happy nor sad, neither angry nor resigned. And his eyes looked neither ahead nor to the side, but inwards, for the world Allan now inhabited lay within himself.

Jock reached his son and held out his hand involuntarily, converting it at once into a movement for the chair-handle. Allan had seen it. He didn't react. The wheelchair moved by itself. At first it looked even to Geoffrey as if Allan were smoking: he had a cigarette-holder in his mouth, connected by a flexible tube to the side of the chair. But this was no hookah. It was the control-pipe which drove and steered the wheelchair. It made an eerie picture.

46

Geoffrey felt a twinge of horror: it was as if he'd only learned for the first time that this miniscule movement, this slight puffing and sucking, this limited turning of the head, was virtually all the movement his friend was capable of making.

Allan Mann was totally paralysed from the neck down. He was a quadriplegic. He'd never again move more than the muscles in his face and neck.

Geoffrey felt the tears rising. He watched as Jock, Charlie and the scout lent their hands to push the wheelchair forwards up the snow-grimed path. Then Allan took his mouth away from the tube and turned towards them.

'Get your hands off!'

The three men recoiled. Charlie made as if to try and help again. But, from the gate behind them, came Melanie's voice. It was clear, quiet, gentle and authoritative.

'Leave him alone,' she commanded.

So they left Allan alone to drive up the pathway, to climb the ramp, to negotiate the front door, to steer into the living room and finally to come to a halt in front of the fireplace. Without any help.

Eight

'Well?' demanded Allan. 'Are you going to offer me a drink or just stand and gawp?'

No one moved. Charlie cleared his throat. Linda looked at the water-mark on her shoes. Wiseman peered into his empty glass. At last Jock stepped forward.

'Of course, of course, lad,' he hastened. He poured a half-glass of sherry, reflected on it, then filled it to the top. Allan had ordered no concessions to be made, Geoffrey knew. Jock put the glass to Allan's lips like a father not yet used to the baby's bottle.

Allan sniffed the glass. 'No Scotch, dad?'

Dorothy drew in her breath. 'You're not *drinking*, Allan?'

'Tilt the damn thing,' Allan ordered. 'I may be a cripple but I don't need teaching how to drink.'

Allan sucked in a mouthful and nodded to Jock to take the glass away. He took the mouthpiece between his lips and reversed the wheelchair so that his back was to the mantlepiece and he faced the room. A half-smile twisted his thin, pale lips. In a quiet voice, he said, 'Welcome to the freak show, friends.'

No one responded. They tried to carry on talking normally and not stare. It was very strained.

Geoffrey looked closely at Allan. His hair was institutionally short. Thinner and greyer than before, it looked as if it had been allowed to grow out for a month before parole from a madhouse. His forehead was lined with creases that fanned out vertically from two deep clefts in the centre of his brows. Geoffrey recalled

48

how his lines had always been horizontal: smile-lines and little flecked crow's-feet lighting up the corners of his eyes when he laughed. His face had changed shape, too. His nose was more prominent, more hooked. His cheeks had grown thin and translucent and his lips were no longer a young man's lips but had become thin, pallid ribbons on each side of a zip. Things for keeping other things in with.

Geoffrey was astonished how Allan dominated the room, however uneasy people felt in his presence. He was the focus of power. It defied the rules of body language. Allan was seated while the others were standing. Allan was deformed and abnormal, while the others were whole and sound. Allan was defenceless, the others strong and active. Yet, even when he sank back into his private world, Allan controlled the room.

'It's great to have you back, mate,' said Geoffrey and laid a hand on his shoulder. There was so little substance beneath the man's clothing. Allan, Allan, he cried to himself. Where's the real you? The Allan who should be coming home from an expedition to the Andes or the Paris-Dakar run or some international trials in Belgrade? Not this Allan, the hospital version, the Allan sitting before him. He forced himself to keep his hand on his shoulder.

Allan turned his head and looked up at Geoffrey. He raised an eyebrow as if to say, Is it really great to have me back?

Allan looked around the room. He knew exactly what was going through everybody's mind. They were looking to him for some kind of absolution. They were guilty they weren't suffering like that too.

It's ridiculous, absurd, pathetic. I'm supposed to be the patient, he thought. Why is up to me to heal the healthy? Why is that my job? It's hard enough being a cripple without having to forgive them all their insultingly childish deceptions and agree that it's a beautiful world, a well-ordered and harmonious world, *when it isn't*. When it's a disgusting, deformed, mediocre, chaotic, savage world.

Why can't they be real? Why can't they leave me alone?

Charlie, Rigor Mortis, Linda, Dorothy, Jock. Covering their embarrassment with false cheerfulness. Cheerfulness, that terrible, suffocating, strangulating British spirit. I had enough of that in hospital. Always 'Keep your pecker up, lad.' And,

'Mustn't grumble, son.' And, 'Look on the bright side of things.' The nurses thought they were Air Raid Wardens and made the whole hospital into a Salvation Army soup-kitchen. 'You're coming along fine' and 'It'll be all right in the end . . .'

It *won't* be all right in the end! This *is* the end!

Allan felt his jaw knotting and aching. He looked up into Geoffrey's face. Maybe Geoffrey understood. He fought to answer him without losing control. His words came out hoarse and cracked, from a point outside him.

'Yes, it's okay being back, I suppose.'

Dorothy held out the mouth-organ to Allan and with it a strange fabric-covered wire frame.

'Look what Arthur's brought you, darling,' she said. 'And Melanie went out and got this frame thing. It's a stand for playing without hands.'

Allan slowly focused on the instrument and in the same hollow, croaking voice, said, 'Thanks. Very thoughtful of you both.'

Geoffrey was watching from the window where he was talking to Wiseman. Without meaning to, he'd adopted the same body posture: his arms crossed and cradling the sherry glass and his legs folded at the ankles.

Linda had moved over to Allan and went on one knee so as to be on the same level. She fidgeted with her rings, perhaps because she wasn't smoking. Allan hated cigarettes. He raised an eyebrow quizzically.

'So, Linda, how's the casting couch? Got to top of the bill yet?'

Linda pulled a face and looked at her hands, a working actress's hands. In a controlled voice she said, 'That's not necessary, Allan. Look, if you're mad at me because I couldn't get up to see you more than a few times . . .'

'Three times,' corrected Allan coldly. 'Once a quarter. Like the gas bill.'

'I've been working late every night. I really haven't had any time for myself. I'm sorry, Allan. Now you're back in Oxford maybe we could see more of each other.'

'No time for yourself? Precious little for me either.' Allan's lips were thin and bloodless and they tightened as he spoke. 'Why did you come today, Linda? Conscience troubling you? Don't tell me. I'll guess. It's a quarter-day.'

'*Allan*,' pleaded Linda. She put out a hand to squeeze his arm. It froze on his sleeve.

'Don't *Allan* me. Say what you mean. Oxford isn't any nearer to London than the hospital. The truth is, you can't bear being near me any more. Admit it. You only came because you thought you had to.'

'Allan, you're not making this easy for me.' Linda's hazel eyes were filling with tears. Geoffrey knew she had loved Allan and wished she could love him still.

'Easy for *you*? Oh, I'm sorry! How should I make it easier for you? Get up out of this chair and do a hopscotch on the floor and say, "Okay, folks, the joke's over, I was only kidding?"' Allan moved his head closer to Linda's. Little flecks of spit settled on her cheeks but she didn't wipe them away. 'You want to know how easy it is for *me*? Listen! Can you hear the motor? That's my cushion. A whole big rippling vibrating cushion to sit on. You should see the sores I get without it.'

'Don't, Allan. Stop.'

Allan's voice was growing harder. People in the room stopped talking and Wiseman went and stood behind the wheelchair. Allan went on, 'Now look down the side of my leg, Linda. Do you see the bulge? *Do you?* That's what we in the wheelchair brigade call a kipper. In a minute my sherry will come trickling down into it.'

Wiseman cleared his throat. 'You've gone far enough now, Allan.'

Allan ignored Wiseman. 'How do I shit? You'll be wondering that. I'll tell you. Shitting is suppositories every day and once a week a hand up the arse. That's shitting . . .'

Linda stood up, white-faced and shaking. Her voice was blocked, hurt, angry. She managed to say, 'I'll get you some more sherry, Allan.'

Allan had begun to laugh. It was a hiccoughing, panting sound, a rictus of a laugh. It became a choking sob. He hung his head on his chest. Melanie got up from the other side of the room and went and knelt down in front of him. She drew her long black hair over one ear and looked at him with worry in her dark eyes. Her voice was subdued.

'You won't remember, but I was a cripple as a child,' she said

51

quietly. 'I had polio in both legs. They managed to cure it and they're better — not perfect, but better. But one thing I learned. There's no use in being angry or taking your frustrations out on yourself or other people. It doesn't do any good. It's fruitless, believe me.'

Allan stared fiercely at Melanie. She held his eye. After a while his face softened and a hint of a smile lit the corners of his mouth. It seemed to Geoffrey like a smile of recognition; Allan had found an echo of his own suffering. With a touch of self-mockery, Allan replied, 'I have my way. You have yours. I'll make out. Okay?'

'I know you will,' said Melanie.

Allan hesitated. His thin lips softened more. He dropped his eyes and said, 'But thanks anyway, Melanie.'

It was late in the afternoon before everyone had gone. Jock and Dorothy faced a long drive back. Linda had taken a lift with John Wiseman back to London. Only Geoffrey and Melanie remained. The nurse, Maryanne, was working in the kitchen. Allan was exhausted.

Their conversation meandered slowly. The central heating gurgled in the pipes and sporadically the headlamps of passing cars sprayed beams of light across the walls and ceiling. The flat was insufferably hot. It seemed already to have acquired the characteristic foetid stuffiness of a hospital.

Melanie was reading a copy of the *Journal of Anthropology*. Every now and then she'd murmur something like, 'What rubbish Piaget talks!' or, 'Do you suppose Levi-Strauss has ever *seen* a gorilla when he goes on about deep structures . . . ?' Geoffrey felt a pang of something close to jealousy. Yes, he envied Melanie her certitude. She never seemed to doubt what she thought. She made such sure-footed judgements, so definitive and straightforward. She was ten years younger than him but ten lifetimes older. If you believed in such things – and he didn't – Melanie was an old soul. She seemed to belong closer to Allan in that respect.

Allan's head was slumped on his chest and his eyes lay hidden within some deep and private internal space. After a while he stirred. In a half-whisper he said, 'Geoffrey, get the mouth-organ and fix it up, will you?'

Allan moved his wheelchair over to the window. Behind the

rouched netting the afternoon was ebbing into night. Geoffrey rigged up the instrument on its stand on Allan's shoulder.

'There we are,' he said, bringing it to Allan's lips.

'Not so close, man. I'm not going to eat the bloody thing.'

Allan bent his head forward and began to suck and blow. It made an awkward, unmusical sound: melancholy and discordant. It was a sound with solitary and tragic associations. Geoffrey felt the mood taking him over. But quite suddenly Allan stopped. He let the instrument clatter to the floor.

'Take it away,' he commanded tightly.

He spun his wheelchair round so that he was facing the mantlepiece. The atmosphere was thick with frustration and suppressed violence. He stared at the array of trophies all over the mantlepiece and wall. In the same tight, fierce voice he said to Geoffrey, 'And get rid of those things too. Get them down and throw them out. Every damn one of them.'

Nine

Geoffrey Fish tried it out. He tried it out the following morning,
alone in the office adjoining his lab. He wanted to imagine what it
would really be like.

He made it into a game he played against himself and spoke to
himself as though he were a child. First he had to spell out the
rules, and then the game could begin.

Right. Are we ready? (He spoke with his eyes half-closed, the
chair bending under his weight.) Okay. Here are the rules.

First, what you *can* do. You can:

> smile; pull faces; stick out your tongue; suck your teeth;
> sneer and snigger; giggle and gaggle; bite your lip; look up at
> the ceiling; half-turn to see who's come into the room behind
> you (no more than a half-turn, mind); wink and blink; sneeze
> and wheeze; sniff and snort; speak and listen; do your
> favourite party-trick, the one where you move your ears
> without moving your forehead.

Get it? Now for what you *can't* do. You can't:

> put this book down; scratch; clean your ears; rub your eyes;
> shave; nip round the corner; fill the kettle; answer the door
> or the phone; blow your nose; dress or undress; undress
> someone you love; wash and dry yourself; boil an egg; write
> a cheque; open a letter; pick up a pencil; pour a drink; get up,
> let alone walk; walk, let alone run; run, let alone win races.'

Geoffrey, you're *smoking*! You can't do that! Who's there to open the pack for you, to take out the cigarette, to put it in your lips? Who's there to light it, to wait and catch the ash before it falls off, to take it out and stub it in the ashtray? Exactly. Smoking is positively out of the question. But that was a dummy run. Now we'll play for keeps, okay?

Think. Think how you are sitting. Upright or lounging? In a chair or on a bed? Let your mind travel over your body, from feet to scalp. Your legs are crossed — where? At the ankles? At the knees? Which elbow are you leaning on? Your shoulders are sloping, already there is a slight pain down your back and your neck needs stretching.

Right. Hold it there.

You use glasses for reading? They tend to get sweaty at the bridge, don't they? You like to readjust them from time to time. It's only a small, unconscious movement to relieve a trifling irritation. But when you can't move your hand it becomes monumental.

Your scalp. Just over the right ear. It's itching. It's only a small itch, but there's nothing you can do about it. Remember when you were on parade in the Army and you weren't allowed to make the slightest movement? You had the same itch then. And you were dying to scratch it. Everything else faded from importance. Note, listen, follow the itch in its progress towards agony. Already it is turning to pain, a pain that is beginning to spread, to spread up the whole side of your face.

Ha! Caught you! You were looking at your watch. Positively out of order. A watch, you have a *watch*? Who do you suppose will wind it up for you at night?

What is left to you, then?

Well, you can still cry. Though after nine months you'll have cried all you can cry. The crying and the howling, the outrage and the disbelief, these must pass in time. But there will still be some indestructible deposit left after the process. Most probably anger. Anger principally at the *event*, that it should ever have happened at all. Anger that there should exist something that has been done and can't be undone. Anger with other people for their fatuity and their pity, their morbid prying, their emasculating helpfulness.

Your back is to the wall and the wall is in the innermost

chamber of your self. Beyond here there is no retreat, except into madness. This point is your own, naked mind. Your head is the only place you can inhabit, it is the only place you have left to go. Maybe, just possibly, from here you can start out again and begin gradually and tentatively to grope your way back.

I, Geoffrey, tried this game this morning because of something Melanie said to me last night over a cup of coffee in that plaza they have in her Department. Oh, you know how to paralyse monkeys, she said scornfully. But do you know what it can be like to be paralysed yourself? Can you possibly imagine? Typical Melanie. Knowing what she'd had wrong with her legs as a child, I couldn't really throw it back and ask how *she* knew. Anyway, I'd made some glib, facetious remark that was meant to be encouraging about Allan. Something to the effect that, with the extraordinary *redundancy* in the human brain, with all that volume of cells unallocated to specific functions and thus available to be set to work, I was sure that, given time of course, it should be possible to regenerate in the brain all the functions the organism had lost. Facetious, because of course Allan hasn't lost his mental faculties, only the physical ones. But it was clumsy, I have to admit. Melanie flew off the handle. I know when she's really angry. She plaits her hair into knots. I expect it's what her gorillas do.

It felt strange sitting there like a stone, playing a secret game with myself. Strange and slightly mischievous and shameful at the same time. I stayed rock-still in my chair for twenty minutes, maybe twenty-five. The phone rang often. Someone tapped at the door and I called, Come in. It was Roach with a bundle of periodicals. He said, Are you okay, Geoff?, full of false concern. My scalp itched like fury. A hair had got caught doubled-up in my nose. It was sheer agony.

Funny thing: in their cages the monkeys had quite suddenly gone quiet. They stayed quiet the whole time. It was Armistice Day in the jungle. I should award a red poppy to each.

Twenty-five minutes is not long, compared with twenty-five years, compared with a young man's lifetime.

Ten

During the first months, when winter gradually gave ground to spring and the University broke up and re-convened, Allan took no special interest in his surroundings. He made no attempt to impose his own personality or taste on the flat but left it just as Jock had made it — part morgue, part monk's cell, part hospital, part prison. It could have been an annexe to the hospital.

The flat was functional in the way that was incompatible with beauty. All the surfaces were made for wiping down, the chair fabrics for resisting spills, the curtains for easy cleaning. And so much was white. Why? You only had to clean white things all the more. Was it to show up germs, as though germs were little visible black specks? Or because white was intrinsically clean and thereby closer to godliness? White vinyl on the floors. White Formica on the table-tops. White plastic lampshades. White plastic knives and spoons, caravan-style. But Allan scarcely noticed. When he did notice, he didn't care. His life was not there, among his surroundings. What life he had was inside, within himself.

The layout of the flat was simple. His bedroom was at the back and overlooked a garden which had been divided down its length and which, at the far end, gave onto the University Parks behind a line of tall poplars. The room faced west and in the summer the sun set precisely behind the trees. Allan would spend long hours at the bedroom window, gazing out sightlessly. He liked to sit in the semi-dark, leaving the fluorescent lights off. Most of the flat was lit by this panel lighting, an idea Jock must have picked up from the hospital.

The bed itself was high and could be tilted by a motor to get him into a sitting position. It had two metal bars that caged him in, in case he had a spontaneous spasm in the night and fell out. It also helped when Maryanne, the contract nurse, came to move his bolsters, to change his position and to fix on the straps from the hoist. The hoist was a steel girder at right-angles to the bed. Having belted him in, she could lift him out and down into his chair. She'd strap him into the chair by ties around his waist and legs, she'd check the battery level and the ripple cushion and then wheel him into the bathroom. The door had a two-way hinge, like a cat-flap, so that Allan could push his way through from either side.

Between his bedroom and the spare room where Maryanne lived for five nights a week was the bathroom. The bath was a kind of modified Sitz-bath. Overhead was another girder and hoist. The straps were of thick plastic and a shower curtain could be pulled loosely round the whole bath. The knobs were chrome, the bath and surrounding tiles white. However, in the way that people associate baths with the sea, the floor tiles were in a pebbled beach pattern: Jock's taste. Every morning Maryanne would wash Allan down. Sometimes he'd had an erection and the kipper-bag had come adrift. There was always something to be cleaned up. In the corner was a large white enamel bin for his night-shirts. And, at the far end of the steel girder, the lavatory. After the wash she'd leave him sitting over it for a while, in the hope that gravity would save him from the glove.

Allan would be dressed in the bathroom, hoisted back into his chair and a car-rug placed over his legs. The flat was kept equatorially hot; not being able to stir his circulation, he had to be kept warm. Then came breakfast, the next step in a highly ordered routine. The kitchen had been made out of two rooms and led, via a back door, into the garden. A vast white washing-machine was permanently churning and regurgitating away in the corner. A white-topped table was fixed to the wall at a height where Allan could be easily fed. Jock had built a nest of drawers in the wall for the cutlery, the pots and pans. There was a special extractor over the stove so that the window didn't have to be opened too often. Above the fridges were shelves and cupboards full of cans of soup and vegetables, many of them the stewed fruit Allan had to have for his digestion. To one side was a medicine cabinet containing his pills and the hypodermics Maryanne would have to use *in case*. One of the advantages of being paralysed, he once said to her, was that you didn't feel injections.

Breakfast was served. Maryanne clipped the head off a soft-boiled egg.

'Not caviar kedgeree *again*,' complained Allan.

'Has my lord lost his appetite?' she asked, spooning the egg into Allan's mouth.

'Your lord has lost none of his appetites, Maryanne. Only the ability to do anything about them.'

'He's still got quite a tongue,' she said.

Maryanne was probably twenty-nine or thirty. She was slim but strong and had short dark hair and lips that were red without make-up. She cooked well and gave Allan a *cordon bleu* dinner on the anniversary of his accident. She smelled good, not starchy like the nurses in the hospital. Whatever mess she had to clear up for him, she always smelled fresh. When they were alone together, he played the part of a lecherous old roué and Maryanne the innocent maid. It was a form of inverted flirtation. He did it deliberately. It hurt, but it was also a catharsis of a kind.

After breakfast, he would go to work. The living room was also his study, less monastic than the other rooms because it was lined with books, but spartan nevertheless. It looked towards the front of the house, through white ruched net curtains and leaded window-panes, down the gravel path to the street. His table was in front of the window but he spent most of his time at his three book-stands in front of the shelves, on which every morning Maryanne put up the books he was going to study: Winfield on Tort, case precedents in Jurisprudence, textbooks on Roman Law . . . By a suck-puff instruction on his Possum, he could turn the pages back and forth on the stands. It was hard, but not as hard as the work itself. Winfield was the best sleeping-drug Allan had ever known. He seriously considered suggesting Wiseman should put it on his prescription list.

On the table lay the tape-recorder and a modified typewriter. Again, by sucking and puffing down his mouth-tube in a particular way, he could move a marker across a matrix to the letter he wanted. But it was slow, agonisingly slow for a man whose mind worked faster than most. And someone else had to put in the paper and take it out. He hardly ever used the machine. For his essays, his tutor, Dr Esther Fry, would send round an emanuensis. Or else he'd dictate into the tape-recorder and get it typed up at the Law Faculty.

There was a sideboard at the other end of the room, which, because of the L-shaped layout of the flat, also had a window onto the back garden, although a privet hedge gone to seed blocked out most of the light. The sideboard housed the sherry (which Jock brought over) and the whisky (which Allan got Maryanne to buy), together with the old cut glasses he'd had in his college rooms. There were invariably flowers on top. People still brought him flowers, fruit and sweets. They meant well, but it was an expression of how they saw him. Geoffrey, however, brought a small pharmacopeia from time to time: special cocktails of Amytal and Preludin, and once even some genuine reserpine from the Himalayas. These were tranquillisers and anti-depressants. Allan wasn't ready yet for a real buzz, Geoffrey calculated.

The chairs were PVC-covered in imitation tweed check: Jock had gone overboard on the effect. The floor, too, was patterned linoleum. Without rugs or carpets, the place felt cold and clinical. From his Possum, Allan could open and close the curtains. He could operate the front door-lock when someone buzzed. He could dial the telephone and, if people rang long enough, receive calls. He could turn the lights in each room on and off. And he had a special alarm system in case of emergency, only it didn't work when it was really needed. Once during the first weeks Maryanne came back from shopping to find him sprawled half out of the chair. Only the body-strap round his waist held him up. He'd had a huge spasm and the chair had almost toppled over. It had caught against the table, with Allan's head a foot from the ground. His face was bright purple and his eyes bulged out of their sockets. He was choking.

Work would be interrupted by morning coffee at 10.45 and lunch at 12.30, very precisely. Then the afternoon nap, in the chair, generally in the bedroom in front of the large window overlooking the garden. With the rug over his legs, Allan felt like a bathchair geriatric. He liked to sleep through the early

60

afternoons, for summer had now arrived and this was the hour he should have been out there on the track, training.

Twice a week he had a tutorial. He could, in principle, get to the Law Library in the St Cross building under his own steam. Melanie had once walked it with him, to work out a route that avoided steep inclines and difficult kerbs. But for the time being he let the ambulance come and deliver him there and back. He'd sit in the back, keeping his eyes down. He didn't want to see the girls in their summer dresses, the joggers in their tracksuits, the cyclists laden with books and racquets. It hurt him to see those teeming, mobile hordes. And to be seen by them.

His tutor, Dr Esther Fry, was a tough taskmaster. She was short, wrinkled and leathery, with a fez of completely white hair. She seemed to be even harder on Allan than the other pupils. She'd tear his essays to pieces in the tutorials in front of the others. She argued hard with him and forced him to defend himself every inch of the way. There was only one concession she made to his disability: she changed the tutorials to the main college hall, for it had a Gothic doorway wide enough for his chair. And she organised a roster of first-year students to read to him in a special room in the library reserved for the blind. Otherwise she was so strict it seemed cruel. But Allan understood. And, grudgingly, he liked her for it.

He would then be returned to his whitewashed cell. He welcomed it. The flat was safe, secure, hygienic, ordered. He had only himself to cope with there. And yet it was about this time of day, the *heure bleue*, that he'd be overcome by another of his violent waves of depression.

And he'd turn to music. The cassette-recorder had an automatic feeder. He would sit there, his head sunk onto his chest, as the chaste sounds of Pachelbel and Palestrina filled the living room. Early music, C. P. E. Bach, Purcell, Telemann. Cerebral music. Music to take the soul out of the body.

61

Eleven

Linda paid Allan a surprise visit one evening. She didn't tell him, of course, but she'd come up with John Wiseman who was attending a dinner of the British Neurological Society in Oxford. Nor did she say they'd booked into the Randolph Hotel together.

She was looking tired but happy, and less pinched than recently. Maybe it was spring in the air, maybe the success of her television series, or maybe it was a man in her life. Allan didn't ask. He avoided her eye, though he could see her in the pool of light from the table-lamp, fiddling with the tassels of an Edwardian shawl and every now and then running a hand through her hair. She tried not to smoke in Allan's flat. At one point he looked up at her, winced and fought back the tears of frustration. He took a breath to speak, then dropped his eyes and let the breath out.

'Tell me,' said Linda tenderly. She reached out her hand a little towards him as he sat with his back to the mantlepiece in the half-light. When he finally spoke, he didn't recognise his own voice. It was rasping, bitter; it rode on the edge of something dangerous.

'Blenheim. Remember Blenheim?'

Linda caught her breath and put a hand to her mouth. 'Oh God,' she said.

'Do you remember what we talked about that time in Blenheim Park?'

'You mustn't think about that.'

'We made a vow together. Do you remember?'

'Yes, but . . .'

'*What* did we vow to each other, Linda? I want you to tell me.'

'Allan, please!'

'*Answer me!* We made a promise which we'd never break. Remember?'

Linda's hands flew to her hair and her bracelets rattled. She said nothing, waiting with horror.

'Linda, I want you to do it for me.'

'I *can't*! We promised, but that was then.'

'Because *then* you loved me,' said Allan. 'And now you don't.' He looked up at the white ceiling, white even in the half-light of evening. White everywhere: white walls, white ceiling, white uniforms. The house that Jock built. A white cell.

Linda said faintly, 'I couldn't do it, not even then. It's wrong. It's immoral.'

'Putting a cat or a dog out of its misery, is that immoral, Linda? Can you imagine what it's like for me, imprisoned in this . . . this useless carcase?'

'Allan!'

'You don't love me enough. You never did,' he said bitterly. 'The fact is, you find me disgusting. And I make you feel guilty.'

Linda got up and shook him violently by the shoulders. Her hazel eyes were wide and angry. 'Stop it!' she cried. 'Pull yourself together, Allan Mann! Snap out of this self-pity. It's self-indulgent. Think what you *have* got going for you. You've got your mind, your brain, your*self*. You'll end up on the Queen's Bench if you only keep going with your Law. Stop talking this defeatist shit!'

Allan turned his head as far away from her as he could. Through gritted teeth he said, 'Okay, Linda. I have other friends, you know.'

'Geoffrey? Geoffrey wouldn't do it either. Don't be such a fool. You're *not* some dog that's been run over. You've come all this way and now you're thinking of giving up. I'm ashamed of you, Allan!'

'Ashamed of me,' he echoed cynically. He felt defeated. He wished he hadn't broached the subject at all. No one understood. He'd come this far by himself, and he'd have to do the rest by himself.

But how? At times seriously, at times as a game, he'd wondered *how* he could end it all for himself. Everyone else had at least some means. They could walk along to the chemist's or start up the car in the garage or jump off an apartment block. Even if he could get to a chemist's, who was going to unscrew the bottle for him? How can a paralysed man jump, God damn it? And everyone else at least *knew* there was a way out if ever they should need it. They had the possibility; he didn't. No one would give him that. It seemed that by removing the possibility of death they had also removed the possibility of life.

Linda bravely tried to change the subject but Alan had switched off. When finally it was time for her to go, she came forward to kiss him. As her lips touched his forehead, he jerked away. '*Don't!*' he whispered harshly.

He decided he shouldn't see her again. It was too painful. It was different with Maryanne. Maryanne only knew him as a cripple; that was the *given* in their relationship. With Linda he was the has-been athlete, reduced to a useless and impotent wreck. A failure who couldn't even succeed in killing himself without help.

The following morning John Wiseman paid Allan a surprise visit. He arranged for a psychotherapist to visit him once a week. And he prescribed a new pink pill for Allan to take after breakfast every day. At the time, Allan made no connection between Linda's visit and that of John Wiseman. He was too wrapped up in his own self.

The psychotherapist belonged to the Let-It-All-Hang-Out school. Curing a patient meant getting him to let go, to open up and bring it all forth. She was a solidly-built woman with an eager manner. The tragedy of Allan's case for her was, quite simply, that he couldn't take part in the ultimate therapy: one of her group feeling sessions. So she had to make do with a tape-recorder. Allan could operate this using the Possum suck-and-blow controls. Whenever he felt a bout of depression coming on, he was to wheel himself over to the table and speak into the recorder, speak anything at all but just let it all come out. The whole notion revolted him.

From time to time he did use the recorder, though it was mostly to shock and spite the therapist. He did an imitation article on the pretty young nurse Maryanne in the style of *Penthouse*. He invented surreal dreams loaded with erotic symbolism in case the woman was a Freudian. He sang lewd rugby songs. But nothing shocked her. She simply paid her weekly visit and emptied the machine like a chamber-pot and said enthusiastically, 'Well *done!*' Allan found her response unsatisfying and after a while gave up the shock tactics.

One day the psychotherapist asked him to describe his early morning routine into the tape-recorder. He started off well.

I wake up before six. It's a habit I picked up in hospital. They make the rounds at six, doing a body-count. I lie in bed and luxuriate. There's no alarm clock to turn off. There's no radio to tell me of the crises of the night. I'm not one to stick my head under the pillow for another few stolen minutes of sleep.

Nor do I get myself up. Maryanne gets me up. I don't wash my face. I don't shave. I don't take out a shirt, sniff the armpits to see if it'll do another day, none of that. I don't stub my toes on the skirting, trip over the cat, knock the alka-seltzer bottle off the shelf. You won't catch me filling a kettle or putting an egg on to boil or getting the toast stuck in the toaster.

I live like a prince. I am waited on hand and foot. I don't lift a finger. My shoes are polished for me. My mail is opened for me and read to me. Did even the most luxurious Roman emperor have the sleep rubbed out of his eyes for him? Did the most uxorious of the French kings have a slave-girl to dig out the wax from his royal ears? Who held the handkerchief when His Imperial Majesty the Tsar of All the Russias blew his nose? Ha! I live better than a prince! They didn't even have it so good on Parnassus!

But that wasn't how the day started. That said nothing at all, nothing of the thousand things that went on before Maryanne came into the room. The process of waking, the little process that everyone else took for granted, for Allan was packed with a myriad of microscopic terrors.

That day, for instance. A dream had woken him, an erotic dream. The girl wasn't Linda, though she had a bit of Linda's mouth. She had long dark hair and loving hands that reached out

65

to him and a smile that beckoned him constantly towards her. They were in an airport one moment, and then on a grassy bank. Her smile said, There's no hurry, we have eternity . . . Because they were each other's there was no urgency, just a slow, sweet, heavy-loaded fusion, so complete, so inevitable . . .

But he woke. It was Maryanne's alarm clock from her room. He tried to pretend that the alarm was the dream and the reality was where he'd been. But the image faded, left him. And then it came. The thick, fat, giddy wave of panic that smacked into him like the first oncoming of a heavy dose of amphetamine. He couldn't feel himself breathing. He became frantic, frantic for air. Frantic to get free.

Then he thought, calmly, Right, I'll just reach up and pull myself out of bed and there we go. He reached up. Nothing happened. The command was disobeyed somewhere along the line.

Then he got angry. He could feel the tears trickling hotly down his cheeks. He beat his head on the pillows, back and back and sideways and upwards, beating himself senseless against the impossibly soft wall that refused to concuss him.

Sometimes he was lucky. He'd got a phantom pain in his right leg. It told him he was still connected to a body. It whispered hints, too. *Maybe*, it said. *Maybe* I'll come back and spread a little round your body, slowly at first, creeping my fingers around your thighs and calves, infusing you with feeling again. Yes, he'd cry to himself. Yes, I'd do anything for that. Name the price! But no one came forward to do the deal. And the pain crept away as it had come.

Sometimes he wasn't even that lucky. Then he'd use his old running trick. He'd imagine the panic was a writhing, oily creature like an octopus. He had to get it into this box and then ram the lid shut. It would only stay shut if he kept talking, talking, thinking, thinking. The noise of his thinking would keep it in there. So he'd start thinking. Not about anything outside. He began with his breathing. He couldn't feel his lungs rising and falling, but he could feel and hear his throat. So he closed his throat to produce a kind of rasping which he could actually feel. Then he'd explore other sounds. He fluttered his epiglottis as if he was snoring. Then he alternated the breath in quick succession between his throat and nose. The vocabulary of breathing sounds was limitless. He could write music. Mann's First Symphony for Nose and Larynx.

Then there were the sounds from Maryanne's room. He imagined he was sitting still because it was a concert and he was the audience. Not a movement, not a cough. The heating gurgled. Maryanne was in the bathroom. He had to listen, but he tried not to imagine what the sounds meant. And yet he did. Shortly she'd be tapping on the door. It was a nice thing to do, suggesting that he did have some privacy to respect, although in a minute she'd be fixing the sheath back on if it had come off in the night and turning him on his side and rubbing spirit onto his back. And then that most unprivate thing of all, which was foreshadowed by the sound of her snapping on a surgical glove to get to work on his bowels while the room slowly began to fill with the stink.

But there were other times when none of these devices worked. The lid of the box opened like a coffin in a horror movie and out crept the tentacles that would fasten themselves around his throat. There was nothing he could do then. He felt he would burst. He bit his lip till it bled. He squeezed his eyes so tight that they saw white. He wrinkled his face so that even the angel of death would fly by and pass him over.

Then he wanted to die. Just *not to be*.

Twelve

And then Jock died.

Once a week he'd come down from Manchester and wage battle with the wilderness of the garden. He'd set his hand to making a crazy-paving pathway down the garden that was wide enough for Allan's chair, so that the lad could travel down to the fairies by himself. This project, on which Jock laboured while other men were at church or washing their cars, was to be his last. The garden won the battle. One Sunday in early July Dorothy was in the kitchen. She heard a cry and the fall of a large stone. She rushed out to find Jock crumpled over the path. His cancer had come out of hiding.

It was a quick passing. Quiet, relatively painless, frequently tearful, but quick. In his struggle to clutch onto life, Jock began to understand for the first time the furious zest which had consumed his son and driven him to excel. Waxy-faced and wasting away, Jock lay in his hospital bed on the day that Allan visited him and tried to tell his son that he *understood*, that life itself was the only thing of any value, that he'd gladly buy back his life at any price, even at the price of being a cripple. But once again Jock was out of tune with his son. The fight had gone out of Allan. It was better to die like Jock, he thought, than to be condemned to live a living death.

The therapist, still paying her weekly visits to the flat, waited for the reaction of shock and grief that a son was supposed to feel upon the death of his father. And for the counter-reaction, the

68

new sense of responsibility, of being the new head of family, of walking in the shadow of no one any longer. But it was not like that. A kind of angry resentment took hold of Allan. It took hold of Dorothy too. For Dorothy it was as if Jock had run off with another woman. For Allan it was more a kind of thoughtlessness, an act of negligence on Jock's part. Why? Because his death meant two things: Maryanne had to go and Dorothy move into the flat in her place.

Jock had commuted most of his pension to buy and fix up the Oxford flat. Even with the small life insurance sum, there was no income and precious little capital left after the mortgages. Dorothy had to sell the Manchester home, put the double bed and lounge cabinet into storage and move in with Allan. Maryanne could no longer be afforded. Dorothy had done a training course years before and could take over Maryanne's nursing job. The District Nurse would now come in every other day and, for the month of September, it was arranged that Dorothy would stay in a small residential home round the corner and learn her new duties from Maryanne. But however much Maryanne could teach Dorothy about the drugs, the apparatus and the routines, she couldn't teach her how to treat her son, the patient.

Allan grew to dread those mornings when it was his mother's turn to come in and change, wash and dress him. She seemed to treat him like a horse she was afraid of. *Don't show your fear*: that was what they told you. *Be forceful, confident, positive.* Allan knew that it was to conceal her fear that Dorothy always talked, talked and kept talking.

'No more bad dreams, dear? You know, I've been discussing it with Maryanne.'

Allan could hear her snapping on the surgical glove as she approached him from the rear. He knew what was coming next. The household routine was so unvaried that the same subjects and thoughts were gone through over and over again. The therapist had let Dorothy listen to the tape-recorder and one particular erotic dream Allan had graphically recounted. Dorothy took it bravely, clinically, but deep down he knew she was shocked. Shocked but somehow fascinated. This was what she was thinking of, he knew, this and not his nightmares, when she spoke of his *bad dreams*.

'I'm sure it's something you're eating, dear. Or something you're not getting. Maryanne seems to think it's quite normal. 'How can it be *normal*,'' I said to her, ''how can it be normal when it's been going on for ages?'' I'll have another word with the D.N. She's so much more . . . experienced.'

Talk, keep talking. Allan bit his lip. Dorothy rolled him onto his back. He shut his eyes. He couldn't feel anything but he couldn't bear to look at his mother's face. Her expression said, This is just a job, a job like any other. I'll get through it if I don't think about it too much. Even when petted and fussed over as a child, the only child, Allan had never felt so suffocated by intimacy and good intentions.

'We'll soon have you cleaned up and ship-shape. When I've done your hair I'll put your books up, dear. Which ones do you want today? No, don't tell me yet. You know I'll only forget.'

Maryanne put her head around the door. She looked pert, bright, pretty. 'Did you sleep well, Allan?'

'He's been having those bad dreams,' answered Dorothy. She finished straightening his tie and smoothing down the collar. 'I'll just go and fetch his spare battery. This one's almost flat. It's amazing how he gets through them.'

When Dorothy had left the room, Maryanne came up and, glancing quickly at the swing door behind her, said in a whisper, 'You've been spitting out your pills, haven't you! I saw a whole pile of them behind the fridge. Dr Wiseman specially prescribed them.'

'Wiseman just wants to make me into one of his vegetables. He wants to institutionalise me. You don't want to tame me, do you, Maryanne? You like me wild and sinful.'

Maryanne smiled and began brushing his hair. She laid her hand on the nape of his neck and brushed with long, slow sweeps. 'I cleared them up. Your mother won't find out.'

There was a silence. Desperately trying to be cheerful, he said, 'So you're walking out on me, Maryanne. Deserting me for another. Faithless, that's what you are.'

'I've told you, my boyfriend's the jealous type. We can't go on meeting like this. Sssh! Your mother's coming.'

Dorothy came back with the spare battery. She stood for a moment in front of him. 'How nice the lad looks today, doesn't he, Maryanne?' she said with delight.

70

Allan looked up and fixed his mother with his deep-set eyes. He could feel two spots of heat rising on his cheeks.

'Mother, I want Maryanne to stay.'

Dorothy faltered. For a moment it looked as if she'd drop the battery. She glanced quickly at Maryanne, sensing betrayal. 'Allan, please. Don't let's go through all that again. It's been decided.'

'I'll chuck up my degree and get a job. Reading for the O.U.P. or reviewing. Something will turn up. But I want Maryanne to stay.'

Dorothy put down the battery and went to open the window. Then she busied herself rearranging the bed and bundling the dirty sheets into the linen basket. She took refuge in talk.

'This is the most sensible solution, dear, we all know it is. Dr Wiseman and the D.N. agree. Of course I'd love it if she could stay. But she just can't and we'll have to make do without her. I'm sorry if you don't want your old mother living with you, Allan dear, but it can't be helped.'

'Oh God,' he said quietly to himself. Then he went silent. It was hopeless. His lifeline was being severed. In a week Maryanne and all that she meant to him would be gone.

Maryanne duly left. Dorothy took over running the house and Allan's life. She carried on the routine with a brave and cheerful front. He was very quiet and introverted and snapped at her much less. She felt on stronger ground and was prepared to give it time. After all, the poor lad had just lost his father.

The Friday afternoon of the following week was wet and grey. Dorothy was out for the afternoon; she'd gone for a job interview in the Personnel department of the main local department store. It would be part-time work, to make ends meet. Allan hadn't finished his week's study. He just couldn't. Instead, he sat staring out of his bedroom window at the blurry outline of the poplars at the bottom of the garden. The drizzle blotted out the pathway so that he couldn't see the place where the crazy paving ended and his father had fallen. The white of his bedroom walls was muted to match the grey outside. The house was quiet.

He sat for an hour, perhaps two. Slowly he reached for the mouthpiece and turned his wheelchair to face the room. He looked it over, inspecting everything in a different way. No, there was nothing there.

He went into the kitchen. He knew it all. The stove was electric. The knife drawer was shut. The medicine cupboard was out of reach. Nothing sharp projected. The table corners had been carefully trimmed with vinyl. Even if he could fill the sink he couldn't reach to get his head in it. The front door was on the latch, too, so there was no chance of charging out into the street.

Slowly he turned the wheelchair round. The kitchen door was held open by a rubber wedge. Down the corridor, on the right, was Dorothy's room. Hanging from the architrave over the door was a jacket and skirt she'd brought back from the cleaners that morning. It was still in its polythene bag.

Mesmerised, he propelled himself towards it. There was a caution printed at the bottom, reading *Danger: keep away from children.* Could it be done?

He manoeuvred his chair so that he was facing the door. The bottom of the bag was just below head-height, but it was hanging too far away. He reversed the chair and charged feebly at the door. It stood firm, closed.

Then he had it. He turned so that now his back was directly against the door. By wriggling his head he managed to get in and under the wide opening of the polythene bag, but it still only covered his shoulders. It was too loose and the air flowed easily in and out. Carefully, cautiously, he took the lining of the skirt in his teeth. He pulled. The wire hanger began to give. It bent further. Suddenly it gave. The whole thing, bag and all, fell like a crumpled parachute over his head and shoulders, enveloping him in a dark, clinging hood.

The mouthpiece was outside. The chair was immobile. Even if he wanted to, even if at the last minute he had a change of heart or some deep life-impulse came out of hiding to reclaim him, there was nothing at all he could do about it.

He wriggled his head deeper into the folds of his mother's skirt. And he sat there, in the dark, listening to his own breathing as he breathed away the scanty air, waiting for unconsciousness and death.

Thirteen

What went wrong? That was the question Geoffrey Fish asked.

Dr Wiseman, who came over from Stoke Mandeville the moment he heard the news, spoke of clinical depression syndromes. He concluded that the pink Tryptazol tablets had been too weak. In future he'd prescribe Tofranil for serious cases of endogenous depression.

Dorothy said it was her fault for leaving the plastic bag there. Allan had been rather withdrawn lately, she said, but there'd been nothing to suggest *this*. Though she was herself in a state of shock, she refused to take sleeping tablets because she wanted to be awake, just in case. And she was afraid of sleep anyway and the nightmares it brought. She would never forget that moment when she came home: opening the front door and calling out to Allan that she'd got the job, then seeing him, dropping her shopping, rushing up, tearing of the bag and the skirt and seeing his face, blue-blotched and the eyeballs rolled upwards . . .

It was lucky it had been raining or she'd have stayed longer in town. It was lucky the interview had been quick. It was lucky the bus had come right away. For Allan, it was unlucky.

He was rushed to the Radcliffe Infirmary where, under oxygen, he recovered consciousness. They kept him in for two days to make sure there was no brain damage. Back at the flat, he was to be kept under observation by the District Nurse. The Tofranil seemed to be working. But if he had a relapse or there was the slightest hint he'd try it again, he'd have to go back to

Stoke Mandeville or to a nursing home where they wouldn't let him out of their sight.

Linda came up from London. For her it was perfectly obvious what had gone wrong and she couldn't understand Geoffrey's question. It was self-evident why Allan wanted to die. 'And it's a pity he wasn't allowed to,' she said.

He couldn't ask Melanie; it was the summer vacation and she was not there to help. She was away doing field-work on her gorillas in Africa.

None of these answers satisfied Geoffrey. 'Suicide,' he said to the monkey squatting on his desk before him, 'is what you might call an extremely dysfunctional activity.'

The monkey sat grooming herself with her fair-haired, agile fingers. Occasionally she'd stop and cock her wizened little head on one side and watch Geoffrey intently. Then she'd go back to her fidgeting. Though in a way tamer than the other monkeys, this one was the rebel. That was what made her special. She had her own mind. Geoffrey glanced at her and, for a moment, regretted he'd used her for testing out the formulation he'd made up from Dr Samuel's cube of brain tissue. She was the wrong one to try out something new on: too wilful, too unpredictable. The results had been disappointing, but whether that was the drug or the monkey was hard to tell. Geoffrey rubbed a hand over his face and went on.

'Suicide runs counter to everything evolution strives for. Survival is an instinct that's wired-in to all forms of life. Yours too, my beauty. Survival at any expense. Last summer in Canada I came across a trap with a wolf's leg in it. The creature had chewed off its own leg rather than die there. It certainly bled to death later. Anyway. But unlike you, my love, a human being can override his instincts. More or less. How? It's because of his particularly highly developed consciousness. Or, more exactly, self-consciousness.'

Geoffrey leaned back in his swivel chair and ran a pinkish hand through his stubbly red hair. The monkey stopped fidgeting to watch him. As he spoke again, she put her head on one side as if to hear him better.

'It's all to do with consciousness, isn't it. Okay. Now, suppose you take a knife and cut out the brain from a cat, a monkey like

74

you and a human being like Allan. Cut away those bits which control the motor and sensory functions and what you're left with is the associative cortex, the bit that only talks to the other bits of the brain and hasn't got any direct projections outside it to the legs and arms and ears and so on. That's where the consciousness lies. In man, that part is both relatively and absolutely enormous. But then you've got to take into account not only the *number* of brain-cells there but the degree to which they're connected, their *connectivity*. In man, that too is absolutely massive. Are you with me? You're not with me. You want to know what's the point of all this. The point is: when a man decides to kill himself, a dysfunctional biochemical event is taking place in this region.'

The monkey had begun to bob up and down and tug at her pinkish face with her small hands. 'I'll express it mathematically for you, if you prefer,' said Geoffrey and rose lumberingly to his feet. He went to the painted piece of hardboard on the wall that served for a blackboard and wrote in yellow chalk:

$$C = f_1(n)f_2(s)$$

He stood back and blew the chalk off his fingers. The monkey sneezed. 'Consciousness,' he said to the creature, 'is a function of neuronal cell number (n) and of connectivity (s). Now you will notice that there is nothing in the equation allowing the possibility of consciousness destroying itself. It can't. It's axiomatically excluded. But, damn it all, Allan *did*! He did try to kill himself, he did make his consciousness attempt its own destruction. Why? You tell me why. And, more important, *how*? How did it occur in his cortex?'

The monkey jumped off the table onto the floor, scurried across and, in a single elegant movement, climbed half up a filing-cabinet and snatched the piece of yellow chalk. For a moment Geoffrey actually thought she was going to write the counter equation to answer his question, but she hopped back onto the table and began picking the chalk to powder. Soon her hands and front were dusted with yellow. She wasn't concerned with the question of life or death. She simply lived. She represented what Geoffrey saw every day of his life through the battery of machines he had for measuring brain patterns, sweat glands, respiration, heart-beat, muscle tension and the rest: the eternal and irrepressible will to live. Now for the first time he faced the will to die. He sat next to the monkey on the table and pressed his forefinger and thumb deep into the corners of his eyes. He had to start from first principles.

'Look at it another way then. Consider the brain as a system. As an organ, it's rather curious. For one thing, unlike the skin or the liver or other organs, its cells don't regenerate. When a brain cell dies, that's it. Not that it matters normally. We lose about ten thousand every day, but over a lifetime that's still only three percent of the total. On the other hand, the body does everything it can to protect the brain. Biochemical defence mechanisms stop it being used as a food reserve practically until death by starvation. Almost every other organ will be sacrificed in preference to the brain. Are you with me?'

The monkey stopped picking at the chalk momentarily and cocked her head on one side. She almost put Geoffrey off his stride. He'd never had pupils quite so apparently attentive.

'Right, then. If the brain is so precious and if it has taken three thousand million years to get it where it is, then how can it possibly also contain the faculty for destroying itself? That runs against every evolutionary device and mechanism.'

He started pacing the room. The fluorescent panels still flickered badly and he reminded himself to get them fixed. In the main part of the lab, the other monkeys were holding their own conference, full of fury and disagreement. *Quot simiae, tot sententiae.* Querulous little buggers. Would a monkey ever commit suicide? They said that dogs did, pining for a master. And there was the case of lemmings . . . But these could be perfectly well explained as being functional for the species. So then *why*?

'We're talking of the brain as a system. A system is defined by the function it performs. Take away the function and you take away the system. Remove the function of a brain and you no longer have a brain. A brain that wishes to destroy itself when its function is survival and self-perpetuation can no longer be considered a brain. And what is Allan except a brain? Allan *is* a brain. That's it!' Geoffrey clapped his hands so loudly the monkey nearly shot off the table in fright. 'Allan wanted to kill himself because the essential function of a human brain had been taken away from him. I don't mean it's not *occupied*: he's got enough to think about, to calculate and learn and recall, to analyse, to conceptualise. No, what he's lacking is the function of *control*. He's a brain without a body to control. What we've got to do is somehow give him a body.'

The monkey had dropped the chalk on the table and was busy grooming herself, occasionally chattering when Geoffrey's voice faded. He scratched his head. 'Shall we get him a pet? Not a dog, for sure. You've got to give dogs exercise. A cat? Too independent-minded. Another human? A child? No, not another child in the house. Something that can be trained. Something that'll give him feedback. Something to match the interplay of mind and the body he's lost. What?'

At that moment the monkey reached between her legs, picked up the chalk and stretched out a hairy arm to offer it to Geoffrey. As he took it he began to smile. He nodded slowly to himself. Then his smile broadened into a grin, the grin into a guffaw. Of course! The answer had literally been staring him in the face!

'You, my beauty! You're for Allan. You're the one for him.'

And, as he picked the monkey up and dusted off the yellow chalk from her front, he thought to himself: Allan's got the time and the patience. Let's see if you'll do better with him than you do with me. I think I'll keep you on the tablets, just to see.

That was how, one week later, Geoffrey came to be standing on Allan's doorstep. It was early in the afternoon and Geoffrey was sweating slightly. He looked quickly up and down the street. What he was about to do was expressly forbidden both by Department and Home Office regulations. In both arms he carried a large box covered in newspaper, though he was conscious that this only made it all the more conspicuous. It was hard to carry, too, for it lurched around with a life of its own.

Allan's voice came thin and reedy over the intercom. 'Oh, it's you, Geoffrey. Push when I buzz.'

He went into the flat. Once again he was struck by the hospital smell: the floor-wax, the disinfectant, the air freshener covering up unwanted smells. Allan was in the living room, sitting in front of his reading-stands. He turned his head when Geoffrey came in. His face was expressionless.

'Hello, Geoffrey,' he said blandly.

Geoffrey moved round so that Allan could see what he'd

77

brought. Allan registered no reaction, so he put the box on the table and started undoing the newspaper, the side away from Allan. It was to be a surprise.

The creature sprang from its package like a jack-in-the-box. It looked quickly round the room, saw Allan, leapt straight onto him and scampered down his front. It was the monkey, a small, fine-haired, honey-coloured little animal.

'Christ, get it off! Get the little bugger off! I can't stand monkeys! What kind of trick is this?'

Geoffrey stood back. 'I brought her along for you. She's yours, Allan.'

'For *me*? What am I supposed to do with it? Chase it around the flat all day? Very funny.'

'No, you don't understand . . .'

'The vile thing is pulling my hair! I hate it! Get it off! *Get it off!*'

Geoffrey reddened and moved towards the monkey. But she was too quick. She slid down Allan's back and scrambled between his strapped legs. He yelled. The monkey was terrified. She sprang onto one of his reading-stands and clutched at a page. The page tore and both monkey and bookstand went crashing to the floor.

'I've fitted her with this pain-pack, you see,' Geoffrey was saying as he lumbered after the monkey. 'It's just that I haven't quite got it working yet.'

The animal took refuge on the mantelpiece and sat chattering and howling as she watched him coming in for another attempt to catch her. Her tiny hands found something beside her to play with and she put it to her mouth and bit. It was a thin electric wire. There was a sharp crackle and a hissing sound from the fuse-box in Allan's Possum. The monkey leaped in terror off the ledge, landed squarely on the tray of drinks and sent the lot flying. The wire evidently worked the electric curtains. Shorted out, they went berserk, swishing themselves open and closed, open and closed, in a ceaseless frenzy. Cowering under the table, the monkey watched with fascination. Suddenly, in a series of rapid hand-over-foot leaps, she was up the curtains and riding them giddily back and forth.

'For Christ's sake, Geoffrey!' shouted Allan. 'What is this? A bloody circus?'

He reversed into a corner while Geoffrey tried to coax the

monkey down with a handful of banana pellets. He was saying, 'She's a *cebus apella*, one of the most intelligent I've got.'

'I don't care if it speaks Chinese, get it out of here! I don't want anything to do with it. Take it back to the labs. Drown it. Anything. But get it out of the house.'

Geoffrey heard the front door opening. It was Dorothy returning. She heard the commotion and dropped her shopping bag and rushed into the living room, leaving the front door open. She screamed, 'Allan, are you all right?'

At the precise moment she entered the room, the monkey took a great leap from the curtain and landed squarely on her head. She screamed again and made futile swatting movements in the air. This was surely some incubus, a demon come to possess Allan's soul again . . . But from her perch on Dorothy's head, the monkey could see the front door open. Freedom! She sprang down onto the floor and with her scarlet bottom held high in the air scampered through the front door, down the path and into the street.

Geoffrey followed in pursuit, but as he arrived at the front door a gust of wind caught it and slammed it shut in his face. By the time he'd opened it and was in the front garden, there was no sign of the monkey. He searched the trees, the pathway, the pavements, the hedges, the lamp posts and the road itself. He dragged a cyclist off his bicycle and asked if he'd seen her. He stopped an old woman who beat him off with an umbrella, terrified by his lunatic questions. But the monkey had disappeared completely.

It was hardly an auspicious way to start a new relationship.

Fourteen

It seemed logical enough. There was Allan, an active brain without a body. There was a monkey, an intelligent, playful and very mobile little creature. And there was Geoffrey who of all people knew how to teach monkeys to do things. True, the monkeys in the labs were only taught to go through mazes, to remember objects picked out at random, to press a button for a reward and so on. All the same, Geoffrey reasoned, you only had to look at the prehensile hands of the monkey to see the possibilities. If organ-grinders could teach them to dance and pass a hat round, couldn't he teach one to pick up a mouth-stick, turn on a light and fetch a drink? Finally, what he was short of, Allan had in abundance: time and patience. This was the vital ingredient in the behavioural conditioning process. It might be very interesting, too, to see how the man and the monkey got on. And there was the drug as well: maybe something might show up there.

The logic was perfect and would have worked in a perfect world. Unfortunately the translation from theory to practice didn't take account of that one little element that was so assiduously excluded from the scientific laboratory: the human factor.

The first, immediate resistance came from Allan himself.

'What are you trying to do? Make me into a freak show?' he demanded when, on the following day, Geoffrey went round, alone, to try and talk him into the idea. But his mind was closed.

80

'For goodness sake, Geoffrey, you can't be serious. The thing's vermin, and you know how hygienic this place has to be kept. And anyway, what will it achieve? It's a savage little ape from the trees. It's hard enough training Mother. Can you see that little thing washing me, changing the sheets, turning me in the night? Give me back Maryanne, sure. But a monkey will only make more trouble and nuisance. I appreciate the thought, Geoffrey, and you mean it well. But it's not on. Anyway, Mother wouldn't hear of it. You should have heard what she said yesterday!'

However, much to Geoffrey's surprise, Dorothy didn't rule it out. He was about to leave and give up the idea when he put his head round the kitchen door to say goodbye to her. She turned quickly and hid a handkerchief in her lap. Her grey hair was disarranged and her eyes swollen and red. Geoffrey held on to the doorhandle, not wanting to have to go in and comfort her.

'We can't go on like this,' she said in a trembling voice. 'We simply can't.'

Geoffrey sneaked a glance at his watch. He hated these situations. He let a silence fall, then said, 'Maybe I could make you a cup of tea?'

Dorothy wasn't listening. She had buried her head in her hands and spoke in a shaky voice into her lap. 'I'm at my wits' end. I try my best to cheer him up and he only snaps at me. The D.N. says I've got to be patient and it'll get better in time. I do try. But I never do things the way he wants them done, not like Maryanne did. He's so fussy. I don't think he realises that other people have feelings too. The tea's always too hot or the juice is too cold. The page-turner thing is always getting stuck. I'm forever running in and out, picking up his stick and changing the tape in the machine. I got offered that job but I can't take it. I'm terrified of leaving him alone, out of my sight. I never know if he'll try it again. I'm even afraid to go out to the shops. I'm cooped up here all alone. He can't work if I'm in the room, so I stay in the kitchen or in my bedroom, waiting for him to ring that blasted bell. I don't know how much more of it I can take, not having Jock here to help, either.'

Geoffrey tiptoed over to the stove and put the kettle on. He kept an eye over his shoulder at Dorothy as if she might spring upon him at any moment. 'I'm putting the kettle on,' he said carefully.

Dorothy had run out of steam. She wiped her eyes, saw the running mascara and said, 'I'm sorry. It's none of your problem. I must look a fright. I'm sorry.'

He stood at a safe distance by the stove and waited for her to rearrange her face. Then he began to tell her why he thought the monkey would be such a good idea for Allan. It really wouldn't cause her much extra work either. 'After all,' he said, 'I've got ten of the blighters to look after and I'm a bachelor.' The monkey could be house-trained quickly and wouldn't make any more mess than a cat. And there would be what he called a pain-pack, a little box strapped on the monkey's back that would deliver a small shock whenever a button was pressed. It worked by remote control and they could use it to punish the animal if she was disobedient. Geoffrey had spent the week fixing the pack up and was pleased with his handiwork. He knew the monkey was misbehaving partly because it felt rejected by him. It would just have to learn, with the help of the pain-pack if necessary.

'Perhaps a pet would do Allan good,' conceded Dorothy. Her mind was receptive.

Geoffrey was heartened. The following day he came round with the monkey again. Tactfully, he left her in the car while he talked once more with Allan.

'Try it for me, Allan. Just give it a try. If you don't like her, I'll take her back right away. I'll give her to you on loan and I'll take responsibility for training her. For God's sake, Allan, give it a go. What have you got to lose?'

Do it for *me*, Allan, he thought to himself. I want to try out an idea. You have all the time in the world, and besides, you're highly intelligent. I might never get a chance like this again.

Grudgingly, Allan relented. The monkey was brought in. For a while she refused to get out of her box. Then she slunk off into the corner under the table and stared uncertainly at Allan with her bright eyes flickering.

This is going to take time, said Geoffrey to himself.

The next problem came from a more expected quarter, though Geoffrey didn't see it until it was too late.

George Roach occupied the adjacent lab. They were both at the same level of seniority, as Senior Readers in Experimental Medicine. The post above them, a chair, was empty. The head of the Department of Medicine, Professor Burbage, was keeping it open until one or other of them produced some really important work, something that would make the Department's name known worldwide, something such as a nomination for a Nobel prize. The chair carried tenure and, in an age of Government cuts and anti-vivisection protest, tenure was going to be important. Although conducted with velvet gloves on, the rivalry between Geoffrey Fish and George Roach was a deadly one.

Roach had the habit of sidling into Geoffrey's office on the pretext of borrowing an EMG printer or some electrode gel, or equally on no pretext at all. Geoffrey played his own game with less political cunning and consequently always felt that Roach had the upper hand. Anyway, Roach and Professor Burbage were of the same school, the Oxford school: reductionists, believers in the knife and scalpel. Geoffrey was in the Cambridge tradition: he saw the brain as a system and he used psychochemicals as the key to it. And Roach's whole appearance displeased Geoffrey. He looked too fluid, too insinuating; he had a mean and hungry look. He also had a slight birthmark on the left of his neck, which made him stand with his right side forward. His nose was prominent and his forehead receded. Phrenologically untrustworthy was Geoffrey's verdict.

Roach came in, shaking a test-tube. Geoffrey knew what he'd been doing. The tube contained tiny scintillas of tissue he'd shredded which had to be kept agitated or they'd coagulate. He was working on noradrenalin, a transmitter substance closely linked with the formation of memory traces. Later in the experiment he'd separate out the transmitter by means of a radio isotope marker and then measure the residue. It was typical of Roach to bring it along, another subliminal thrust in their constant duel. He picked up various papers from Geoffrey's desk and scanned them without apparent interest. Then he caught sight of a book lying open on one side. It showed a full frontal anatomical drawing of a large primate. Geoffrey had been studying muscle and bone structures to see just exactly how much he could reasonably expect the monkey to be trained to do. Could it, for instance, stand on a chair and turn on a light switch with one hand? What weight could it readily carry? What biomechanical abilities did it have which could be adapted to Allan's living conditions? The picture in the book was explicit, with everything including its large male genitalia dissected and labelled.

'Bulling up for Melanie, eh?' said Roach. 'You'd better look to your laurels, boy. She'll have been spoiled by the gorillas out there.'

Melanie was due back from Africa in a few weeks. Geoffrey had tried not to think about her. The last thing he wanted now was Roach's snide, prying remarks into his private life. He looked up from his work and felt his hand clench into a fist under the table.

'George, is there anything specific? If not, I've got work to do.'

Roach shrugged, ran his eye over the bookshelves to see if he'd missed anything and went to the door. There he turned.

'We've had a death in the family, I see,' he said.

Geoffrey started. Of course. There was one monkey missing from the cage on the right. It was strictly against rules to let an animal off the premises. This was not only because they cost a small fortune from the dealers but because of what Professor Burbage called "political repercussions". This was just the sort of thing Roach would pick up and use.

'Yes, I'm afraid so,' said Geoffrey quickly, without thinking of the consequences. 'I've got it downstairs in the autopsy room on ice.'

'Spare me the testicles, eh?' asked Roach. He glanced pointedly at the ape drawing in the open book and added, 'Unless you're keeping them for yourself.'

'Piss off, will you,' said Geoffrey and turned back to his work.

Roach left. Geoffrey should have guessed that he would pass by the autopsy room later and find only two cats and a dog.

The monkey stood just twenty inches from head to toe and weighed less than six pounds. She was, nevertheless, a live coil of energy. Her teeth were sharp and her bite vicious. Her eyes were dark, bright and constantly flickering and moving, set deep in pinkish rims which matched her lips and nose. The hair on her face was short, soft, and paler than her coat and turned a dark inky colour from the crown in a line down the spine. Whenever she frowned or showed alarm, she looked very human. She was skinny (Dorothy immediately resolved to feed her up); her bones and ribs showed clearly though the fine hair of the coat.

She was a female Capuchin, not quite yet mature. The stomach hair was pale like the face and turned pink around her small dugs and genitals. Her rump bore two flat pads that showed up pinky-red when she walked. And she had a baby smell, because Dorothy at once took to bathing her in Johnson's Baby Shampoo. The monkey bit and clawed, for she hated water, and let out terrifying, strident shrieks. Allan got Geoffrey to explain patiently to Dorothy that monkeys didn't bathe in the wild, let alone shampoo themselves, and she'd do far better to leave the animal to her natural habit of grooming herself.

The flat may have been a prison-cell for Allan but for the monkey, used to the confines of a cage, it was as free as the jungle. By the end of the first week, the light in the centre of the living room was down and the shade torn to pieces. The standard lamp had fallen onto the typewriter and bent some keys. The curtains had torn around the hooks. The medicine cabinet had given under the monkey's weight and chipped the enamel of the basin. And she had jammed Dorothy's hairbrush in the wheels of Allan's chair so that a specialist had to be called to free it. Even the pain-pack was no use to begin with, since the monkey fiddled with it and got it off her back twice before Geoffrey made it tamper-proof. Allan could deliver a shock through his Possum, which had a touch-board as well so that Dorothy also could administer punishment when it was needed. Allan didn't use the pain-pack, though. He wasn't having any part of this crazy, rampaging little devil who had come to upset the routine and quiet of his thoughts.

The monkey was impossibly restless. She fiddled, she scratched, she picked her ears, she nibbled her toenails, she scratched her coat and then picked her nails and ate whatever she had caught under them. She chattered and cackled, she shrieked and muttered. She ate dead flies on the window-sill. She unpicked a cassette and pulled the tape in a stream all over the floor of the living room. Allan was in despair.

Then she was forever copying things. She watched Allan prodding the Possum with his mouth-stick and then copied him, only succeeding in pressing the alarm which brought Dorothy running. She watched Dorothy pouring out the ketchup on Allan's plate and later doused the kitchen in the red paste. She loved unravelling things. She took apart Dorothy's knitting, her crocheted shawl and her raffia shopping-basket. She ate everything she could. Within the first few days the houseplants were chewed to stubs. She raided the larder and ate herself sick. She nibbled and chewed at the cushions. Once she got hold of Allan's duck-down pillows and scattered feathers everywhere. And she hoarded things like a magpie, bright shiny things like boiled sweets and buttons and a ring of Dorothy's.

She also had her own property. She had found a small, pink, plastic baby doll. Her busy fingers had picked out the eyes and the flossy hair and her sharp teeth amputated its chubby toes. No one knew where it had come from, though Allan suspected it was a memento of his childhood from the bottom drawer of Dorothy's cupboard. It became the monkey's Thing.

But slowly the basic training took effect. Geoffrey had made up the preparation he'd been giving the monkey in the lab, but in tablet form. This was derived from the composition he'd synthesised a long while back from the girl's ablated brain tissue. But he'd added his own cocktail of drugs and, although he'd gone onto other work for the lab monkeys, he thought he'd carry on giving the original tablets to Allan's one. All these drugs were designed to improve learning ability and they needed all of that they could get for *this* monkey.

Before long the monkey slept in her own basket and was no longer put back in her cage at night. She had learned the "no-go" areas of the house — electric plugs, the kitchen knife drawer, the freezer, the loo, Dorothy's room. She no longer destroyed things out of carelessness or curiosity. But Dorothy was worn out. She told Geoffrey it felt like going through the first two years of Allan's childhood, rolled into the space of two months. She was on the point of giving up the experiment. They were getting results, but the creature was really more of a pest than a pet. They'd promised to give her a trial period, and the period was almost up. This time, however, it was Allan who gave the monkey her reprieve.

Fifteen

Allan was strolling in the bright sunlight on a white gravel path between formally-trimmed box trees. He was in France some-where, perhaps Malmaison, perhaps the Trianon. With him was a girl, a blonde with bare arms and Linda's eyes. Her hand was stroking his face, stroking his cheek gently, softly . . .

The light was getting brighter. It went from red to orange to white. Allan realised his eyes were shut and this was the daylight through the lids. No, his mind whispered, don't go there! Don't wake up! Slip back with me. He allowed himself to drift back into sleep. But there was something strange. The blonde girl with the gentle hands had vanished, yet her soft caress remained on his cheek. It had the grainy, insistent quality of belonging to the waking world. Allan half-opened his eyes.

It was the monkey. The creature was sitting on his chest and stroking the side of his cheek with the back of her hand. He could feel the soft warmth of the skin and its fine delicate hairiness. The monkey held her head on one side and was looking intently at him through bright beady eyes.

Allan moved his cheek into the caress. He closed his eyes. He could feel a smile lighting up the forgotten creases at the corners of his mouth. The monkey began muttering in a low voice. Allan opened his eyes fully. He was awake. From the corridor he could hear his mother padding around and, a white later, the sounds of flushing and washing. Then he realised that this was the first time since he dared remember that he'd woken up without the terrible, overwhelming sense of panic. He'd simply woken up. That was all.

It was at that moment, just after six o'clock on a frosty November morning, that the monkey became Ella.

'Ella,' said Allan. 'Ella.'

He didn't know if he meant it as a name at first, or a corruption of a Greek or French word, or just as a sound. He simply said it because it suited the monkey. As he whispered the word, she spread her supple pink lips and opened and shut her toothy mouth in perfect imitation. Allan repeated the word and she mimicked his lip movements exactly. He began to laugh. The monkey swung herself up onto the steel girder above the bed and began to dance up and down, screeching in a duet to Allan's laughter.

Dorothy came hurrying into the room, her face full of alarm. She wore a shower-cap and tried to hide her unmade-up face in a damp towel. 'What's the matter, dear?' she cried.

'Mother,' said Allan when his laughter had subsided. 'I'd like you to meet Ella. Ella, this is Dorothy.'

His mother looked uncertainly from her son to the monkey and back. 'What's that, its name?' She towelled her ears dry, putting her head first on one side and then the other. On the girder the monkey copied her movements exactly. Dorothy had to laugh. 'Funny little tyke,' she said.

'Ella Mann,' said Allan. The tears were still wet on his cheeks and his mouth ached. 'It's got a certain . . . ring, don't you think?'

'But the little mite's all thin and skinny. *Ella* makes me think of big fat black ladies.' Then Dorothy added, comfortably, 'Anyway, it's company for you.'

It was on the morning of Ella's christening that Allan learned the news about Linda. Dorothy had washed, changed, dressed and buckled him in. She'd cleaned his teeth and combed his hair. Now it was breakfast and she was feeding him his egg. She liked to spin this time out as long as possible, for she knew that afterwards he'd lock himself up into his studies and he'd be inaccessible to her.

She had taken over the rôle of head-of-family after Jock had gone. A key ritual was the reading of the morning *Telegraph*. She read it aloud for Allan, first the headlines, then the inner pages for University news. Sometimes she'd describe the cartoon to him, as if he couldn't read either. It was very hard to make a cartoon sound funny that way. She avoided the Sports pages. Finally she'd skim the Births, Marriages and Deaths columns. From time to time Jock would find someone he'd known in the Army or at school in the lists. Dorothy never did, but she followed the habit. This day she struck lucky.

'Oh look,' she said and put her coffee cup down. 'Your Linda. Wasn't she called Linda Aikman?'

'She *is* called Linda Aikman,' said Allan.

'Well, not for long, dear. It says here she's engaged to a man called — where is it? — John Maurice Wiseman. That couldn't be *our* Dr Wiseman, could it? Who did your op?'

Allan but his lip. Quietly he said, 'Let me see, Mother. No, hold it further away. I may be a cripple but I'm not blind.'

He read the short notice under Engagements. There was no doubt about it. Linda Aikan was to marry John Wiseman.

'Thank you, Mother,' he said. Then, 'I don't think I can finish breakfast today. Maybe you could set up my stands before you go out.'

Dorothy put the paper down and looked at the half-eaten egg and toast. 'You should finish it up, dear. You need your strength.'

His look withered her into silence. She busied herself collecting the plates and stacking them in the sink, working noisily to cover up the silence. At the sink she shook her head. She swept back a loose strand of greyish hair with her rubber gloves. 'I'm sorry about Linda, dear. I suppose it was bound to happen sometime.'

There was no response. Dorothy turned. Allan had reversed his chair and was already moving down the corridor towards the white swing-door of the living room. The tyres of the chair squelched quietly on the vinyl floor. Ella rode along in his lap.

Linda, engaged.

It was bound to happen sometime.

Was it? Couldn't she have waited? In Stoke Mandeville he'd promised himself he would become the top Queen's Counsel in the country. The foremost barrister in the nation, and in a wheelchair too. He'd do it. He'd show them. He'd turn his misfortune on its head and get to the top in spite of it. And there, at the top, lauded and applauded, quoted and interviewed and publicised, he would once again be a head above Linda and Linda would be proud to be with him.

But she hadn't waited. She hadn't given him the chance. Two months before, he'd tried to end it all because Allan-the-athlete was dead. Now what was there for Allan-the-barrister to live for, Allan-the-brain-without-a-body? And worst of all, she hadn't told him. She hadn't broken it to him alone, so that he could cope with it piece by piece. He'd had to read it in the *Daily Telegraph*, along with the rest of the nation.

Allan squeezed his eyes tight shut. He took hold of the welling pain and placed it apart, in the small box where it belonged, away and out of reach on the table. He willed it with all his force to stay inside and he clamped the lid hard down upon it. After a while it subsided and he opened his eyes. There, with her arms spread out, was Ella. She was sitting on his lap and hugging him. He couldn't feel it, but by the way she buried her face in his chest he was sure she knew what he was going through.

By her naming, Ella became a member of the family. She made it a household of three, not two. And with that came all the complexities of a *ménage à trois*.

It was, as Geoffrey neatly observed, the law of the excluded middle. Ella, the unspeaking middle in the threesome, became the focus of the relationship between mother and son. As Allan began to accept the monkey, Dorothy took the reverse position and began to complain about her. As a result, a certain closed pattern developed in their conversations. These could be about anything — Ella's training, Dorothy's job-offer, Allan's weekly essay, Ella's privileges. Thus one evening Allan said:

'I've been thinking.'

Dorothy looked up from her knitting. 'What's that, dear?'

'It's time Ella went outside to do her messes. We'll get a cat-flap fitted. It'll save all the business with her litter-tray.'

'I don't mind cleaning out her tray. I'm not complaining about that.'

'The point is, it would be more hygienic. You're always on about the importance of hygiene.'

Dorothy put down her knitting. 'I keep this place spotless.'

'Ella should get out and about a bit. It's unfair to keep her cooped up indoors all the time.'

'She's Geoffrey's animal. We can't do anything without asking Geoffrey first.'

So Dorothy asked Geoffrey, confident in his reply. He was against the idea. Sure, they could tag her like a dog, but imagine if she got lost! Geoffrey imagined, and winced: the police calling Professor Burbage at midnight, Burbage in a suit over pyjamas collecting the stray animal, Burbage bittern and clawed and his wife making saucers of bread and milk, then the scene in the labs next day . . . No, it wasn't on. Not yet, at least.

Thus, a day or two later, Dorothy resumed: 'Geoffrey won't have her let out of doors. I asked him.'

'I don't give a damn when Geoffrey says "She's Department property" and all that crap. Who's been training her? Who looks after her? Who does she live with?'

'Well, she may not be here for very much longer.'

'What do you mean by that?'

'We'll just have to wait and see.'

Allan let his breath out in exasperation. There was a long silence, punctuated by the clicking of Dorothy's knitting-needles. Ella was sitting on the table, playing with something she'd found. It was Dorothy's purse. Allan said nothing. The radiators belched. He wheeled himself over to the Possum and drew the curtains. His mother looked up; it was only four o'clock and not quite dark. She put down her knitting, got up and turned the lights on. Allan went on.

'Another thing. I want Ella to come and sleep with me from now on.'

'She's to stay where pets sleep, in her basket on the floor. Geoffrey wouldn't hear of her sleeping in your room.'

'She hates it in her basket. You have to give her the pack every night to get her into it. Don't you?'

'Anyway, it's not safe. She'd jump up onto you. My mother's Aunt Josephine had a Great Dane who slept on her bed. One day they found the poor woman suffocated to death.'

'Mother! Ella's as light as a feather. Anyway, I'd make her sleep at the end of the bed.'

'She'd only interfere with your circulation, dear. She'd make a nuisance of herself when I wanted to turn you.'

'For heaven's sake, she never stays in the same place for more than a moment. I can't see how she'd get in the way.'

'Then she'd stop you getting your sleep, dear. You know what Dr Fry says about that. *Make sure Allan gets plenty of sleep.*'

'She sleeps on my lap in the afternoon. No one seems to mind about that.'

'Anyway, I don't think it's . . . *clean.* She may be a clever little devil but she's really from the jungle. See how she's always scratching herself. Scratch, scratch, all the time.'

'She's cleaning herself, Mother. That's to make her clean.'

'Well, I don't know. People don't scratch if they're clean. They scratch when they're dirty.'

And so the arguments went on. But this last bout Allan won and Ella was finally allowed to sleep at the bottom of his bed. This kind of routine, however, permeated all discussions about Ella. The small tasks Geoffrey taught her to do were, for Dorothy, merely party tricks: amusing, entertaining but really rather a nuisance. Even Ella's constant grooming of Allan's hair began to irritate her. She would have to turn away whenever the monkey got the comb and started going through his hair, probing and grubbing around and picking out bits of fluff and dried skin. That made Allan enjoy it all the more.

Sixteen

Tclick-tclick.

This was the clicking sound Allan made to attract Ella's attention. She sat on her haunches in her favourite place, high up on the top bookshelf by the window in the living room. It was her tree-top. Dorothy was out, working part-time at the local department store. Outside, a fine December drizzle fell silently and ceaselessly. The leaded panes were steamy; with the light on, it was hard to see out. Ella had taken her morning pill, the large yellow tablet Geoffrey had made up for her. Allan looked up at the clock on the wall. It was time for the training.

Ella looked up at once at the clicking sound. Now the command would follow. The tube controlling Allan's chair was mounted on a panel at chest height. Beside this, Geoffrey and a friend in the Department of Electronics had rigged up a cunning spider's-leg rod like a small joy-stick that Allan could rotate with his mouth. By means of a flexible cable this could pivot and point a small beam of light from a unit fixed just below the arm of the chair. It was a kind of mini-laser that directed a thin pencil-beam of orange light. It made a moving spot which Allan could direct onto whatever he wanted — the door, a cupboard, the fridge. This solved the main problem of training Ella, the problem of pointing out the particular object she was supposed to deal with.

Allan worked the joy-stick until the tiny bright spot of light was on the ON knob of his radio, which also controlled the volume. Ella hadn't been shown it before. As soon as she saw the

93

light-spot, the monkey swung down from her perch and hopped onto the table. In front of the radio she turned and cocked her head on one side. Allan gave the joy-stick a light tug.

The bleep meant that Ella had to do what she'd been taught to do with the object pointed at. But what? She took the knob in one paw, then both. Then she hopped back, turned once round in a circle and scratched her fair, hairy, small face. Her pink lips began to part. She plucked at the knob as though it were a walnut.

'Turn it,' said Allan.

Ella pulled. It wouldn't come off. It should: it was round and round things came off and had to be put into round holes, like Allan's polythene beaker that went into his food tray. She began to chatter.

What was he to do? The great behaviourist Skinner could train a pigeon to walk a figure-of-eight in fifteen minutes. Geoffrey had told him that, to encourage him. But who the hell wanted a giddy pigeon? He wanted a monkey that could turn the radio on and off. *Turn* it. He caught her attention again and began to rotate his head. Her eyes opened wider. After a while she began to copy him, revolving her head round and round.

'No, the *knob!*' he cried. 'Turn! Twist! Rotate! Revolve! God, why can't they teach them something useful in the labs, like English?'

Ella went back to the radio and pushed the knob. The whole unit fell backwards onto the Formica table-top with a crash. She leaped back and swung herself off the table and fled out of sight.

Tclick-tclick. Allan called her to attention again. She didn't respond. Then he saw her slinking on all fours towards the door.

'Ella,' he called in a warning voice. She froze in mid-stride, but then crept forward again.

Tssss!

This hiss was the signal that the pain-pack was coming. She had quickly learned to associate the hissing with the electric shock to her back, and often just the hiss was enough. But now she was angry, frustrated. She began to dance up and down and bare her pink gums at him.

Allan picked up his mouth-stick in his lips and jabbed it at the Possum control-panel. Zap! At once Ella let out a howl.

'Now go back and do it again,' he said sternly.

He went through the routine again: *tclick-tclick, bleep, tclick-tclick, bleep* . . . And then, *tssss!*

Under alternate pain and cajoling, she gradually found what to do. The moment she turned the knob correctly, he fed her a banana pellet out of a special dispenser under the other arm of his chair. Then he went back over the ground again, and again. Each time Ella got it right she received a pellet — what Geoffrey called a *reinforcer*.

The first time she turned the knob and the radio went on, she leaped backwards in fright. For a long time she wouldn't come out from under the table but sat chattering and clutching her Thing to her breast. Then curiosity overcame her and she crept up on the radio from behind and began to prowl round it to find the humans who were talking inside. It made Allan laugh aloud, but he went on with the training and eventually taught her to switch it off again. It took several days and a lot of what Geoffrey referred to as *aversive stimuli* to teach her this trick properly, but soon she was getting it right over ninety percent of the time.

The monkey had to learn. Allan took upon himself the job of trainer. But there was only one way to learn anything properly: the hard way. He would allow no slacking, no short-cuts, no compromises. This and all the other tasks were things she simply had to learn.

Looking back, Allan knew that even his old trainer Charlie Cunningham hadn't been as hard on him as that. Only he had been that hard on himself. But it was right. It was the only way to get results.

One wet and wild Sunday afternoon in December, Geoffrey came round on one of his visits. Dorothy climbed painfully down from the kitchen chair on which she was standing to paint the living room and went to open the door for him. He was rain-blown and shook himself off in the hallway like a burly mongrel. The whole house smelled with the acrid, suffocating smell of emulsion paint. As always it was hot and slightly airless.

Allan sat in the centre of the living room under a naked bulb, like a judge in his chair. Dorothy cast a glance at Geoffrey but said nothing; the practised patience in her face said it all. She went back to her painting. Allan's voice rang out. He was in high spirits.

'Good timing!' he cried. 'The very man we need. What do you think? Is it too dark? Too *depressing*?'

Dorothy had finished the wall over the mantlepiece and was working on the plaster beside the windows. The colour was a rich terracotta. The table and bookstands had been moved to the other end of the room and the typewriter, radio and the Possum to Allan's bedroom. The naked bulb caught the glint of enthusiasm in his deep-set dark eyes.

His mother said, without turning, 'It needs a second coat.'

'Well?' he demanded again. 'Mother wanted to keep it white. It was getting me down. The whole place was a mausoleum. We need some *colour* round here. Mother, you're dripping it. What do you think, Geoffrey? More red?'

'No, it's nice. It's okay. It's very colourful,' said Geoffrey.

Allan read his tone. 'Nonsense! You don't like it one bit. You'd rather it was a delicate hospital *eau-de-nil*, or chocolate-and-cream like a borstal, or magnolia like Mother's room. Eh?' He turned once again to Dorothy. 'Mother, aren't you going to offer Geoffrey some tea?'

'Yes, dear. I'm just finishing this bit.' She dabbed a few more brushstrokes at the cornice and got down off the chair, sweeping the back of her hand over her face. 'Oh, drat,' she said, getting paint on her cheek. With a sigh of annoyance she left the room.

Allan leaned his head towards Geoffrey and whispered, 'Come here.' He wheeled his chair back a few feet. Underneath he had been covering up a paintbrush which had made a puddle of terra-cotta paint on the vinyl tiles. Around it were monkey-prints. 'Ella stole the brush. Mother couldn't find it anywhere. She'd skin her alive if she caught her — you know how intolerant she's getting these days. I had to get her to shut Ella up in my bedroom. Do me a favour, Geoffrey, and clean the thing up before Mother comes back.'

Geoffrey slipped off his jacket and got to his knees. In a moment he had cleaned it up and hid the brush carefully in the folds of the newspapers beside the paint-tray where Dorothy would eventually find it. Then he turned to Allan. Only then did Allan take in his friend's face. It was as long as that wet winter's weekend.

'Hey, what's up, mate?'

Geoffrey shrugged his broad shoulders and let them subside in despair. 'Oh nothing. Well, work really. It's just that I've been on a particular line of research for three months or more now and it's come to a dead end. A cul-de-sac. If I fool around wasting much more time I'll be out of a job. I was replicating some work done fifteen years ago at Princeton on magnesium pemoline . . . well, anyway. Still-born. That's all there is to it.' He sat down in the chair. It was a tight fit.

'I'm throwing that out too,' said Allan. 'I can't bear plastic furniture. The whole place is geting a face-lift. No, I'm sorry about the work. But what about the odious man Roach? Is he getting results?'

'You can't tell with Roach, he plays it so close to his chest. But I've had a couple of offers from Canada. Maybe I should seriously think about them. Roach has got the knives out, I'm well aware of that. If he knew I'd loaned out a lab monkey, he'd go straight to Burbage. It's not *that* much of a crime and Burbage would probably just give me a carpeting, but it's all part of the picture. Roach will use any ammunition he can get his hands on.'

'Cheer up, Geoffrey. There's Melanie's lunch party tomorrow and the vac's coming up. Anyway, maybe we can arrange for Roach to have a skiing accident. I know! Get me one of Jeremy Marsh's Indian blow-pipes and I'll do the job. Who'd ever suspect a quadriplegic of murder? Anyway, I could defend myself in court, couldn't I?'

Geoffrey smiled painfully. Allan went on, brightly, 'Come on, let's go and get Ella. But keep an eye on her with the paint.'

He wheeled himself into the corridor and swept past his mother as she came out of the kitchen with a tray. 'Put it in the living room,' he called. 'We'll be right back.'

Ella was curled in her basket at the foot of Allan's bed. At the sight of Geoffrey she got up and slunk away, skirting the walls until she could hop onto Allan's lap. Geoffrey, preoccupied, just nodded when he saw her there and went over to the window. It was pitch dark outside and the panes were wet and black. Yet he stood there, hands in his pockets, staring out into the evening.

'How about some music?' suggested Allan. 'What's on Radio Three? Let's see, shall we?'

Geoffrey was miles away in his thoughts. Softly Allan made the *tclick-tclick* sound. He swivelled his chair round and a moment later let out the *bleep!* A full orchestra suddenly flooded

97

the room with Beethoven. Geoffrey took a while to hear it. Coming out of his reverie, he turned and stopped short.

Allan was by the bed, as before. Ella was sitting in his lap, as before. And the radio was on. The Possum was disconnected. Allan's mouth-stick lay beside the radio on the dressing-table, out of reach. And Beethoven was filling the room.

'Jesus!' said Geoffrey carefully. 'How on earth . . . ?'

He looked from Allan to Ella, from Ella to the radio and back again. As he settled finally on Ella, a different look came over his face.

'Allan,' he began uncertainly, 'would you mind very much if I . . . I wonder if I could . . . Allan, I'd like to do some tests on Ella.'

'Tests?'

'Oh, not *that* kind of tests. No, just simple straightforward routine intelligence tests. Maze-learning tests. The Wisconsin box. Nothing harmful, nothing that could hurt her. Allan, it might help me.'

Allan paused. He considered it carefully. 'Ella's very precious, you know. And you make her very nervous these days. I suppose if I were there all the time . . . yes, well, if you didn't do anything without agreeing it with me first, it would be all right. But she stays here in the flat with me. Okay?'

Geoffrey shifted his weight from foot to foot. He looked once again at the radio and then at Ella. Finally at his watch; he had to be going.

'Okay,' he said.

Dorothy had gone to her room, complaining of a headache from the smell of paint. Allan was in the kitchen being given a drink by Ella. He, too, was sleepy. He shut his eyes; they smarted from the paint fumes. He was wondering if he should have agreed so readily to let Geoffrey do tests. He didn't want to create precedents. Ella was his and she was growing very special.

When he opened his eyes he saw that Ella, sitting on the table, was toying with two small objects in her tiny dark paws. They were her oval yellow pills, the ones Geoffrey made up for her: her "clever-pills", as Dorothy called them, of which she was allowed only one a day. She'd either been at the wall cabinet or else she'd hidden them when she'd made Dorothy spill the bottle all over the floor. Then an idea hit him. Why not? They'd worked wonders for the monkey.

He made the clicking sound to attract her attention. She cocked her hairy little head from side to side. He opened his mouth and made eating movements with his lips.

She didn't understand at first. Then with a little whimper of comprehension she swung down off the table and up onto his lap. With a quick, deft movement of her skinny arm, she reached up and popped one of the pills into his mouth. The other she put into her own. She looked into Allan's eyes. He winked. She winked back.

Seventeen

In the early hours of that morning, Allan had a strange dream.

He was in a large baronial house (which he recognised later as an old Scottish manor he'd once stayed in for a dance). It was enormous in every proportion because he was very small. Small and hairy and sinuous and very quick. He was terribly hungry and he'd crept quietly out onto the corridor of the first floor. The house was in darkness but for a dim light in the large, high central hallway below. The light glinted dully on the massive polished bannisters and the gilded frames of portraits high up on the walls. The house had only the sounds of night: a clock ticking, a voice on the telephone in the library, an owl in the grounds.

He began to hop down the wide staircase but his toe-claws scratched the wooden boards, so he leaped onto the bannisters and began to swing himself down the outside, hand over hand. Suddenly the library door opened. A shaft of light streaked across the hallway. For a second he thought he'd been spotted. He vaulted to the ground and tucked himself behind the bannister post where he fitted neatly and safely. He held his breath. Steps approached. Heels clicked across the marble floor of the hall, becoming muffled as they stepped onto the rugs and the carpet leading up the centre of the staircase. Feet passed just inches from his head, feet as big as his whole body. But they went on upstairs and passed out of earshot. Quick!

He scampered across the hallway on all fours, his bottom high, his eyes alert. It felt so easy and quick to move that way. Ahead was a door covered in baize and brass buttons. He pushed. It swung back. The rugs and carpet stopped and instead there were just cold flagstones. The corridor was full of obstacles, old leather riding-boots, golf-bags, canvas suitcases that smelled of mould. The kitchen lay ahead. It was almost as huge as the hallway, only it smelled of roasted meat instead of lavender polish. The kitchen seemed to be humming to itself all the time. He could hear mice scurrying away in the far corner by the larder, but he'd leave them alone. He hopped over to the fridge and tried to prise the door open. But it was the old-fashioned kind with a big handle you had to turn, too high up and probably too stiff anyway. He skirted the Aga and made for the larder. There the door was ajar. He slipped inside and put up a long slender hairy arm and felt the ease with which he drew his body up onto the shelf above. Everywhere there were tins, jars, bottles and packets. And a packet of peanuts! He bit open the wrapping. Nuts spilled to the floor. Some he caught with an agility that surprised him. He filled his mouth with all it could hold. Then he swung down again, slipped past the Aga and the fridge into the corridor, through the baize door, up the bannisters on the outside, over and onto the landing carpet and finally back into the bedroom. There he hopped up onto the foot of the bed, squatted on the covers and began to spit out the peanuts onto his forearms, holding them out like a tray. One by one he picked up the nuts and chewed them properly. They were delicious and salty. He looked up. The man at the top of the bed was stirring. The man was moving his head. The man was blinking. The man opened his eyes.

Allan stirred. He moved his head. He blinked and opened his eyes. When they adjusted to the bedroom darkness, he saw Ella sitting crouching at the foot of his bed, chewing at something and staring intently at him.

The Monday morning was the last Monday of term. Allan had finished the necessary work but there was a point of law on criminal injuries he wanted to look up. He'd disagreed with his tutor Dr Fry over the point and he wanted to check it out before lunch, for his tutor might well be at Melanie's lunch party. It involved looking up a particular case precedent in one of the books on the shelves. But he'd forgotten to ask Dorothy to put the book up before she left for work. Damn, he thought.

He shut his eyes. By concentrating as he had done as a boy he found that slowly the image of the particular page he wanted was coming to him, at first dimly, then more clearly. There it was, the exact passage, in front of his eyes. As a young boy he'd had photographic memory; as with such gifts, it had waned in adolescence. Maybe it was now returning! Perhaps that was *Nature's way*, the phrase Dorothy used to explain to herself the inexplicable. (Jock would attribute such things to the Almighty; he'd now be in a position to know if he'd been right). Maybe it was like a person who loses his sight and gains far greater acuity of hearing, one thing compensating for the loss of another. If he was developing his mental faculties to make up for losing his bodily ones, it was just about bloody time.

It was nearly twelve when the phone rang. Linda! She was around the corner. She'd love to pop in and see him, there and then. She'd be round in five minutes.

It was so sudden that Allan didn't have time to think of an excuse. Besides running out of time before having to leave for lunch, Linda was the last intrusion he wanted in his life right then. He hadn't heard from her since learning of her engagement. Linda, his past life with her and all his feelings for her, were still imprisoned tightly in the small box to which he'd committed them. They had withered without light and air. He didn't want to re-open the box, but it was too late. Linda was on her way.

Ella suddenly grew very agitated after the call. She threw the comb down on the floor and began howling and swinging from the stands and shelves. Allan became angry and sent her to the corner. She sat there cuddling her Thing and sucking her thumb.

But the moment he pressed the Entryphone button he knew there was trouble. Behind Linda's 'Hello' he could quite clearly hear a high-pitched yapping. God, she'd brought the dog!

Before he could warn her, Linda had swept into the hall and was complaining about the traffic, the shopping, the crowds, the cold weather. The mongrel, however, at once smelled *primate* about the house. It let out a yelp and started snuffling out the monkey's scent down the corridor, in and out of the kitchen and finally into the living room. Dog saw monkey and monkey saw dog. Ella screeched and leaped forwards, coming to a halt on her hind legs two feet from the dog. But then the dog's manner changed. It was curious. It wanted to make friends, to sniff hindquarters, to play. Ella wasn't having this. She swung herself up onto the table and grabbed a pencil. Holding it in both hands like a lance she made for the dog. The dog fled at the first stab. The two streaked around the floor, under the table, around the wheelchair, upsetting one of the bookstands, and out into the corridor. There was a flurry of scrawling and barking.

'Oh God, I'm sorry. I forgot!'

Linda dropped her handbag and went after the animals. When she'd separated them she hauled the dog off to her car outside.

She came back shaken and flushed and sat down in the chair opposite Allan. She'd changed. Her hair was shorter and more practical. Her mouth, which Allan used to think of as generous and sensual, seemed to have grown slacker. Under faded denim dungarees she wore a collarless workman's shirt. She smelled of cigarettes — Allan guessed she'd been heavily at it in the car before coming into the flat. She wasn't wearing her usual rings, though one hand kept fingering the other as if trying to find them.

'God,' Linda repeated. 'I *am* sorry. I heard about the monkey but I guess I assumed you'd keep it in a cage or something.'

'It doesn't matter,' said Allan coldly. He looked at the clock on the wall. It was twelve-fifteen.

'You must think I'm a right idiot,' she went on hopefully. 'Anyway, here I am. Actually I came to apologise about something else. You know, I wrote you a letter before the engagement was announced. I must have left it in some other clothes because I came across it just the other day and when I saw it I thought, My God, I know what Allan will be thinking! I'm so sorry. I'm hopeless at practical things like that, you should know that.' She looked at him for support, for recognition. He didn't respond. 'You must have felt terribly hurt.'

'I've got over it.'

'Well, anyway. I suppose you know John and I are getting married here, in Oxford. A June wedding. Ridiculous, isn't it? We've talked it over and we really hope you'll come. Please, Allan. I brought your invitation myself. I don't trust myself posting things any more.' Linda smiled in self-deprecation. There was a silence. She fished the invitation out of her bag and opened it carefully in front of Allan, as if that was how he would

103

have done it himself. 'Well, where shall I put it?'

'Over there, with all the others,' said Allan and nodded towards the mantlepiece. It was empty.

Linda sat down, spread her hands on her dungarees, looked at them, didn't like the look of them, lifted her head and scanned the room. 'I like the colour,' she said. 'It's much more homely. Are you going to do it all this colour? Won't that make it terribly dark?' There was no reply. Then, 'Tell me about the monkey. Does it have a name?'

'Ella.'

'Short for Barbarella, I suppose. Neat, that. Does it like stroking?' She put forward her hand. Ella crouched under the table, watching her with her gums bared.

'I wouldn't,' said Allan.

Linda withdrew her hand quickly. 'Does it always go for people? My poor dog, his ear's all torn. You should keep it on a lead. I wouldn't want to live with a little vampire like that around the place.'

'She keeps me company. Better than people do.'

Linda paused. Then she started again, brightly, cheerfully. It reminded him of the way Dorothy talked in the mornings when she came in to do the messy jobs.

'Would you like to see what I've brought for us? I bet it's ages since you've had lunch like we used to. I've got all your favourites here.' She brought the bags in from the hallway and unpacked them. 'Do you remember that fat old Austrian *hausfrau* in the market? She's still there, same as ever. She sent you her love. Well, look what we've got here. I remember you don't eat onions but paté's okay, isn't it? I got some plastic spoons and things. I thought we'd have an indoors picnic. Oh, and there's some wine too. It's too cold — it's freezing outside — but I'm sure it will *chambrer* in here. Where's the corkscrew, in the kitchen? Where's that monkey? He won't jump up on me, will he?'

She returned with a corkscrew, tablecloth and plastic cups. She cleared Allan's work off the table and began laying it in busy silence. Ella had taken refuge on her vantage point on the upper shelf. Linda kept glancing up nervously. She had just uncorked the wine with a loud pop when Allan asked her an abrupt question.

'Is the clock right?'

She put down the bottle and looked at her watch. 'I make it twenty-five past. No, twenty-six. You're a couple of minutes slow.'

'The minicab should be here any minute,' he said. 'Would you get me my rug over there?'

'Minicab? Are you expecting someone? Allan, you should have said. I expect we can stretch the food, though.'

He looked at her squarely. 'I've got a lunch engagement, Linda,' he said.

Linda's hand flew to her face. She bit her lip. Spread with the indoors picnic, the table suddenly looked absurd.

'Well, let me take you then. Save on the cab,' she volunteered. They both knew that her old red mini estate was far too small.

'That's not necessary, thanks all the same.'

There was nothing more to be said. The hired ambulance came to collect him. He called Ella who hopped onto his lap and snuggled down, keeping a wary eye on Linda. Allan drove himself down the pathway in the frosty midday air. He turned his head. His breath made clouds of steam. Linda stood forlornly on the porch.

'Nice to see you again, Linda. Would you mind letting yourself out? Oh, and thanks for the invitation. I don't think I've got anything else on that day.'

He turned away and didn't look back once as his wheelchair was placed on the hoist and lifted inside the ambulance. He saw nothing of Linda's desolate little wave as he was driven off.

Eighteen

Melanie's father died when she was five and her mother sent her from school to school across the United States. When she was just fourteen and still not fully recovered from her polio, her mother ran off with her lover to Columbia. At twenty-one, Melanie came into the remains of a badly-invested trust. She paid her way through Princeton, left the States and sank the rest into a small terraced house in that part of Oxford just over Magdalen Bridge known as the Plain. She'd had builders in to re-vamp the whole house. What to the previous owners had formed the front room, the parlour and the kitchen was now knocked into a single large area on two levels.

The house gave Geoffrey the feeling of being Lawrence of Arabia in a casbah. Kelims hung on the walls, in the centre stood low fretted tables with inlaid brass tops and on the shelves brass pestles and beaked coffee-pots served as book-ends. He sat on the arm of a settee covered with camel-hair rugs, waiting for it to snap under his weight, toying irritably with what looked like a patchwork quilt of antique yashmaks. Why hadn't she gone the whole hog and tented the place from floor to ceiling? And where were the souvenirs of her field-work in Uganda, the spears and gourds and neck-rings? Where was the genuine gorilla scalp for the next fancy-dress party? Geoffrey would have to tackle her on that. He began to recognise the signs: *dementia alcoholica*. Easy on the hot wine.

At diametrically the other end of the double room stood

Professor Burbage with George Roach at his elbow. Why had Melanie invited them? Ambition, that's why, he concluded. Her work had been getting *exposure* — not only in the professional journals but in the popular press as well. Gorillas were suddenly all the rage. The academic world had fashions, like anything else, and it was just a question of being in the right place at the right time. And Melanie was. More, she'd begun to look like the right person too. Gone were the lank curtains of dark hair from which her interesting, ironical pale face peered. Now her hair was short, bouncing with waves, and her lips were painted a definite red. She was bronzed and she moved around the crowded room with the proficiency of a practised hostess.

He swilled the orange-peel around the bottom of his empty glass and tried not to feel so resentful. She had grown so attractive. He felt like some great fleshy stone which had been bearing down on her; relieved of the weight, she was rising and flowering. But his mind kept coming back to Allan's monkey, *his* monkey. *Christ*, how the creature had picked up the tricks. And the radio! Twisting a knob demanded enormous control from the motor cortex. How long had it taken Allan to teach her? He began to wonder if he'd missed something when he'd first given Ella the drug, something which was only beginning to show itself now.

'How's your glass, Geoffrey?'

It was Melanie. He looked up, feeling a flush rise to his cheeks. 'Thanks. It's a nice party, Melanie.'

'People seem to be enjoying themselves, but you never can tell with your own parties. I had a good talk to Harold Burbage. He's really very interesting, whatever you think of his approach.'

'He's got power, that's all. Power's always interesting.'

Melanie smiled and was about to say something when there was a call from the door. Allan had arrived. She touched Geoffrey briefly on the arm to say she'd be back. He got up and followed her to the front door. Allan was coming up the concrete ramp she'd had made beside the front steps, driving his chair backwards. He said something to Melanie which Geoffrey couldn't catch. With a light laugh she said, 'Allan, you're not the only friend I've got who's in a wheelchair, you know.'

'Touché,' said Allan and steered himself into the house. Once inside he turned round and faced the gathering.

Only then did Geoffrey see what his friend had in his lap. His jaw dropped and he heard the wine from his glass spilling onto his shoes. For God's sake, Allan had brought the monkey!

He looked in desperation at Burbage, but Burbage had his back to Allan and was lecturing a group of Department graduates. Roach, however, was by his side and Roach spotted the monkey at once. He held back for a moment, then tapped Burbage lightly on the arm, whispered a few words in his ear and pointed with his little finger. Burbage looked and saw. His face changed and he cast around the room until his eyes rested on Geoffrey. He held them there, saying silently, We'll be talking about this.

From then on, the party could only go downhill for Geoffrey. He slipped a couple of Tofranil tablets into his mouth and washed them down with the hot spicy wine, although he knew it was a fatal mix. He kept out of the conversations.

Professor Harold Burbage was a well-fed man with a round face, a shiny bald head and a rich gingery beard that was trimmed exactly so that it grew only below the line of his jaw. For all his weight he was agile and dexterous and his delicate hands fluttered like a magician's as he talked to Allan, the centre of attention, with the interrogatory persistence of a policeman. Allan, innocent of the implications, was answering truthfully.

'It's one of ours, you say, and yet I don't see the tag,' Burbage said and checked round Ella's neck for the small tag all Department monkeys carried. Ella bared her gums.

Under his breath, Geoffrey whispered, 'Go on, *bite him!*' For once, however, Ella behaved with courtesy. She took Burgage's hand and shook it. Everyone laughed, even Burbage. He asked Allan whether he'd given her a name.

'Ella.'

'Ah, Ella for *cebus apella*. Very good, eh, George?' Burbage turned to Roach for acknowledgement, then went back to the monkey. 'Tell me, Ella, what's he been getting you to do? De-louse the cat, eh?'

But the food began to arrive, plates circulated with portions of chicken and salad and a basket of baked potatoes went from hand to hand. Burbage retired to a table to attack his. Melanie brought a plate for Allan, knelt down and cut the food into pieces. Ella sat close to her while she was carving and from time to time laid a paw on her hand. Melanie fixed the feeding-table in its slots on

108

Allan's chair and then Allan made the clicking sound. At once Ella hopped up onto his lap and fed him piece by piece. When he'd finished she wiped his mouth with a paper handkerchief.

Burbage was watching from the wings. Geoffrey saw him nodding to himself. An idea had clearly come to him. He was speaking in low tones to Roach and Geoffrey thought he heard the phrase *marketable proposition*. He kept away from Burbage for the rest of the party, except for a brief word at the end during which the monkey was not once referred to. But he knew that later, as quickly as it took to type it up, he would find a memo in his pigeonhole requesting his presence in his Departmental Professor's office.

'Well, Geoffrey, what do you have to tell me?'

Professor Burbage sat at his desk. Under his white lab coat he wore the waistcoat of a suit and a golf-club tie. His rounded face bore that headmasterly look that said, This is going to hurt you more than it hurts me. Before Geoffrey could answer, he went on, 'I don't need to remind you about the rules concerning animals taken off the premises — particularly at the present time with all this irresponsible anit-vivisection nonsense around. It only draws attention to our work. The Press blows these things out of all proportion.'

Geoffrey said nothing, waiting for the Professor to unburden himself.

'You're going to tell me the man's a cripple and we should do what we can to help,' Burbage continued. 'Geoffrey, what do you suppose we have charities for? Or perhaps the monkey's some kind of *field study* you're doing? Then where's the proposal for it? I recall nothing passing this desk about allocating scarce Departmental resources to teaching our monkeys to spoon-feed cripples. Unless I'm greatly misinformed,' he added heavily. He leaned back in the sprung leather chair and put his hands behind his bald head.

'Geoffrey, don't get me wrong. I'm all for lending a helping hand where we can. But let's not forget what our function here is. We're an establishment for pure research, not applied studies. We're scientists, not technologists like your friends in America and Canada.' Geoffrey remembered the memo he'd written on his return from visiting his counterparts in Montreal and

Columbia. He'd overdone the praise; Burbage would have read that as implied criticism. It was the kind of mistake Roach would never have made. But Burbage was still talking.

'I'm worried about your work, Geoffrey, I don't mind telling you. Why didn't you consult me before going off on that tangent with pemoline? The pemoline myth was exploded years ago. I don't understand the purpose of replicating old work that showed no results anyway. And now we have this business with the chap in the wheelchair. I think it's time we had a little chat about things.'

Geoffrey edged to the front of his chair. 'Look,' he said, 'I admit the pemoline idea didn't work, but the theoretical framework of introducing it into a peptide chain looked promising. And as for the monkey, do you realise that Allan Mann tried to commit suicide earlier this year? Here was a sick organism trying to destroy itself for lack of a means to fulfil its function. Okay, the monkey was a one-off crazy idea. But you saw it yesterday. And I can tell you its learning rate performance knocks spots off anything we're achieving in the Department by tissue ablation or psychochemistry or anything else.'

'Are you telling me that one wheelchair case is getting better results than the whole of my Department? If you are, I'd like notice of that.' Two white blotches had appeared on Burbage's cheeks. 'Let me repeat. We're not concerned here with the *uses* of science. Leave that to the commercial drug companies. Or, in your pet case, to the physios in Out Patients in our hospitals. Our purpose, Geoffrey, is simply to *understand the biological process.* No more, no less. Who does what with our findings doesn't interest me in the least. Take my advice. Get back to the RNA templates you were looking at. And for God's sake get that bloody monkey back here before it does some damage to the Department and let there be an end to that nonsense.'

'Now wait a minute.' Geoffrey half-rose in his chair. 'The end application *must* concern us. We've got to do more than just understand the workings of Nature. We've got to go out there and *use* our knowledge to change things, to improve the conditions of life. We've got to bend Nature to our will. We've got to take it on!'

Burbage leaned even further back in his chair and inspected the ceiling. He tugged at the fluff of his underchin beard and gave his favourite quotation from Engels. '"Let us not flatter ourselves overmuch on account of our human victories over Nature. For every such victory it takes revenge on us". No, Geoffrey. Your Mother Nature is a bitch. She's unpredictable, unmeasurable and pretty damn incomprehensible too. So let's just stick to measuring what we can, observing how biosystems behave and work, and not try and change the world, shall we?'

'I'm not so naïve as that, of course. But I am saying we have the chance to change the world for one particular human being at no cost to ourselves. And, I believe, learn something from the exercise too. In fact, I propose to run some tests on the monkey as soon as I can.'

'Tests? Absurd! The animal's been away from lab conditions for far too long. Anyway, what good is a sample of one? You've got no control group either. Okay, so you put the creature through a Y-maze a few times and it does well. What have you got? Can you isolate the factor responsible for its performance? No, I'll tell you why that little bugger knocks spots off our work here, *if* it does, and that's because it spends all day with a creature of somewhat higher intelligence than itself who gives it a good deal of parenting. A fat lot of good that'll do us here. Try telling Roche or Dow Chemical to formulate a love-and-affection drug. Or publish that you've isolated what improves learning and announce that it's simply a *happy home environment*. Sorry, Geoffrey. Let's try and be scientific, can we? There's nothing we can get out of an experiment like that. I want that monkey back here like today.' Burbage paused. 'If you want tests done on it, then I'll get Roach to look into it. His work's going smoothly and he's got time on his hands.'

Geoffrey swallowed. He nodded as if to agree and folded his legs casually. He appeared to be weighing up everything Burbage had said. 'There is *one* way the Department could benefit, though. I was struck by how everybody at lunch yesterday responded when the monkey started feeding Allan. The anthropologists were as green as hell. That couple of zoologists from Harvard wanted to start a full study right there and then. And, who was it, that fellow on the Hebdomadal Council, who went on about *this* being the face we ought to be presenting to the public. To show our work is socially useful and responsible. As a kind of public relations exercise.' Geoffrey levelled his eyes on Burbage's. 'I'm thinking of this as a *marketable proposition.'*

Professor Burbage sat upright and looked sharply at Geoffrey. It was clear he'd been thinking on the same lines all the time.

'Go on,' said Burbage.

Geoffrey could feel the sweat rising under his arms. He took a breath and began to lay hostages to the future which he might later regret.

It was a deal. But could Geoffrey deliver?

'What do you mean?' demanded Allan angrily when Geoffrey broached the idea to him in the afternoon. 'You'll take Ella away unless I agree to do an interview for a television documentary? It's blackmail!'

It was blackmail, and Geoffrey knew it. But he was merely responding to Burbage's blackmail. You had to pass it down the line. Geoffrey waited for Allan's fury to subside, but he was far more difficult to deal with than the Professor, far more rigorous. With him there weren't the trade-offs that were possible with Burbage. Allan railed on, livid.

'I will *not* be blackmailed! I won't give Ella up, for starters. Just see what a stink I'd make if anyone tried. *University Deprives Cripple of Loyal Pet.* How would that look in the *Oxford Times* or the *Daily Mail*? As for appearing on television, why do I want the world prying into my privacy? I'm just getting myself together at last and I don't want any interference.'

'It *is* the Year of the Disabled,' suggested Geoffrey gently.

'Oh, thanks. It's one year for all of you. For me it's the rest of my life.'

Geoffrey frowned in silence. He rubbed the back of his neck. He could feel himself getting angry too. Hell, whose idea was it to get Allan a monkey in the first place? Hadn't he taken enough risks with the Department already? Hadn't he spent hours helping Allan and Ella get accustomed to each other and devising methods of training her? He deserved a favour in return. This was business, like Burbage's business. Favours were given, favours were called in.

'You owe me one, Allan,' he said.

Allan looked at Geoffrey for a long minute before he softened 'Okay, okay,' he said wearily. 'But understand why I'll do it. Not because Burbage threatens to take Ella back, because he shan't. Nor because it gives me any pleasure thinking of twenty million viewers out there ogling at me in their armchairs. No, I'm doing it for you, because you asked me to. That's all. Okay?'

'Okay. Thanks, mate.'

Allan wheeled himself back to his reading-stands and carried on working. He interrupted his study for a moment to ask, 'When do you want to fix it? You'd better give me notice so I can book the minicab.'

'Well, actually, the idea is to come and do it here, in your flat.' Geoffrey avoided Allan's eye. 'In fact, Burbage was on the blower to the editor of Horizon before I saw him. It seems they'd like to fit it in during the first week of January. If that's okay with you.'

'It's okay with me,' said Allan in a dull tone. 'It'll give me something to do over Christmas, thinking up the answers.'

Geoffrey went to let himself out of the flat. As he put on his overcoat he said again, 'I appreciate this, Allan. I'm rather on the spot, you know.'

Allan turned and smiled. He spoke in a gentler tone. 'Sure, I understand. Take care how you drive and don't forget your seat-belt. We don't want to have to look for an Ella for you.'

After Geoffrey had gone, Allan reflected that he did indeed owe his friend one. And for the tablets too, which were already producing results in his work.

Nineteen

They arrived with the first snow, one bleak January morning. Geoffrey was shocked when he opened the door, for there were six of them. He'd imagined there would only be a cameraman and the interviewer. Allan wouldn't like it. Already he'd holed up in his bedroom and was only coming out at the last minute.

As the crew brought in the lights, stands and power cables, the flat began rapidly losing its heat. Geoffrey was close to panic. But Tony, the producer, understood and told his assistant Timothy to control the front doors to create an air-lock. Tony was short, shy, and had pink piggy eyes and a nervy, intimate manner. He'd brought a change of shoes in a plastic bag and made Rick, the cameraman, take off his snow-covered boots and go about in stocking feet. Everyone was behaving with care and something close to an uncertain kind of awe. They knew what they'd come to film but they didn't know what to expect.

'We'll have to move that easel,' said Tony in his quiet, close-to voice. Geoffrey had brought the easel and flip-charts and set it up in front of the fireplace.

'Well,' said Geoffrey, 'I thought you might like to know a bit about our work in the Department. Let me show you. We're dealing with the effect of various psychochemical compounds on associative memory . . .'

Tony held up a hand. 'I'm afraid this is television; when they call it mass media, they mean media for the masses. We're here to film a quadriplegic and his monkey.' He caught Geoffrey's look

114

of disappointment and said quickly, 'Well, I don't see why not. Rick, set up over in the corner there, will you, and we'll get a take of Dr Fish before we begin.' He mumbled something to Rick which Geoffrey didn't catch and Rick, with his dark oiled hair and black kid jacket and stocking feet, led Geoffrey over to the back window and fixed up the camera. Meanwhile Tony had decided to turn the interview into a fireside chat; he drew the curtains and lit the gas-log fire. The arc lights went up, the central heating blasted away and soon the whole place was melting.

'Take one!'

There was silence in the room and Geoffrey began to deliver his lecture. He was only half way through the first chart when he caught the sound of rubber wheels squelching on the vinyl floor. In the doorway, beyond the searing arc-lights, sat Allan in his chair. Allan said nothing. Tony looked around to see what had made Geoffrey falter in his delivery and saw Allan. 'Cut!' he ordered. To Geoffrey he said, 'We'll have to leave it there for the time being. Maybe we can come back to you if there's time at the end.'

Allan wheeled into the room and fixed them all with a baleful eye. Tony introduced the team one by one. 'This is Jerry, the lighting engineer. And Felicity, who'll be asking you the questions. Rick, behind the camera. And Rose, to make you up. Rose, you'd better get down to it right away. I'm Tony and this is my assistant Timothy.' A skinny young man with a keen manner came forward and held out his hand before realising his mistake.

Tony cleared his throat and went on, talking softly and directly to Allan. 'I think we'll have you beside the fire, Mr Mann.' He signalled for Timothy to wheel Allan there, but Allan drove himself. Everyone stopped what they were doing and watched. Turning to Rick, Tony said, 'We'll want footage of that.'

The lights were set up but had to be changed because they showed up Allan's lean face as gaunt and hollow. Rose was squatting beside him, rubbing foundation into his cheeks, holding the stick with the pads of her fingers to let her own nails dry. One of his hands slipped off his lap and she put it back, her face registering shock at its lifelessness. She held her body further away then, as though he had something contagious.

Tony turned to Geoffrey. 'I believe you said he was some kind of star athlete.'

115

'Yes, he was a Blue.'

Tonly clapped the palms of his hands like a flamenco dancer. 'That's the angle! Doesn't he have any trophies around, cups and badges and shields and so on? I can't see anything.'

'And photos too,' said Timothy keenly.

With hesitation, Geoffrey replied, 'Well, actually there's a whole lot of stuff in the cupboard . . .'

'Fine,' said Tony. 'Let's have them out.'

'I'd rather you didn't,' said Geoffrey, turning his back to Allan in the hope he wouldn't hear. 'I mean, it might upset Allan.'

'Then I'm afraid some of our questions may upset him too. No, I'm sure he's proud of his achievements. It's quite something to run for your University. Timothy, go and fetch what you can.'

Jerry, the lighting engineer, had lit up a cigarillo. Geoffrey bit his lips and touched Tony on the shoulder. He said, 'Actually, Allan doesn't like people smoking in the flat. Otherwise he has to open the windows and that lets out the heat.'

'Of course,' said Tony quickly and went over to Jerry. Jerry whipped the cigarillo out of his mouth and ground it out on the floor. Then he quickly stooped and picked up the pieces and wiped the floor with a handkerchief. He moved a cable junction-box over the spot where a scorched stain remained. Everyone was on edge. Allan hadn't spoken a word yet.

Timothy set up an array of silver cups on the mantlepiece and placed a photo in Allan's lap. It was the picture of his final Varsity race. Tony caught Allan's look and returned the photo to the mantlepiece. But he went over to Rick and in his intimate tone signalled that the camera should come in close onto the photo, then slowly pan across to Allan's head in close-up, then track back until subject and interviewer were both in frame. Geoffrey understood: it was to be the Before and the After.

Geoffrey went to fetch Ella but as she came in she took fright. She scrambled for the door and when Jerry involuntarily reached to grab her, she bit him sharply. He howled and cursed under his breath. As Geoffrey went off in pursuit he heard Jerry say to the cameraman, 'Gawd, I'd have skinned the little bugger before now.' Rick replied, 'He didn't get you in the nethers, you should care.'

Geoffrey retrieved Ella and placed her on Allan's lap. Allan looked up and spoke in a voice loud enough for the room to hear.

'You told them to get tetanus jabs before coming, didn't you?'

Jerry let out a small whimper and began sucking his wound like a snake-bite. Everyone turned to Allan. It was almost as if they'd really only just discovered his presence.

The filming began. Felicity, the interviewer, was an eternal youth of forty-ish with agony-aunt glasses and a manner that said she was fearless in confronting unpleasant issues. She took off her glasses for the more sensitive questions. She deliberately used blunt language in an effort not to sound patronising. She covered Allan's family, his father's death, his schooling, his sport. Then she moved onto questions of social relevance.

'One of the main criticisms levelled at society today, Allan, is that it frankly doesn't *care* enough. It treats the disabled as outcasts and sweeps the whole problem under the carpet. It locks them away in institutions as if they're *unsightly*. Would you agree this is true, Allan?'

Allan said quietly, 'I don't get out to meet society as a whole, so I can't say.'

'In your own experience, I mean.'

'My friends treat me as I am. That's how they stay my friends.'

'But surely more could be done to improve public awareness of the *issues*? For instance, at the educational level.'

'You mean, O-Level courses in Disability Studies? I think the less people have to confront the *issues* as you put it, the happier they are.'

Felicity put on her glasses and took them off again. 'Yes, indeed. Now about your monkey there, young Ella. She's obviously a very original solution to the basic problem of *coping*. Let me ask you: is there scope for using animals in this rôle on a wider basis, as home-helps for the disabled?'

'Monkeys on the National Health?'

Rose, the make-up girl, tittered. Tony frowned, looked at his watch and called, 'Cut! Let's take five. Felicity, it's going nicely but let's keep it informal, chatty. And you, Mr Mann, it's not easy I know, but it would help if you could make your answers more . . . constructive. Get a conversation going. Is there anything we can get you?'

'I'd like some tea,' said Allan. 'Geoffrey knows where everything is.'

Tony called to Timothy. 'Get Mr Mann some tea, would you?'

Timothy said to Geoffrey, 'Does he take milk and sugar?'

Geoffrey nodded. Timothy asked, 'How many spoons?'

From the fireplace, Allan said curtly, 'Two.'

'I'd like to film Ella giving him the tea,' said Tony.

Geoffrey overheard Rick saying to Felicity, under his breath, 'Go on, ask him how he *gets it up*. Can he or can't he? That's what the viewers really want to know, not all that crap about society caring. Jesus, it's hot in here. Jerry, open a bloody window, for God's sake.'

'Don't,' intervened Geoffrey. 'Ella's not trained to go out alone.'

Rick turned to Jerry and muttered, 'Poor creature, cooped up here all day with a cripple. Phone the RSPCA, I would.' Geoffrey was not out of earshot. He heard and winced for Allan. It was getting sticky.

Filming had begun again and Felicity was speaking with a new conversational tone. 'Allan, I'm going to ask you about your relationship with Ella. How would you describe it? To people who don't know you, who don't know the background, it must seem rather . . . unusual.'

'We respect each other,' replied Allan, speaking slowly and enunciating his words carefully. There was a growing menace that Geoffrey was perhaps the first to pick up on. 'Ella takes me just as I am. She doesn't see me as a cripple, just as myself.'

'Do you mean that this is something *more* than just a human and his pet?'

'What are you asking?'

'I mean, do we have here just a man and his pet monkey, or . . ?'

'Or what? Or something unnatural?'

'Unusual was the word I used, Allan.'

'Well, I'm pretty unusual, aren't I? The whole set-up's pretty unusual, isn't it?'

Tony intervened and moved forward. He knelt below the camera line and said, 'Hold it there, Felicity. This is great. We've got a real conversation going here. Rick, I want both their heads in the frame if you can.'

'Like two real people talking,' added his beanpole assistant Timothy from the side.

A silence fell like the silence between lightning and thunder. Allan looked at Timothy, then Felicity, then Tony. His face screwed up with hurt and disgust. He said, almost inaudibly,

'*Real* people?'

He made the clicking noise to Ella and reached his head forward to the mouth-controls. He aimed his chair straight for the door, riding over the cables and upsetting the reflector umbrellas and aluminium cannisters of film. He went through the doorway and down the corridor to his bedroom.

Tony turned on Timothy, 'Idiot! I told you these people are temperamental. Go and get him back. We haven't finished yet.'

Timothy, agitated, said to Geoffrey, 'Can we get him back? You know how to.'

This was a disaster. Trembling, Geoffrey went down the corridor and tapped on Allan's door. There was no reply. He knocked again. Then Allan's voice, shouting:

'Get them out! Get them out of my flat! The whole pack. And you too. I'm not moving until the place is completely empty. You've got your pound of flesh. Take it and go. Go!'

Geoffrey went back into the living room, but Tony had understood the interview was at an end and he'd already given the order to pack up. 'But what about finishing off my little talk?' said Geoffrey to Tony.

'I'm sorry, Dr Fish, but time's against us,' said Tony firmly.

'Well, I suppose you got a bit,' said Geoffrey.

As he was leaving, still nursing his wounded hand, Jerry murmured quietly to Geoffrey, 'Sorry about your bit, mate. The camera wasn't loaded. Tough.'

Geoffrey stayed until the whole team had packed up and left. Then he went back to Allan's room and tapped. There was no reply. He walked quietly back down the corridor, paused to collect his easel and flip-charts and let himself out. He kicked the snow in the path with sudden savagery and cursed everyone, the world in general, Burbage, Roach, the BBC, life itself. He'd created more problems than he'd solved. That seemed to be the run of his luck.

119

Twenty

One morning, a few weeks later, on one of those bright February days that hold out a false hope of spring, Ella invented a new game.

As usual she had waited for Dorothy to leave for work. Then she went back into the kitchen to get her tablets for Allan. She had it all worked out. First she climbed onto the top of the fridge by way of the sink; from there she could stand on her hind legs and pull herself up onto the top of the wall-mounted cabinet. Next came the difficult bit. Sitting on top of the cabinet, she opened the door and reached for the bottle. Normally she'd unscrew the plastic lid, take out one of the oval yellow tablets, replace the bottle and close the door. She was getting good at putting things back in their places: Geoffrey made a lot of fuss about that in his training sessions. Today the bottle was empty. She shook it, puzzled, and then brought it into the living room and put it on the table in front of Allan. She upended it so he could see it was empty.

'Geoffrey's coming later,' he said. 'I'll get some more off him. Now leave me alone. I've got to think.'

He leaned his head back until it rested on the chair back and stared at the ceiling for inspiration. It was a ridiculous case he had to deal with today. A Torquay salesman had stabbed a man in the heart with a large pair of packing scissors. The man had grabbed him by the hair and the salesman was claiming self-defence. But refer for a moment, Gentlemen of the Jury, to the case of Regina v. Palmer (1971) and Lord Morris' judgement (AC 814, 831–2).

When did self-defence become actual aggression? Was it not relevant that the assailant weighed twenty stone and had three previous convictions for GBH? Twenty stone. That was heavy. At his training weight Allan had never been over ten stone eight. Now he was what? Seven? Seven-five? Are you aware of the fact, m'lud, that a child's brain at birth is ten percent of its entire body weight? And that by the time it has reached adulthood, is only two percent? Very well. Suppose the brain of Allan Mann weighed 1500 grams, a kilo and a half, roughly three generous pound-jars of jam. Now, converting pounds into kilos and stones into pounds and dividing by long division . . . The ceiling's terrible. It's got to be painted. Mole grey would look good. Mother would probably choose Naples yellow to go with the terracotta. And that lamp shade must go too.

Allan felt his eyes closing and the world drifting away. His head lolled forward suddenly and woke him. He blinked. This was no good. He had so much work to do. It was only three months to Finals and Dr Fry had been piling on the pressure. This time two years ago he'd also been working for the exams. Then, whenever he felt stale and congested, he'd put on his tracksuit and go for a run round the Parks or the streets. Go for a run! Just like that. On with the tracksuit, tie up the shoe-laces and out into the open in leaps and bounds. But that was not him, that was about someone different, someone else with a different life, it was not about *him*, not about this Allan Mann. No, and again *no*!

He gulped in air and clenched his teeth. After a while it subsided.

Ella was bobbing up and down on her haunches on the shelf, holding her tiny hands over her eyes. She wanted to play peep-bo. She loved it. He would shut his eyes tight and little by little he'd open one. Just a fraction. Ella would cover her eyes too but she always cheated and peeped. When their eyes met, she'd shriek with excitement and terror. Then she'd cover up her face again quickly. But if she peeped out while his eyes were still open, then she was *had*. That was how the peep-bo game went. It could go on for half an hour. Ella never got tired of it.

'Not now, Ella,' said Allan. 'I'm trying to concentrate. Do give me some peace.' He'd have to make a start somewhere. He turned to the typewriter and reached forward for his mouth-stick. It wasn't there.

Damn, he thought. Had it rolled under the typewriter? It

hadn't. Was it on the floor? He reversed his chair to look, but it wasn't there. Had he let it drop into his lap unnoticed? No, there was nothing in his lap except those white bony things he knew as his hands, folded in the curiously pious attitude in which Dorothy arranged them. Ella meanwhile was hopping up and down in huge excitement, cackling and rubbing her head with both her hands simultaneously. Ella!

'Ella!' he demanded. 'What have you done with my stick?' She swung down onto the table, rocked her head giddily from side to side and leaped back onto her shelf.

'Oh I see. It's a game. Hunt the mouth-stick.'

He couldn't be cross. Besides, it was a far better game than last week's, when she locked herself in Dorothy's room. Twice she did it. Both times they'd had to break the door down. Now the lock was blanked off on the inside and it could only be locked from the outside.

'Now let me see. I wonder if it's behind the tape-recorder. I wonder. No, it isn't. How about behind these books? No. I'm guessing that it is still in this room, isn't it. I guess it's . . . on your shelf up there with your Thing and those cotton-reels I saw you pinch from Mother's mending-basket and God knows what else too. Is it? If it is, it's too high for me to see, so it can't be. How's that for logic, Ella? It's in the drinks cabinet. All right, it's not in the drinks cabinet. How about behind the bowl of fruit on the sideboard? Or the window-sill at the back window? No. Oh come on, I give up. Okay then. I'll shut my eyes and just try and imagine where I'd hide it if I were a monkey.'

He shut his eyes. He began to un-think. This was what he used to do before a race or exams. People thought he was meditating but he was merely allowing his mind to float free of his body, to float out and above it and then look down on it from high up, maybe as a speck in a tracksuit in the grass or, as now, a dark-haired, bent, lean figure sitting motionless in a grey vinyl and chrome chair.

His eyelids were lightly closed. To shut them tightly brought whorls of emerald and black. Now all he could see was a dull reddish-brown hue, occasionally shot through with wriggling traces of light that reminded him of the colour spectroscope photos of neurons Geoffrey had once brought to show him.

122

When he wanted to float free, he'd sit like this for a moment, wait for his eyeballs to turn back and upwards and then cast himself off. Sometimes he'd imagine letting himself fall off a bridge, but instead of falling he'd float out on the air and rise higher and higher until he was above the topmost spires of the bridge and everything lay mapped out small below him and he became as infinitely wide and expansive as the skin of the sea.

But this time he wanted his mind to concentrate and he held it back from its flight. He just went on looking into the dull reddishness of the light coming through his closed eyelids. Then, very slowly, like an old sepia vignette coming up in the developing tray, a picture began to form in the centre of his field of vision. It was unclear and kept flickering. But a shape like a whitish square began to emerge. It was divided in the centre and bordered by a straight rod-like things. The square was being held up on a kind of pole which stretched down out of view. Then, suddenly, the picture disappeared. The dull reddishness closed over. Allan opened his eyes. He blinked, for the morning was bright. Then he realised what he was looking at. Ahead of him were his reading-stands, on one of which a large book had been pinned open.

'I've found the mouth-stick!' he chanted in a child's sing-song. 'I've found the mouth-stick!'

Sure enough, alongside one of the vertical arms, neatly camouflaged, lay his mouth-stick. Ella whooped and swung down and retrieved the stick. When Allan had stopped laughing enough so that he could hold it in his mouth, he made the clicking noise and Ella hopped up onto his lap and put the stick between his lips. Then he drove himself into position in front of the typewriter and began to compose the first sentence of his essay on the point at which counter-attack becomes assault.

It was only later that he realised something. He'd had his eyes well shut. Trying it again, he found he could see nothing through them when he got the reddish-brown hues. Even so, from where he'd been sitting the reading-stand directly facing him had been one of the two empty ones. The one with the book set up was over to the right, nearer the window and Ella's shelf.

Geoffrey had his own key to the flat but when he came by in the afternoons he preferred to ring the doorbell just like any other visitor. Dorothy always greeted him with a report on Allan. 'He's been good as gold,' or 'It's not been one of his days.' She still saw her son as a patient. Today, however, she said, 'He's been a joy. Like his old self.'

From the living room came the slow movement of the Beethoven Triple concerto. Majestic, luscious music. Geoffrey was aware of the change. He no longer heard the sepulchral Telemann adagios or the cerebral Bach Partitas. The new sounds went with the redecoration of the living room and the flowers in vases all over the flat and the new pictures on the walls. They also went with Allan's forgiveness for the television interview. They now joked about it.

Geoffrey pushed open the swing door and threw down a bulging briefcase on to one of the two new armchairs Allan had got in. He loosened his knitted tie and took off his tweed jacket; the place was like a greenhouse. But it smelled less of institutional wax polish and pine disinfectant and more like a home.

'How's tricks?' Geoffrey asked as he upended the briefcase into the chair. 'Can we turn the music down?' he shouted.

Allan made the *tclick-tclick* noise and beamed his spot of light onto the cassette player. He gave it a *bleep* and Ella hopped up at once and switched the tape off. Geoffrey took this so readily for granted now that he didn't turn round. He was busy sorting out what he'd brought: an ophthalmoscope, a stethoscope, a small blood-pressure pump and sleeve, some forms and computer input cards, and finally a whole collection of small toys — London buses, road tankers, toy soldiers, farm animals.

'What's the Toytown for?' Allan asked.

'Junk objects,' said Geoffrey. 'For the Wisconsin box.'

He had begun to take the Ella experiment seriously: there *was* something he'd overlooked previously. But this meant running tests scientifically. Science was measurement, precise measurement, and this meant eliminating as many of the extraneous variables as possible. It was no good measuring Ella's talents at learning how to comb Allan's hair, fetch drinks and turn off a tape cassette. The scientific world would only accept results obtained under arid laboratory conditions where distractions and outside influences had been eliminated. Hence the Wisconsin

124

box. This was a larger version of the apparatus used by Geoffrey's colleagues working on rats in the Psychology Department. It was like a giant shoe-box, with a sliding panel in the centre and a two-way mirror at one end. You put the monkey in one half of the box and a number of random objects in the other compartment, pulled out the screen so that the monkey was exposed to the objects for a defined time and watched its performance through the mirror at the end.

'I'll bring it in while your mother makes the tea,' said Geoffrey.

'Want a hand?' asked Allan.

'I think I can manage,' replied Geoffrey with a grin.

Ella's tests were going well and her performance was quite staggering. At first Geoffrey had used simple mazes, the simplest being the Y-maze. Here you put the monkey at the broad end. You put a reward (usually a banana pellet) at the end of one of the forks and a punishment (usually a mild electric shock) at the other. George Roach liked to use a concealed bunsen burner to provide the aversive stimulus; monkeys, like most animals, are terrified of fire and a singed *singe* (as Roach would say) learns pretty damn quick. In this way you could readily measure how quickly a monkey learned to find the reward and how long he retained the knowledge under various doses of different psychochemicals. There were more sophisticated variations, of course. If a particular lever, for instance, had regularly yielded a reward in the past, how much of an electric shock on the paw would a monkey tolerate in order to get the reward it expected? And then how long would it go on doing this if the reward were withheld? And so on. It was a wonderful labyrinth of theoretical constructs, as subtle as the human mind could devise.

'I really think you're crazy,' said Allan as Geoffrey heaved the large plywood box into the living room and started clearing a space on the table.

'Ah, but this is different. Here I'm testing for Ella's *memory association*. I'm going to put a pellet under, say, this red bus first time round. Next time maybe the blue pick-up truck. And so on, sometimes repeating, sometimes doing something quite diffe-rent. Then I'll look for such things as primacy and recency. Humans, for instance, tend to remember the first and last of a series given to them, better than the middle items. Does Ella show a predisposition of this kind?'

'The suspense is killing me.'

'Then when she makes errors, why is it? Look, here are two red buses. One's got no wheels. Say I put the pellet, the reward, under one and she consistently goes for the other. That's what we call an error due to interference. There are other kinds of interference. If I teach her a range of tasks, does her doing task A mean she forgets to do tasks B, C, D and so on?'

'That's all very well,' Allan said, yawning. 'You're teaching her parrot-fashion, if that's the phrase. She's far more intelligent than that. I mean, has she failed any of your tests yet? Except when she's bored or wants to tease you?'

'She's very remarkable,' agreed Geoffrey quietly. It was true. He'd been synthesising the results of the various tests he'd been giving the monkey and had built up a single graph of her overall performance. It was consistently, and astonishingly, high. That was why Geoffrey was excited that she might, at last, provide him with a clue to the right direction to take in his research. He had six other monkeys in the lab now on a course of various different formulations of the same concoction he'd made up for Ella. But Ella, who had been on the drug far longer, was way ahead of the others. This way he hoped to isolate the element in the drug that was responsible.

Allan went on, 'I mean, what about teaching her to understand the *consequences* of actions. Teaching her, for example, that there's no point in bringing me my beaker from the fridge if it's empty. You can teach her to sweep the floor, but what if Mother's just done it and there's nothing to sweep up?'

'Ah, you're referring to *purposive* action. No, that's strictly in the human realm,' said Geoffrey and stretched himself upright. He ran a hand through the reddish stubble of his hair and went on, 'Right, I'm ready. Ella, where are you?'

Geoffrey looked around the room. It was then he saw her bottle of tablets on the window-sill. 'That shouldn't be there,' he said and picked it up. At once he noticed it was empty.

'They're finished,' Allan said, 'You'd better bring some more.'

Geoffrey frowned and turned towards his friend who had a bland expression on his lean face. 'Now wait a minute,' Geoffrey began. 'I made her up a hundred, let me see, six weeks ago. They should have lasted three months. Or maybe Dorothy's put some in another bottle? I'll ask her.'

'There was a slight accident,' said Allan easily. 'Mother dropped the whole lot in the sink. She rescued some but I think a lot went down the drain. Imagine what it'll do to the rats in the sewers!'

Geoffrey said nothing. He lobbed the polythene bottle up and down in his hand thoughtfully. Then he said, 'I should have warned her. They're coated with a dye that's the very devil to get out.'

'Oh, we got it out all right. Mother spent hours scrubbing the sink. It's as good as new.' Allan paused. 'But surely you've got lots more in the lab?'

Geoffrey put the bottle carefully down on the table. He felt a cold sweat spreading all over him. He went and stood directly in front of Allan, who stared defiantly back. Geoffrey's throat was dry. He didn't like having to use a trick to get at the truth.

'Allan, that isn't true. You're lying to me. The dye on those tablets is perfectly water-soluble. It doesn't stain.'

Allan arched an eyebrow. 'Am I in the witness box? Shall I swear the oath?'

Geoffrey felt his face turning red and he tightened his damp palms into fists. 'This is not funny, Allan. You've been letting Dorothy give Ella a double dose, haven't you!' He spoke in a whisper. 'She's been having two tablets a day instead of one. Hasn't she! *Christ!*'

He let out a small cry, shot out a hand to grab hold of Ella by the nape of the neck and held her roughly on the table top while he shone the ophthalmoscope into the pupils of her eyes. He peered first into one, then the other, then checked them both again. Finally he let her go and she scampered away into the corner.

'Well, there doesn't seem to be any lasting damage there,' he said. 'I was afraid her retinas might be permanently damaged. As it is, they show slight signs of pigment alteration, but I think she'll be all right. One of the components in the drug changes pigment colour and can cause blindness. We're not absolutely sure.'

'Blindness?' Allan drew in his breath.

Geoffrey rounded on him. Allan had screwed up the project by giving Ella the overdose. He should never have allowed Dorothy to do it. How could proper scientific measurements be taken if the single most important variable wasn't held constant?

What good were Ella's fantastic results if he couldn't tell *why*? The whole project was cock-eyed, unscientific and a waste of time. If he couldn't produce some sound results from Ella, he'd get the boot from Burbage. At the very least he'd damn well take Ella back and keep her in the labs under his nose. Perhaps he could salvage something by doing that, perhaps not. Basically, Allan had *fucked it up*.

At that point Dorothy came in with the tea. Geoffrey took a breath and was about to have a go at her too. But as she put the tray down she saw the bottle of tablets. 'What's that doing there?' she asked and picked it up. 'It shouldn't be out of the cupboard. Ella's had her one for the day. I don't know, things seem to have a life of their own in this flat.'

Ella's had her one for the day. So Dorothy hadn't been feeding her the double dose. Allan couldn't. Who had?

'Dorothy,' said Geoffrey tightly, 'Are you *sure* Ella can't get at the kitchen wall-cabinet?'

'Sure? You can't be sure of anything with that little wretch around,' she said. 'The pranks she gets up to! Anyway, what's the matter?'

Geoffrey didn't answer. Another idea was forming in his mind. Dorothy hadn't put the bottle in the living room. Ella must have. But if Ella was feeding herself from the bottle, why did Allan invent the transparent lie about an accident? And why would Ella trouble to bring the bottle into the living room if she was feeding herself in the kitchen?

'Allan! Allan, look at me!'

Allan looked away. He began to wheel himself over to the reading-stands.

'Christ, Allan!'

Geoffrey had understood. He grabbed his friend by the shoulders and spun the chair round. He snatched up the ophthalmoscope and shone it into his eyes. But Allan shut them and held them tight shut.

'What's going on?' asked Dorothy in a quavering voice.

Geoffrey tugged at Allan's eyebrows but he jerked his whole head aside. Geoffrey grabbed him by the hair and forced his head right back against the back of the chair. He dug his foot into the spokes so that the chair wouldn't budge. Allan began rolling his eyes round and round and wriggling his head to throw Geoffrey

128

off. He bit into Geoffrey's hand. Then Ella joined in. She went for Geoffrey's wrist but he fought her off for long enough to get his thumb and forefinger in each side of one of Allan's eyeballs. He dug deeper and held it there just long enough to shine the torch onto the retinas. One look told him everything. Already there were hints of brownish flecks appearing in the dark blue. God only knew what other damage there might be.

'For Christ's sake, Allan, what are you playing at?'

'Will somebody tell me what's the matter?' cried Dorothy. She'd taken up a position with one hand on the telephone.

But Allan said, 'Leave us, Mother. Please. It's nothing. Geoffrey's had a nasty surprise, that's all. We want to talk about it alone.' When Dorothy had left the room, although he knew she'd be listening in the corridor, he went on, 'So, you see. What's making you angry? Shouldn't you be pleased your precious project isn't screwed up after all?'

Geoffrey raised his hand. He was about to hit him. 'That's a shitty thing to say! It's *you* I'm worried about, you bloody fool. How long have you been taking them? How often? Jesus Christ, you don't know what I've put in the damned things!'

'They don't do Ella any harm,' said Allan, still challenging.

'Maybe, but they're *untested*. Ella *is* the test. God knows if I hadn't caught it now what might have happened. You might be going blind. Blind, Allan! I'd be responsible.'

'You'd be responsible. That's all you care about. They'd point the finger at you, Geoffrey. Blinding a cripple. Burbage wouldn't like that.'

'Allan, what are you doing? Are you trying to kill yourself again? Because, if you are, believe me, I can give you something a whole lot more effective.' Geoffrey's hands were trembling and he leaned on the table for support. He was shocked how close he'd come to hitting him.

'I don't want to die,' said Allan more quietly, lowering his eyes. 'I've worked out a way of doing it if I ever want to. I know I can succeed another time. In a way, I don't need to because of that. No, Ella's pills seem to help me with work. I'm so tired, stuffed up, stale. Concentrating wears me out. What do *you* do when you're tired and worn out? Go for a stroll? Pop out for a drink? Go for a drive in the country? Take Melanie to the movies? Okay. Then tell me. What do *I* do?'

Geoffrey felt his body's tension ebbing. But he was still angry. He came to stand in front of Allan where he had to face him.

'I know what I *don't* do. I don't go dosing myself with drugs I know nothing about, drugs which haven't been tested for human use. I'd need to know a whole lot more about how they work. Just remember, Allan, your brain is your life. You should consult me before you take things that tamper with it. I wouldn't like to see you becoming a cripple in brain as well as body. You just think about that.'

Twenty-one

The fool, cursed Geoffrey. The bloody idiot.

He hunched his blue duffle-coat and got out of his car. The Department car park was pitch black. It was midnight, cold and moonless. His foot caught an empty can and sent it rattling viciously across the black ice. The concrete cube of the laboratory building was as bleak as Colditz. His key wouldn't turn in the frozen lock and he bruised his numb fingers getting it open. From the basement the heating plant hummed on stand-by. Geoffrey didn't like lifts at night, so he took the stairs. His lab on the top floor was as he'd left it, in darkness except for the low blue safety lights. The monkeys stirred as he passed but they wouldn't wake up properly until he turned the lights on. It was their midnight hour too.

He shut himself in his office; it was cold and airless. He rubbed his hands as they regained sensation and swung his arms back and forth. Briefly he wondered about the calorific value of tandoori chicken. He'd taken Melanie to an Indian meal after a Wajda film. It had been a curiously easy evening, perhaps because he had work to do afterwards and so there were none of the questions like 'Shall we take two cars?' or 'Won't you come back for a drink?' with all their latent tension and hurt.

He took off his duffle-coat and jacket and turned on the small Belling stove, officially laboratory equipment, which everyone used for heating coffee. Slowly it glowed red and gave out a glimmer of heat. He particularly didn't want to be cold. Low temperatures reduce the electrical activity of the brain.

He unlocked one of the glass-fronted cabinets that lined the wall. In it were several large polythene tubs in a line, each labelled with the names of the monkeys: Lincoln, Washington, Roosevelt, Nixon, and so on. The names offended visiting biochemists from mid-Western universities, but his friends from UCLA and Berkeley found it normal: they chose Nikita and Mao and Tito. Geoffrey felt his mind wandering. He shook himself and concentrated. Ella's tub was simply marked 'Ella'. He took out three oval yellow tablets from his tub and made a note on a record-card. Then he locked the cabinet. Three should give some indication, although Allan had probably taken fifty over a period of time. Indications, or contra-indications. He eyed the tablets in the palm of his hand uncertainly. What the hell *were* they? A bit of this and a bit of that. Derivatives of imipramine to interact with the limbic system and the reticular formation, giving a kind of 'lift'. Derivatives of tranylcypromine, his old friend Parnate, which inhibited monoamine transmitters in the central nervous system. Derivatives of the datura plant, mainly scopolamine, to do the reverse and stimulate synaptic activity in the hippocampus region of the brain, the region associated with short-term memory. And all of this in a base synthesised almost two years before from a section of ablated human brain tissue, from the girl who had screamed when the surgeon probed a bank of memory cells. These were the ingredients. The cocktail had been shaken, incubated, added to a neutral chalk-based substance, centrifuged dry and finally compacted, with a yellow dye, into small oval tablets. What were they really? A bran tub. Scientifically, a bloody bran tub.

He pushed a space clear on the desk top and pulled out from the lower drawers a tangle of small round plastic discs with a series of wires attached. These were the basic electrode sensors he used on his monkeys. With a bit of adaptation, some different conductive gel and stronger tape, he could probably get them to work on himself. It was going to be one hell of a job, wiring himself up unaided. The instruments and recording apparatus were in the lab next door, among the monkeys, but he'd get wired up in his office. If he could. He toyed with the idea of calling it off until morning, until he could get a student to help him. But that was too risky; this was the only way. Alone, at night, in secret.

He separated the equipment. The EKG sensors, measuring heart rate, went on the back of the ankles. The EEG receptors were relatively easy: they went on the temples and the back of the neck. So were the EMG sensors, for measuring muscle tension. He'd leave the sweat-gland receptors to last. These plugged into an SLC machine and went onto the finger-tips. That would be damn tricky; his fingers were those of a rugby-player, not a nimble monkey. He'd probably end up with the whole lot in one almighty mess.

But first the drug had to be correctly prepared. It would take too long to work into the metabolic system if he ingested it orally like Allan. It would have to be injected. He got a pestle and mortar, a bottle of sterile saline and a hypodermic. For several minutes he ground the tablets until they formed a powder as fine as rouge. He shook the powder into a culture dish and added a measured amount of saline. This he stirred slowly and carefully until he was sure all the particles were evenly suspended, and he put the dish aside to let any bubbles rise to the surface.

Now he was ready. He had only to fill the needle, get himself wired up, plug into the instruments next door, take readings before the injection, administer the injection, and wait. He got up and fetched himself a coffee from the machine in the corridor. In the distance he heard the first of the college clocks striking one.

At one o'clock Allan fell into a light sleep.

He had specifically asked his mother to prop his bedroom door open so that he could see the light from the hallway. She had kept a light on in the hall ever since Jock died; she believed a light deterred burglars.

Towards three o'clock, he woke. Darkness! Everywhere it was dark. He couldn't see the end of his bed. He couldn't see the merest glimmer of white from the ceiling. The room extended in all directions to black infinity. What time was it? A car passed, far away. Was it morning, were they going to work, was everyone up and getting going? Was it daylight?

So this was it. This was blindness. A total blotting-out.

'Mother! Mother!'

Dorothy heard the cry and called back from the darkness. Allan heard her stumbling to her feet, throwing open her door, padding fast down the corridor, then opening his door, swinging it open, swinging it so that the light from the hallway came in, dim as it was yet as bright as a miracle. His bedroom door had swung closed while he'd been asleep. That was all.

'I'm sorry, Mother. It was just another dream. Go back to bed. And please wedge the door open this time. Thanks.'

The dim hall light swamped his room. He moved his head as far as he could to see everything, to remember and record everything as though it were his last chance. He'd been reprieved. But he couldn't chance shutting his eyes. They might catch him this time. The wind might change, as his mother used to threaten him when he pulled faces as a child. The wind might change and you'll be blind. A blind cripple.

Jock's old shaving mirror was still there, on the dressing table beside the clock. If he could get to it, what would he see? His hair more salt than pepper now. His lips clamped tight to hold in the panic, as tight and thin as the seam of a weld. But what about the eyes? Yes, the eyes. Were they already going brown, flaking inside like rusty railings? Or opaque white like the eyes of a baked fish?

Oh dear God, what had he done?

Allan was panting. What could he do? He couldn't wake Dorothy again. He would just have to wait and contain himself until morning. Until daybreak. Until first light. With his eyes open.

The last of the results came off the computer terminal before daybreak. Geoffrey glanced quickly at them. He'd go over them all more thoroughly when he'd had some sleep. Muscle tension and brain-wave activity consistent with any mild psychochemical stimulant. Sweat-gland functioning within the normal parameters for an enhanced state of physiological arousal. Reflex motor action unimpaired. In general the figures showed an increase in attentiveness, alertness. This was a familiar feature of drugs to enhance learning. In fact, it was often mistaken as the direct cause. Alertness and attentiveness were obviously important conditions for learning, but it was wrong to conclude that they *caused* it. He pushed the print-outs to the side of the desk. It all looked okay. Quite normal. Nothing to get alarmed about.

Before leaving, he flipped through some basic perception

test-cards. The phenomenon he'd observed in Allan's and Ella's eyes was worrying. He had no proper apparatus for measuring eyesight, but he shut one eye after the other in turn and read the volume numbers of several journals on the shelf. Not bad for a tired thirty-nine-year-old. Then, to check the eye-brain link, he went through some perceptual trick cards. First the Necker cube, a drawing that could be seen as a cube one way but also inside-out. Next, the Ponzo railway-lines that converged with two rectangular bars of equal length placed separately across them; correctly, the upper one seemed longer than the lower. Close-together parallel lines that appeared to converge, dots that jiggered themselves into squares, the Muller-Lyer arrows, the trick figures of Orbison and Poggendorf, of Zolner and Penrose. Fine. Okay. No trouble there.

He sighed with relief. Maybe he hadn't done any perceptual damage to Allan. After all, eye pigmentation had nothing whatsoever to do with sight. Nothing was without its risks, but maybe if he kept a close check on Allan's visual acuity, there would be no real harm in letting him carry on taking the tablets. Allan could be reassured and he might go back to taking them of his own accord. That could be very interesting. Geoffrey needn't know about it, officially that is. Besides, Allan *had* said they helped him with his work. Yes, thought Geoffrey, I'll refill Ella's bottle.

He got to his feet and shadow-boxed the air for a moment to loosen his shoulders. He rubbed his face; it felt dry and scaly. He stumbled through the lab for another coffee. On the way back he flipped off the switches of the oscilloscopes and the ink-pen charting instruments. Back in the office he cradled the plastic cup between his hands for warmth, leaned back in the spongy swivel chair until it groaned, shut his eyes and thought.

Damn! An image flashed across his mind. Nixon was at his food-dispenser again. He'd fiddled it free and now the floor of his cage was full of banana pellets and the other monkeys in the cage were feasting on them. Damn, damn. He'd better go and fix it.

Geoffrey spilled coffee on his trousers as he got up. As soon as he'd seen to the cage he'd be home to bed. He disconnected the dispenser from the main hopper; the monkeys in Nixon's cage had enough there for the night. He'd fix it properly later.

Back in the office he stopped short. Nixon. How had he known

135

what Nixon was doing in the cage while he was in the office? Of course. He must have seen it out of the corner of his eye coming back from getting the coffee. You're dog tired, Geoffrey Fish, he told himself. Everything is taking ages to filter through the reticular. You noted it subconsciously but it's taken until now to percolate through to the conscious level. That's how déjà-vu sensations occur. You'd better get some sleep.

He put down the mug and turned out his office lights. He said goodnight to the monkeys as he always did (it was called environmental enrichment) and paused at the lab door to see that everything was switched off and in order. He had his hand on the light-switch when he realised that he couldn't see Nixon's food dispenser from there. He stopped. He retraced the line he'd taken to the office door. There was nowhere along that path in a line of sight with the dispenser. He frowned. He walked the route again, then a third time. There was no doubt at all about it. He'd imagined it, or he'd *seen* it.

He found himself going over the computer print-outs again in case there was some hint of hallucinogenic behaviour. There was none. He sat down in his chair as before and shut his eyes. The image was fugitive and would not return. He sat there for another hour in the cold room, thinking. It was only when the first threads of a steely February dawn lightened the laboratory windows that he decided to go home. He'd made his mind up. He'd get Allan to continue taking the tablets and he'd watch him very carefully. Allan made the perfect subject, being all brain and no body. Yes, this could be *very* interesting, he thought as he started up his car and drove slowly home through the empty city streets.

Twenty-two

Geoffrey waited a week before making his move. He visited the flat every day and watched and listened. He wanted it to come from Allan.

On the fifth day he knew he was on the right track. Allan almost broke down in front of him. His Finals were barely ten weeks away and he was desperate. His concentration had grown weaker and weaker since giving up the tablets; he'd spend hours on end playing with Ella or just daydreaming. Dr Fry was sending back his essays. His photographic memory had fled. Since his accident these exams had become the goal of his life, and he was thrown into panic at the thought of failing them. He looked on it as a race to be won, and won by sheer force of will. And so he threw himself into bouts of frenzied work until he felt his brain would explode, only to find he'd forgotten what he'd learnt just an hour earlier.

There were other problems at home during those difficult March days too. Dorothy, for example, was alternately the skivvy and the gooseberry. She complained to Allan she felt like the Other Woman in her own home. Ella had begun to behave like a jealous wife. She wouldn't let Dorothy touch the comb, and anything to do with the tape-cassettes, the mouth-stick or the feeding routine was strictly her own province. Dorothy began to refer to the monkey as the 'cuckoo in the nest'. Geoffrey understood: widowed, without friends in a new city, nursing a crippled son, the woman had to stand by and see her only

137

function in life being usurped by the interloper. He also understood why Allan so often sided with the monkey; Dorothy was always predictable, but Ella was constantly novel and surprising. Ella was simply better company.

On the seventh day Allan raised the subject Geoffrey had been waiting for. It arose because of a problem Ella herself caused. She'd recently begun to bite. Though slight and skinny, her bite was vicious and terrifying. It was because she was approaching sexual maturity. But three days before, the District Nurse had come by on one of her visits and picked up the brush to tidy Allan's hair when Ella went for her. The Nurse had to have stitches. She'd laughed it off herself, but earlier in the morning of the seventh day a young man with a pale face and long fingers came to see Allan from the Area Health Authority. Allan, furious at the interruption, was terse and uncooperative and sent the man packing with a flea in his ear.

'He threatened me with having her put down as a public nuisance,' said Allan to Geoffrey. 'I'd like to see them try.'

'They could, you know,' said Geoffrey quietly. Inside, he was seething. This was the kind of publicity he did *not* want.

'I'd take the case to the House of Lords. Only I'll have to teach her not to go for ermine.'

'Allan, this isn't funny.'

Allan was sitting by the window. He looked up suddenly, his eyes brimming with tears of frustration. 'You're damn right it isn't funny! She's all I've got to keep me sane. As it is, I don't know how much more I can take before I crack up. The work's going to pot. I can't concentrate, I can't remember dates or rulings or precedents. I wish to God I could go back to those pills. Ten weeks! I don't care if I go blind then.'

Geoffrey said gently, 'Did they really help with the work?'

'They — I don't know — they just seemed to make everything so clear, so lucid. Oh *hell*.' Allan twisted his head to the side and bit his lip.

It was then that Geoffrey mentioned in a roundabout way that he'd sampled the tablets himself the previous week. 'I ran a complete scan on myself. There was absolutely no sign of any physiological ill-effects. None whatsoever. Mind you, I wasn't testing the effects over time.'

138

'What about your eyes?' said Allan harshly. 'You said I could go blind.'

'Well,' Geoffrey hesitated. Should he nudge Allan closer? 'As I said, we simply don't know. There's some suggestion of an alteration in eye colour, but that's perhaps only a question of the pigment, not actual sight.'

'I'd settle for green eyes if I'd be sure of getting my degree.'

'I must warn you, Allan, as a scientist and as your friend. The tablets are quite untried on human subjects.' Geoffrey would not look Allan in the eyes but pretended to be busy with some papers in his briefcase. You will be the first human subject, he was thinking. A willing subject: more than willing, *wanting*.

Allan said nothing. Geoffrey felt a small kick of elation.

'Well, anyway, I see Ella's getting her daily dose properly. I'll keep the bottle in the kitchen cupboard topped up.'

'Do what you like,' said Allan in an offhand voice. But Geoffrey read the tone and he knew that the point had gone home.

As he returned from the kitchen and gathered up his briefcase and duffle-coat, he said, 'By the way, I think Ella can be trusted enough to be let out of doors now a bit, don't you? Keep her within earshot and I don't suppose we'll have any trouble. It'll do her good.'

'Yes, maybe,' said Allan uncertainly.

'Don't worry. She won't run away. It's just an idea anyway. So long, Allan. Don't work too hard, you'll only get stale.'

As he walked through the crisp March air, Geoffrey couldn't help smiling to himself. He'd played with open cards. Allan was in possession of all the facts, and if he went on taking the tablets, it was his own decision.

Buzzing.

The buzzing came from inside Allan's head. He'd dozed off. Ella had started feeding him his tablet again but his mind was sluggish because of the stifling heat of the flat. The buzzing continued. He tried to ignore it but it rose like a bubble to the surface, bringing him with it.

He half-opened his eyes. The midday sun drowsed the room and fell dazzlingly onto the open pages on the reading-stand. The buzzing stopped abruptly. Then it started up again, deafeningly loud. There was a *smack* and for a moment silence, then once again the buzzing.

It was a bluebottle at the window, one of the year's first crop, incubated by the central heating. It was knocking itself against the pane. Phototropic suicide. Would it kill itself before Ella ate it? He didn't want to watch. He stretched his eyes open and tried to focus on the close-printed lines of the Law case-book set up before him. In the case of *Rex v. Regina* . . . No, it was no good. That bloody buzzing. Concentration was impossible. He'd go mad.

Allan looked in desperation at the windows. They were all shut. Couldn't he will the fly to go off somewhere else? A normal person could just get up and let it out. Get up and go to the window and take hold of the handle and give it a half-turn and push it ajar and let the fly out. Could he turn the handle with his mouth-stick? It was hopeless.

He closed his eyes. If he couldn't get the fly out of the room he'd have to get it out of his mind. He concentrated hard on removing the buzzing out of the room, out into the front garden, out and away into the street.

Minutes passed. The buzzing had stopped. He'd done it. He could now concentrate on the Law reports again. He began to read. After a while he was conscious of a draught round his neck. He turned.

There was no buzzing because there was no bluebottle. The window was open just an inch. Ella hadn't eaten the fly. She'd let it out.

She sat on the window-sill looking at him. She cocked her head on one side and he felt sure he could see her smiling.

The young man from the Area Health Authority made his recommendation: unless all doors and windows in Allan's flat were wired up and a warning notice pinned to the front door, the monkey would have to be destroyed. But it was a Department of Medicine monkey: in whose jurisdiction did the matter fall? It all depended on whether Allan's flat was adjudged a private residence or an appendage of the Department in which an extra-mural experiment was taking place. On this also hung the question of what the Department was doing loaning out licensed lab animals as though they were books in a library. The correspondence went across Professor Burbage's desk, and

Burbage called Geoffrey into his office.

The Professor stroked his fluffy beard and said, 'My first inclination is to let them have their way. Send the pest to the chloroform bag. However, the BBC have written, effusively, thanking us for the interview. The programme goes out in ten days or so. Who knows, maybe we will receive deputations from the universities of the world, from disabled war veterans associations and medical research establishments. I will not be the one to stand up in front of the Press and say, 'Sorry, gentlemen, but our star turn bit a nurse and had to be destroyed.' How about *you*, Geoffrey?' He banged a fist on the table.

The two men hammered out a new bargain and, with his political skills, Burbage got the Area Health Authority to agree. In fact, everyone agreed, except the most important party who hadn't even been consulted. It fell to Geoffrey to break to him the news of the collective decision. He took a shot of Amytal before driving to Allan's flat. Even so, he was shocked by the ferocity of his reaction.

'*Have her teeth out?*' Allan shouted, incredulous.

Geoffrey tried every angle but the answer was always a definitive 'No!' But a letter three days later from the Health Authority tipped the balance. It appointed a day on which Ella had to be presented at the County Pest Control Centre where the chloroform bag awaited her. Allan's fury redoubled under what he saw as blackmail. But when he finally yielded, Geoffrey fixed up an immediate appointment with the Department's vet. That wasn't the end of it.

'A *vet*?' exploded Allan. 'I'm having none of your hamfisted butchers near Ella! If it's got to be done, I want a proper oral surgeon.'

To pacify him, Geoffrey found one who would do it, a colleague of Dr Samuels, the man who'd given him the brain cube. The surgeon worked at the John Radcliffe hospital and his fee was half a dozen bottles of Glenfiddich. The only stipulation was that it was done on the quiet. A nurse would be sent to meet Allan and Ella and take them through the back ways to the operating theatre.

On the fine late-March day it happened, Geoffrey collected both Allan and Ella in the ambulance and took them to the hospital. In all, the operation took twenty minutes and at the end the surgeon made it clear he'd undercharged. All Ella's small

141

sharp teeth were drawn and the cruel trenches sewn up. Cleaned up, she was wrapped in swaddling blankets and handed back to Allan. He hung his head and barely nodded.

Geoffrey was vastly relieved. He insisted on wheeling Allan himself down the corridors and through the swing doors. 'Well, that wasn't too bad, was it?' he said. 'It's all over. We'll give her something for the pain and I'll prescribe a special soft-food diet and, you'll see, in a week or so she'll be as right as rain.'

But nothing could cheer Allan up. As Geoffrey helped the driver lift the wheelchair into the ambulance, he could see two wet lines running down his friend's cheeks.

Twenty-three

Dorothy was out at work. Ella was curled up in her basket on the table in the living room, breathing fitfully and occasionally moaning to herself. She'd been kept lightly sedated since the operation two days before. It was late afternoon and the sky outside was already quite dark. Allan had turned his back on the reading-stands and dozed off. His brain literally hurt with the work and with containing the panic. He let his head loll backwards and stared at the ceiling until it receded infinitely far away. It was then he began to notice it. At first it came dull and elusive, perhaps one of the vestigial pains he was still getting in his legs, perhaps a muscle somewhere twitching for no particular reason. It grew sharper. It synchronised itself to his pulse. so that each pump of blood brought it closer. Pain. A dull undercurrent of ache, peaking with small sharper spikes. But where? In the dead outposts of his body? Inside his brain? In the imagination?

Then all at once it came, searing, tearing through his mouth like a hot wire, blazing through the roots of his teeth and coursing deep inside his gums. He let out a howl and jerked awake. But he didn't recognise the howl. It came from within him, from his voice-box, but it wasn't his.

Ella was huddled in her basket, hugging her Thing and howling.

Ella's recovery took longer than it should have because, on the third day, she caught Dorothy using the comb on Allan and went

143

for her. The soft clap of her toothless gums did no damage to Dorothy but it opened the stitches and Geoffrey had to come and apply an anti-coagulant. But she fiddled and scratched her mouth and wouldn't let it heal. Dorothy suggested a solution: a baby's top modified into a kind of strait-jacket. And so the monkey spent most of her convalescence with her arms trussed behind her back.

Allan cared for her with all the love he had. When he thought she was getting too hot or too cold, he'd come over to her basket and take her rug off and on with his teeth. He gave her her morning tablet by sucking it up on the end of a straw; taking his own was more difficult, but he managed that too. He tried grooming her with a comb in his mouth, but that didn't work. He also tried feeding her and once managed to spoon some thin cold porridge into her mouth. Otherwise she was given peeled grapes to suck, which she could roll around her mouth without needing her paws. Allan gave her more attention than ever, to his mother's patent dismay. If Dorothy had hoped to claw back some of her lost influence in the household while her opponent was out of action, she was disappointed.

Most of all, Allan spent hours just talking to Ella. When he told Geoffrey she'd be talking soon too, he laughed. The world's most advanced chimps, Washoe and Sarah, could form simple sentences through a voice synthesiser, but after years of intensive training their linguistic capacity was still below that of a two-year-old human being. It couldn't be done.

But it could, thought Allan. And, in a way, it already was. True, the monkey couldn't talk English, but the more he spoke to her the more he felt sure she understood. It became his form of relaxation from work. Between bouts of reading and essay-writing, he found himself chatting away to her on all kinds of subjects. He reminisced about his childhood. He told her comic anecdotes. He laid plans for the future: they'd go to football matches when she was better, or to London, or abroad. He'd specialise in international law and they'd travel the lands and the seas. Most of all, he talked her into getting better.

'Fight!' he'd say. 'You've got to keep fighting. Don't leave it to your body by itself. You've got to push. Geoffrey says you don't remember the past and you've got no notion of a future. That's rubbish. You're too clever for him. He doesn't know you as I do.

It hurts right now, but soon it won't. In a few days you'll be up and scampering about. Trust me. But you've got to fight for it. *Will* yourself better!'

It happened to be Easter Monday when, all of a sudden, Ella was well again. Allan woke to find her tearing round his room. To celebrate, laughing so hard from relief that his chair jerked and hiccoughed, he took her on a wild rampage through the house.

Geoffrey was delighted too. More: when he ran the first set of Wisconsin tests he was stunned. A fortnight had passed without any reinforcing and Ella had forgotten nothing. He spent a full day at the flat and went through every piece of equipment he'd brought along.

'Well,' he said towards the end, rubbing his flattened nose with his fist. 'I'm proud of my pupil.'

'Oh?' Allan turned round from the reading-stands. '*Your* pupil?'

'I've done all the standard tests for memory,' Geoffrey said, sinking into an armchair. 'Active avoidance. Operant behaviour. Visual discrimination. And maze learning, though I haven't done much on mazes with her; I can't hump them over from the labs. But I'd guess she's pretty damn maze-bright.'

'She's extraordinary,' said Allan fervently.

'Oh?' Geoffrey said casually. 'Anything particularly extraordinary happened?'

The two men looked hard at each other. Geoffrey remembered quickly looking into the pill bottle earlier and guessing Allan had begun them again. Allan changed the subject, pointedly.

'Anyway, what's so significant about all these tests? So you find a drug which improves a monkey's learning ability. Big deal.'

'We use monkeys because we can't use humans,' Geoffrey said, avoiding his friend's eye. 'The mechanism of the human brain is one of the last remaining biological mysteries. What I'm trying to do is to discover how the learning process works, how the memory trace arises in the first place and how it's recalled. Maybe in years to come it'll help you learn up your Roman Law.'

'You're so clever with drugs, can't you make a pill with the whole syllabus in it, somehow?'

'Actually, that was tried once.' Geoffrey laughed. 'It didn't work. Let me explain where we are and maybe you'll see the real purpose behind what I'm doing with Ella. Okay?'

'Yes, Dr Fish.'

'The first thing to realise is that memory is, almost literally, a *thing*. To move from learning to recall must imply there's something physically present which represents a memory once it's learned and before it's recalled. That's known as an engram, or a memory trace. With me?'

'I think so. But what *kind* of thing is a memory trace?'

'Well,' Geoffrey began. 'At first it was thought to be some kind of electrical impulse. That was disproved. You can stop electrical activity in the brain by drugs or by cooling it right down, but the memories remain intact. So it's not like switching the power off in a computer memory bank. The same way, speeding up electrical activity in the brain — by electro-convulsive treatment, for instance — doesn't give you new memories or improve your recall of old ones. Although that's not entirely true. Short-term memory, say up to half an hour, is electrical. It can be wiped out by concussion, for instance. But after that it goes into deep store, into long-term memory.'

'So what is it then?'

'We know what it's *not*,' Geoffrey continued. 'It's not anatomical. It's not a new synaptic pathway in the brain, one for each new memory. If it were, you could cut it out and the animal would lose the memory. Lashley tried that with rats. He cut out vast chunks of brain and then put the rats through mazes he'd previously taught them. They'd limp and hobble and stagger along, but they hadn't forgotten the route. So it looked as if memory inhabited several places in the brain at the same time. Okay, then maybe it is physical. Maybe memory is a molecule, one specific molecule for one memory, perhaps repeated several times over in different parts of the brain. Certainly the nucleotide sequence of an RNA molecule, for instance, is capable of storing enough information to cover the memories of a lifetime. But then, theoretically, you should be able to extract these molecules and implant them in another brain and so give it a new set of memories.'

'Well, can you?'

'No, you can't. It looked good with earthworms and later with

146

rats. But the memory transfer experiments simply couldn't be replicated properly and they're now considered spurious. Nice idea, inadequate evidence. Then lots of other things were tried. Peptide chains, for example. Straight RNA too. No joy.'

'So what are *you* looking at?'

'I start from a different point. I take the whole mammalian brain — yours, mine, Ella's — and ask, What are its most striking features? Why are mammals so highly intelligent? I think the answer lies in the fact that so much of our brain cortex is associative: that is, it's not committed to motor or sensory activities but it's only plugged into itself. And so much of that is uncommitted, what we call redundant. It is available for learning by experience, in contrast to being already wired-in for specific functions. In the mammal's brain there are very many duplicate pathways by which information or instructions can pass from A to B. In learning, a large number of cells, which may not be necessarily interconnected, alter in the threshold levels of their synapses — and even in Ella's brain a single cell can make over 10,000 synapses with its neighbours. So you can see that a memory is a kind of firing-pattern coded over many cells. That's why you don't find a particular memory localised in a single place but rather duplicated all over the place. At least, that's my hypothesis.'

'So the drug you're giving Ella is supposed to do what exactly?' Allan's voice betrayed an edge of urgency.

Geoffrey stretched. 'It's *supposed* to stimulate the uncommitted cortex in such a way as to make it more receptive to assimilating new codes of cell-firing patterns. And so far it's looking very good.'

Allan went on in a controlled voice, 'And could there be any . . . side-effects to what's happening in her brain?'

'I've really put myself in the dock. As I've said, the answer is that I don't know. Ella's brain is very similar to a human's, structurally speaking, only the motor and sensory areas are relatively larger and the association areas correspondingly smaller. But I can't forsee any *physical* changes there. I expect any changes will be behavioural, simply as a result of vastly speeded-up learning. Don't forget, I've got another six Capuchins at the lab, on various dosages and variants of Ella's tablets. So you see, I'm keeping a very close eye on the whole thing. If anything looked like going wrong, I'd be the first to know.'

'I'm glad to hear it,' Allan said and dropped his head in thought. 'She's very precious to me.'

'I know.' Geoffrey rose to his feet. He'd understood the true line of Allan's questions, and was pleased. He didn't want to spoil it by lingering. 'I'll go and tell Dorothy we've finished and she can come in now.' He started packing up his briefcase.

'No, don't go. I'd like to go on talking.'

Geoffrey looked at his watch. 'I can't stop. I really have to get back to the lab.'

'Geoffrey, Geoffrey, you work too hard. Play a little for a change.' And in a quieter voice he added, 'Seen Melanie lately?'

'My Nemesis,' Geoffrey groaned theatrically, but inside he could feel the hurt rising. 'I think she finds monkeys beneath her. I'll change to orang-outangs.'

'You're always quarrelling, you two. It must show there's something there.'

'No, it's over. Well, it certainly is for her.'

'Geoffrey! For God's sake, you're the bloody alchemist around here. Mix her up one of your cocktails.'

Geoffrey held onto the side of the table; his hand was trembling. 'Anyway, it's more fundamental than that. She's an ethologist and she sees me as some kind of scientific pervert. She's always asking about you and Ella, and the same thing keeps coming up: I should harness Ella's natural instinctual behaviour patterns, not pump her full of psychochemicals.'

'Come on, it's spring! Give it another chance. Take her out somewhere romantic. Tell her you love her madly. Slip something into her drink. After all, you're an expert on stimulus and response, aren't you?'

Geoffrey laughed. It was spring, true. It had crept up unawares. He'd only realised it that morning as he walked up Parks Road from the labs to Allan's flat. All that crude vitality, everything in adolescence. And he, feeling old and flakey-faced and scrubble-haired and very, very tired.

Allan was right, though. There was nothing to lose. The old season's skin had to be sloughed off before the new could grow. He clapped his friend on the shoulder and went to the door.

148

'Okay, I'll give it a crack. If I blow it, I'll want my money back. See you, Allan.'

Spring. Allan's second spring in the flat. It was easier than the first, though it was hard enough. Sometimes it was very hard indeed.

When it got too hard, he would leave his work and drive himself to his bedroom. There he'd sit, staring out of the window into the long narrow garden, to the tall poplars at the end and the distant Parks beyond. Sometimes he'd watch the poplars standing out against the sun until it sank below the skyline. He liked to look into the middle distance, beyond the line of trees, into the emptiness. Focusing out there he would let his eyes fall lightly shut and find he was looking deep into himself, half a mile into himself. In this state he could let his mind fly free of his body. Up, up and out, away over the grass and up the trees and along the hedgerows. He liked to imagine he was Ella and she was out there, exploring, encountering, scenting, seeing.

Several days after his talk with Geoffrey, the spring panic hit him hard. It hit him so he gasped. Weeping, he hurried down the corridor into his own room. Dorothy was out shopping. Ella rode with him, nestling against his jersey and butting her face under his chin. He came to a halt in front of the window. Christ! The greenness, the hope, the vitality, the squirming, wriggling bursting life out there! He closed his eyes. Slowly, very slowly, his mind calmed down. He held it there, suspended, floating, ready to attach itself to whatever it fancied.

He didn't feel Ella as she hopped down off his lap. He didn't see her climb onto the window-sill, look back, clasp the latch in both hands and turn it. He didn't see her hop out and drop lightly to the bed of weeds below.

He fell into a light daydream. He'd got up somehow. He'd passed like a ghost through the wall, through the window. He was walking down the crazy paving. He was small, low to the ground. He looked round. Something told him he shouldn't be doing this. He stopped, felt his back arching, reached round, lit bright and lurid against a dark thundery sky. It look menacing. He turned and moved a few paces down the path. He wanted to go to the trees and explore.

A butterfly, the tenderest blue, landed on a bunch of

149

primroses. He peered closely at it. He couldn't remember seeing anything so fine and fragile. He put out a hand. The butterfly took to the air and fluttered away, over the fence, to somewhere else.

The grass growing between the paving-stones was full of its own life: ladybirds and woodlice among the clots of weeds, ants among the dandelion roots, tiny spiders swinging from their safety-wires. The dandelion stalks tasted bitter. But in the verge was cat-mint which felt good on his body. He went in among the tall weeds. There were dead Michelmas daisies and juicy daffodils, mats of periwinkles and shoots of dog's-spit. He rummaged through this low jungle until he came to the foot of the garden. There, cladding a garden shed, were the first shoots of a large honeysuckle. He pulled one trailing stem towards him and nibbled a bud. It was delicious. The wind ruffled his back and he knew that rain was coming. But this was fun. He looked about him.

Above the shed a chestnut tree leaned over from the next garden. He shinned up it, arm over arm, sometimes jumping, sometimes swinging. It was wonderful. Free. Loose-limbed and free. A pigeon crashed suddenly out of the foliage and he nearly fell off. He watched it fly away over the grassy park beyond and knew what it was to move through the air, to flap the wings and cross space, to soar and float and coast and travel free.

Hssss! He spun round. Below, on the shed roof, was a black cat. Its back was arched and spined and its tail fluffed up in aggression. It advanced crabwise, spitting. He screeched and began jumping up and down in a counter-display. The cat flung a fistful of claws at him and he leaped higher up the tree, along a branch, down another and took a flying leap onto a poplar. He looked back. The cat had slunk away into the other garden.

He jumped from the poplar onto the fence. It smelled of creosote, but the view! The Parks stretched for acres, dissected by gravel paths and dotted with tall trees. In the far distance rose the spires and towers of the colleges and city offices. They were already partly blurred by the curtain of rain that he could see approaching. Distant cyclists began to pedal faster. People started putting up their umbrellas. Runners in tracksuits began to sprint. It was time to be getting back. Quick. Run for it.

'Allan! Allan! Are you all right?'

150

Dorothy was shaking him. He brought her into focus: there was terror in her face. Her grey hair was everywhere. Her raincoat was wet.

'Don't do that,' she said, breathing deeply. 'I called. You didn't answer. I came rushing in and found you . . . found you all slumped back with your eyes open. Oh, thank the Lord. I got quite a turn. You looked like . . . like when I found you that time you tried to . . . end it all. Oh Allan, dear.'

His mother pressed her plump cheeks into his face and he could smell the town exhaust fumes in her hair mingling with the face-powder. She straightened. 'And you've got the window open! Where's that little terror?'

Ella was sitting in the corner of the room, quite quiet. She didn't move until Dorothy had left the room to tidy herself up and make tea. Then she came forward and jumped up onto his lap. She held out her hand. In it lay a primrose. He shut his eyes. He could feel the tears coming, but different tears. The dove had returned with the olive-leaf.

Twenty-four

Geoffrey returned home exhausted. His shirt was soaked with river-water, he'd pulled a muscle in his shoulder while punting and he was in a filthy mood. He'd taken Allan's advice and staged the grand re-seduction of Melanie. He'd ended up acting ferryman to Linda and John Wiseman as well. Far from protesting his love in the idyllic setting of a punt on the Cherwell, he'd almost felt a gooseberry. He sank into an armchair with a large scotch and cursed life. It had been one lousy afternoon.

It had been doomed from the start. He'd scoured the city for cold roast duck and an old Macon Viré, smoked oysters and a light salad: the most special things he could think of, for that day he was to win back his love. Melanie came round to his rooms; she wore an open blouse over a petticoat-dress and her dark hair was swept back in the way she now wore it. But as they were leaving, the phone rang. She insisted he took it. It was Linda, up for the day with her fiancé John Wiseman. It took no more than ten seconds to destroy the tryst he'd planned; Linda and John were to come along too. There was a problem with the punt: Geoffrey hadn't booked one and they had to wait for one to return. Then Wiseman had brought champagne (which made Geoffrey feel upstaged) and wasn't dressed for punting, so that Geoffrey had to do all the poling himself. Wiseman sat back with his arm round Linda and relished being chauffeured while Geoffrey sweated and got the pole stuck and was clipped over the head by low-hanging willows and ended up so drenched and foul-smelling that he refused to sit next to Melanie but took his lunch apart at the stern. And he had a row with Wiseman. It had been coming for months.

Wiseman was saying emphatically that Allan should not be told Linda and he were up in Oxford; it would hurt him. Melanie disagreed: Allan was just like any of them and it would do him good if they visited him. Wiseman smiled indulgently and said he couldn't agree. Allan was *not* just like them, he was a cripple and a pretty rum one at that, what with his curious fixation with that monkey of his. Therapy was one thing, but an overdependence on pets was spurious and faintly unhealthy.

Geoffrey remembered feeling his cheeks reddening. 'You should qualify that,' he said. 'Allan's taking part in an experiment that's breaking important new theoretical ground.'

'Quackery,' Wiseman pronounced. 'Medicine is not about handing out monkeys to the disabled of Christendom. It may keep the lad entertained, but that's only treating symptoms, not causes. Let's try and cure the thing at the root, shall we?'

Geoffrey knew when he was losing his temper — he'd speak with slow venom in a voice he didn't recognise. Punctuating every syllable he said, 'Tell us, then, your record in curing Allan. You had him in your charge for nine months. I'm sure you did everything *you* could, but he came out a total cripple. A vegetable with a brain. Then what happens? You put him on a course of anti-depressants and psychotherapy and what does he do? Six months later he tries to kill himself.' Melanie tried to intervene but he went on regardless. 'But look at him now. Since he's had Ella, he's got a new lease of life. He lives for the creature. Damn it, he *lives*. Full-stop.'

Wiseman merely nodded as if he'd been listening to a dry academic paper on a topic of marginal interest. Addressing the water as he trailed a hand through it, he said, 'Some people would wonder if Geoffrey isn't just using the chap as a convenient baby-sitter. I mean, either the monkey is there to help Allan, in which case a medical justification is called for, or it's there because Geoffrey believes something of scientific value about brain functioning can be learned from boarding out a lab animal with a friendly local cripple. Which is it?'

'It's both,' he'd said, fixing his eyes on the surgeon. 'Allan's happy. I'm happy. My Professor's happy. Only John Wiseman is unhappy. I wonder why!'

Linda jumped up to intervene and rocked the shallow boat so

that a wave sluiced on board. Wiseman's fawn suede shoes were ruined. Geoffrey felt that won the argument for him.

Back at home, he smiled into the empty whisky glass at the memory. He reached for the telephone. He'd give Allan a call and tell him the story.

Dorothy answered. 'Allan's in his bedroom. Shall I get him?'

'No, don't trouble him,' he said. 'Everything all right?'

'He's fine. But the monkey's filthy, *filthy*. Isn't there something we can do? I know you said she could go out and about, but goodness knows what she gets up to. She must have been all the way down to the river this afternoon, she was so wet and smelly. And she's always bringing things into the house. Today it was a whole lot of willow-leaves. Is there something wrong with her basket?'

'I know she brings dirt into the place but Allan won't have her cooped up all day, you know that yourself.'

'Well, I don't know. Anyway, I hope you enjoyed yourself. How was Linda looking? Allan said he thought he'd seen her and Doctor Wiseman on the river with you. I don't know what he's on about sometimes.'

We'd agreed not to tell him, thought Geoffrey. He said, 'Oh, did they call?'

'No one's called. I've been in all afternoon and it's been as quiet as a church hall. Are you sure you won't speak to Allan? All right. Can I give him a message then?'

Geoffrey stared into his glass and said nothing for a long while. He could hear Dorothy on the other end calling, 'Geoffrey? Are you still there?' But he was thinking: that's strange, that's not possible, or am I going off my rocker? There must be a perfectly straightforward answer. The lousy afternoon, the exhaustion, the scotch, jumbling everything up into nonsense patterns. He cleared his throat.

'Yes, I'm still here. Just tell Allan that the afternoon was a complete fiasco and I want my money back. He'll understand.'

In the run-up to Finals, Allan escaped more and more often into his daydream world with Ella. It was always the same. He'd get a block. He'd redouble his efforts until his brain hurt and he felt dizzy, until Real Property became unreal and he could no longer

154

spell Jurisprudence. Then he'd go off into his bedroom and sit, quiet and still, in front of the window. If it was warm, the window would already be open and he'd watch Ella hop onto the sill and slip through out into the garden. Then he'd fix his eyes on a point beyond the line of poplars and allow them to close gently. In a moment the floating feeling would begin. Then the first of the images, the private cinema in his mind's eye.

His 'rests', as he referred to these times to Dorothy, became the best part of the day. He lost interest in Ella's hide-and-seek games. He'd grown out of them. He always knew where she'd put the mouth-stick or the cotton-reel. He only had to close his eyes gently and he'd see in his mind's eye exactly what she was doing with them.

As for his work, he was almost in despair. He'd driven himself pitilessly ever since he'd come back from the hospital and yet he felt he knew nothing, that his mind was congested and yet empty, empty of the facts he really needed. The tablets helped him concentrate and, if he really *pushed*, he could make his childhood photographic memory work again. But there was just so much in his head, all clamouring for attention, and yet so much more outside in the textbooks and reference works that he had no hope of covering in the three weeks that remained.

One hot afternoon in late May, with just ten days to go, he sat in the special room in the Law Library equipped for blind students. He was alone, except for Ella who sat as patient as a cat on the sill by the open window, watching everything. His brain mutinied. It screamed, *no more room!* He wheeled himself away from the reading-stands and let his head drop onto his chest. It was too hard. He gave up.

Dr Esther Fry, his tutor, put her close-cropped white head around the door, saw him and came in. Her eyes were ringed with puffy bags like myopic glasses but could convey great kindliness as well as severity. She perched on a desk and put out a hand to touch him on the shoulder. She let him speak first.

'I feel like Socrates. I only know that I don't know anything. I think I'd prefer the hemlock to Finals.'

'I know how you feel,' she said gently. 'You think you can't make it.'

He nodded. He couldn't hold it back. He looked up at his tutor, then at her hands with their copper bracelets and arthritic knobbles and then at his own hands lying useless in his lap. 'I can't go through with it,' he said, choking. 'I really can't. I'm exhausted and drained. I haven't even begun revising Tort. I physically can't cope. It's hard enough coping with the basic business of living . . .'

She let him go on. Finally she said, 'You have a brilliant mind, Allan. You of all people mustn't waste it.'

'I'd rather my brain had gone than my body. I could live with that better.'

Dr Fry said nothing for a while. She looked down and smoothed her skirt and said, 'If it's any help to you, there's something I'd like to tell you. I don't normally speak of it.'

'You're going to tell me a cripple story,' he said sullenly. 'Everybody has one.'

'No. This is not a cripple story. It's about myself. I took my Law Finals here in 1941. During the Easter holiday I was married. Secretly. The man I married was shot down and killed in the second week of the Finals term. Two weeks later I lost the child I was carrying. And during exams we received the news about my brother; he was killed in the front line. But I took the exams and I got them. Believe me, the spirit can overcome *anything*.'

Allan looked up and met her eyes. They were shining. She went on, 'I know you won't flunk it now, Allan. You wouldn't have come this far otherwise. Look at me and tell me. You're going to do it, aren't you? Do it and win.'

'Yes.'

'But you must be clear *how*. Where does your strength come from, Allan? Is it from prayer? From God?'

'Oh no, not prayer. Nor God.' He gave a short, bitter laugh.

'Hope, then?'

'What do I have to hope for?'

'Love?'

'I'm without love too. Except for Ella. I love Ella.'

'Very well. Anger, then? Resentment? Hate?'

'No,' he said. 'I've spent all the anger and hate I've got.'

'Then *what*?'

He thought for a moment. What really was it that carried him through, that made him know, deep down, that he wouldn't flunk the exams? He spoke carefully.

156

'I suppose it's just that I'm obstinate. I *refuse* to fail. It's sheer wilfulness. That's how I won races and school prizes. Some kind of fury of will.'

A smile broke across Dr Fry's face. She eased herself off the desk and picked up her bag. 'You have it,' she said. 'You'll make it. Now I must go. I'm chairing an examiners' meeting and we're finalising the papers. Keep in mind what we talked about. Goodbye, Allan.'

'Goodbye,' he replied. 'And thanks.'

That evening, Dorothy went out and Allan was left alone. He'd had supper and watched the news on television and was settling down in the living room to begin revising Tort. He'd sent Ella out of the room; he wasn't to be disturbed. But she kept creeping back in. She'd suddenly taken it upon herself to rearrange all the small objects in the house. She ferried the spare keys from their peg in the hall and put them on the mantlepiece. A bottle of ink from his desk and two biros were traded in the kitchen for a cupboard knob that had come off and some bills pinned on a magnetic clip. This went on until he could stand it no longer.

'For Pete's sake, Ella, I'm *working*! Go and play somewhere else.' He turned round. She was in the doorway, on her hind legs, ready to run off. There was a letter in her hands. He clicked and she hopped closer.

He could see the envelope was marked "Dorothy" in big print, in Jock's writing and very private-looking. Despite himself Allan longed to read it, but if he got Ella to open it up he'd never get her to put it back. She'd obviously pinched it from Dorothy's room one day when she'd forgotten to lock it and she'd get a walloping when Dorothy returned. He turned his chair and blipped the letter in Ella's hand.

'Take it back!' he whispered urgently. But she misunderstood. She'd seen his mother opening letters and knew how it was done. She hopped up onto his lap and began pulling the letter out of the envelope. He craned his head away. He didn't want to see. He had work to do.

But he caught sight of a phrase in the letter. He started. What was this? He saw a few more words. He linked them up in meaning. He felt his scalp prickling. He wheeled his chair backwards until he could blip the typewriter. Ella knew what to

157

do; this was straight-forward. She jumped onto the table and inserted the bottom of the letter in the machine. He turned it on with his mouth-stick and pressed the carriage return until the whole letter was up in front of him. It came out upside down, so it wasn't easy to read. But he managed.

It was Jock's parting letter to his wife. As Allan read he felt his eyes stretched and bursting with horror. He read it over and over again until the tears blotted everything out.

> My beloved,
>
> There are some things it's hard to say face to face and so I'm putting down a few thoughts closest to my heart in a letter. We both know the doctors are right: I don't have a hope and I'll be gone in a short while. Don't grieve when I go, my darling. It's a release and we should be thankful for His mercy.
>
> I face the end with only two regrets. The first is to leave you behind, especially with Allan to look after. But keep going, darling, and get out and about and live life to the full — God knows it's short enough.
>
> My other regret is Wiseman. Every day I ask myself, did we do the right thing? We could have sued. The lawyers said we had a strong case. There was enough evidence to show that if Wiseman hadn't messed up the operation by trying out that new technique, Allan would be walking today. But you know why we decided not to press the case. It would have destroyed Allan's morale, and the lad needs every ounce of that he's got. I still believe we did the right thing. Don't torment yourself any more. You've got to accept what is and look to the future with hope.
>
> He's a wonderful lad and I love him very much. Take care of him, as I know you will. He'll need all the love you can give him. Bless you, my darling. Whatever happens to me in these last days to come, don't forget how much I love you. Always.
>
> God be with you.
>
> Jock.

Twenty-five

Allan would be walking today.

Walking.

Walking. Or just sitting. Sitting in an armchair. Lifting my hand to scratch my nose. Reaching forward for a pencil. Reaching out to stroke Ella or to feed her one of her pellets. Picking up a coffee cup, sipping it, putting it down. Getting up. Getting up out of the armchair and going over to the bookcase. Taking out a book. Flipping through the index. Putting it back and taking out another. Carrying the book to the table. Sitting down and spreading the book open. Making notes on a pad. Moving a pencil or a biro over a pad to make notes. Twisting my wrist to look at my watch. Dialling with my index finger. Dialling a friend. Dialling Geoffrey. Dialling Melanie. Dropping the biro and reaching down to pick it up while the phone rings at the other end. Holding the receiver to my ear. *Hello? Melanie, is that you? Free for lunch? How about the Sorbonne? Fine. See you there, one o'clock.*

Walking. Walking down the street. Pausing on the edge of pavements to let cars and cycles pass. Thinking of going to the track later. Crossing the street. Greeting friends. Turning down St Giles. Doing a child's hop-scotch on the paving-stones. Strolling down the Cornmarket. Brushing past women with prams and children dragging. Turning up a lane into the market. Selecting a rose from a stall. Picking it up and smelling it.

Turning down a narrow passage way off the High. Stepping

into the restaurant. Looking up to see Melanie already there at the top of the stairs, all in white, dark hair against white silk blouse. Reaching out to draw her close. Kissing the side of her cheek. Handing her the rose. Feeling her squeeze on my arm. Going into the restaurant. Waving to a friend in the corner. Holding the chair for her. Sitting down myself. Opening the menu. Pointing a finger at the wine list. Holding the wine glass to my nose. Clinking glasses. And afterwards, when the rain has cleared and the sun is out, strolling out into the bright wet streets. Strolling. Strolling to the library. Browsing in Blackwells. Walking to Melanie's house over Magdalen Bridge and sitting on her Moroccan cushions taking Turkish coffee. Reaching out for her. Kissing her, now on the lips. Finally walking back home. Rolling up my umbrella and swinging it as I walk. Swinging it in time to my step. Walking. Walking.

Walking.

I don't walk. I don't run. I don't make tea or shake hands. I only puff and suck. That's my way of walking. One puff is chair forwards. One suck is chair backwards. My life is measured in sucks and puffs.

Wiseman. *Messed up the operation by trying out that new technique.*

How he messed it up doesn't matter. The man is guilty of living murder. Who's in prison? I am in prison. And Wiseman? Wiseman walks free.

This is not justice. There is a balance in the nature of things. That balance has been upset; it must be restored. There must be an equivalence. There must be an evening-out. I will put myself on one side of the balance. On the other will be Wiseman. His practice, his reputation, his ambition, his expectations. His marriage. And in the evening-out these will be brought down, as far down as I have been brought.

Twenty-six

Dorothy came home that evening, slightly tipsy, to find Jock's letter facing her on the table like a writ. Coldly, distantly, Allan made her sit down. He began to cross-examine her. Who had admitted him to hospital? What were the names of the doctors who did the diagnosis? Who decided on the laminechtomy? Names of the O.D.A. and the theatre staff? Copies of all correspondence? What had she and Jock signed before the operation? What had Wiseman told them about the operation, the new technique and its risks? What were his precise words? What explanation did he give when they confronted him afterwards? Did they *not* confront him afterwards? Which firm of solicitors, which chambers, which counsel were consulted? Names, times, dates?

Leave it in the past, Dorothy implored; what's done can't be undone. It was Jock's decision. She'd been for suing, but she'd given in to him. He'd done it with the best motives.

After that night, Allan withdrew into himself. He wouldn't leave his bedroom; he'd only talk to Ella. For hours he poured out his heart to her, about his anger, about Linda, about Wiseman, about his impotence to reverse the past. She listened. Meanwhile his mother, excluded from his life, worked to exonerate herself. She gave the flat a complete spring-clean and filled the place with flowers. She managed to send Geoffrey away when he turned up on the doorstep, despite the urgency of his manner. She gave excuses; she was too ashamed to tell the truth. For four days this

161

went on. It seemed as if Allan had at last given up.

Then, on the morning of the fifth day, he asked to be dressed. He set off down to the Law Library where he asked for a case-book of precedents on professional negligence to be set up. He felt a new driving force within him. He'd come close to opting out of the exams. They now became crucial. He *had* to get them. They were the qualifying round.

John Wiseman would find himself receiving a rather special wedding present. And the exams were the first step towards that.

Exams started at different times for different Faculties, but for the undergraduates themselves the pattern was always the same. Every step that led to the Jacobean inquisition-house called Examination Schools had its own ritual, like the Stations of the Cross.

The men wore *sub fusc* — white shirt and bow-tie, dark suit and shoes, mortarboard and gown. The women, too, wore only black and white. Breakfast had the significance it does for condemned men the world over. Those who liked to take leave of the world in style went to the Randolph Hotel, the less choosey to a café in the Market. Either way the cheerfulness was artificial. Then followed the procession to Schools. On this last walk a friend might accompany you; that was an act of a true friend.

In Allan's household the pattern was the same. His mother made kidneys for breakfast. She'd taken his dark suit to the tailor's to be shrunk to his new size. She'd even learned from the personnel manager at work how to tie a bow-tie. She worked hard to make him feel at ease. She told him, 'Exams aren't everything in life. You can only do your best. Other people in your condition wouldn't even be sitting them.' Allan merely nodded. Exams *were* everything in his life.

Just before the ambulance arrived, Melanie turned up. She'd come to see Allan off. She brought him a vermilion carnation the colour of her lips and under her arm she carried a small parcel. She smiled. He looked up into her soft dark eyes and smiled too. She's grown so damn beautiful, he thought. Her scent came to him on a breeze from the window, very womanly, very capable, very comprehensive.

'I've brought you something,' she said, opening the parcel.

'Oh, just look at that!' exclaimed Dorothy.

It was a miniature black gown and a tiny mortarboard, just the right size for Ella. Allan burst out laughing.

'That's wonderful, Melanie! I was wondering how I'd get her in without the proper dress.'

He clicked and the monkey came over. Melanie put the cap and gown on her and suddenly she looked like a tiny version of the college Dean. Allan burst out laughing. He wheeled himself over to the window. Outside the day was fine, with a rich cerulean blue sky.

'It's such a lovely day,' he said to Melanie. 'Shall we walk?'

She smiled. 'I think the cab is here.' As she followed him down the path and watched him being loaded into the ambulance, she said quietly, 'I just want you to know I think you're great, Allan. I used to think I was a hero, coping with my legs. But you, you're okay, Allan.'

She said no more but stood back beside Dorothy and they both waved him off.

Finals lasted a week. There was evidently nothing on the University Statute Book to ban assistants provided they were correctly dressed and served a necessary function. Under the title of emanuensis, Ella was allowed in. Every day a gowned invigilator would take Allan and his monkey to a private room where a scribe was waiting to take down his dictated papers.

But as certainly as the moment of truth arrived it also passed. At the close, under a barrage of popping champagne corks, Allan fell into despondency. He was sure he'd failed at least two papers. The scribe had fidgeted throughout and that had distracted him. He'd been thinking obsessively about Wiseman, he wasn't sleeping and his food had upset him. And yet the world decreed that the trial was now over and it was time to relax. There were parties. He went to cricket-matches. He watched the Head of the River race. He still avoided the Sports Ground, however. Between these diversions he spent long hours in the library reading every possible precedent on negligence and indemnity. There was little time to sit in his bedroom and daydream.

Ten days after the end of exams, a letter arrived. It was marked "Oxford University Board of Examiners". It was too early for the

Class results to be published and Allan knew what it must mean. It was a Viva. Oh God, he thought.

A Viva was an oral exam held before the full panel of examiners. It was the Inquisition. It meant he was on the borderline between two Classes. True, you could only better your Class, but what was his anyway? You could get a Pass and be called for a Fourth; a Second to a First was also possible. Allan remembered his Tort paper. So it was to be a Pass. That was no good. That wouldn't pass the qualifying round. His life was a complete wreck.

'Never mind, dear,' comforted Dorothy. 'It's only a bit of paper.'

The Viva was in four days' time. Allan turned his back on the party invitations and the matches and Geoffrey's constant offers to take him punting. He threw himself back into work, revising, reading, going through old lecture notes, attacking the set questions from every angle. He even let Geoffrey give him some Drinamyl, an amphetamine mixed in with a barbiturate, so that he wouldn't need to sleep.

The day for the Viva arrived. This time the ambulance took him to the gates of the Examination Schools where the interrogation was to take place. One of the porters saluted him and wished him luck. 'It'll be over before you know it, sir,' he said. Allan waited outside the large carved oaken door of the room and tried to empty his mind of the mass of learning he'd been stuffing into it. Ella sat upright in cap and gown in his lap, like a little Victorian. She knew what was at stake.

He tried to hear what was going on inside. Were they testing the manacles and sharpening the pliers? But there was no hint of what they were concocting for him. Cooking smells floated down from a nearby college refectory; they seemed to carry with them centuries of Gothic tribulation.

At long last an usher came to the door. 'Mr Mann, sir? If you're ready . . .'

Allan went into the tall, wooden-raftered room. Yellowing windows let in a pall of cold light. At the far end of the long room, sitting at a table on a dais and gowned like the judges of the damned, sat the six examiners. Their faces gave nothing away, no hint of their attitude, no hope for pity or compromise. Each of them had a pile of papers in front of him. They were Allan's own

164

papers, he knew for sure. They looked so insignificant, so pitifully unimpressive. He took a breath. There was nothing else for it. He began to move slowly down the chilly flagstones.

As he reached the edge of the dais, first Dr Esther Fry stood up. She looked at her colleagues on each side of her. Then, on her right, Morecambe, the only one with a barrister's wig, rose to his feet. On her left, Jessop sidled off his chair. Then Hodgkins got up too. Then Page and, finally, the heavyweight of Jurisprudence, Dr Hewett.

And they began to smile.

Taking their cue from Dr Fry, all six examiners drew their hands from the folds of their gowns and began to clap. They clapped and clapped. The applause rose to the rafters and left Allan sitting there without a word, gaping.

He had been awarded a Congratulatory First.

Twenty-seven

Allan took it as a sign. His chosen course was meant for him and he was now set to rise to the top of the legal profession. Linda would be sorry she hadn't waited for him. It was a triumph. Now, whenever his depressions came, he had only to think back and recall the applause. He could still hear it ringing in his ears, just as he could still see Ella standing up on her hind legs and clapping her tiny hands in imitation.

Geoffrey threw a party for him. Melanie gave him a rare engraving of Oxford. Dr Fry wrote to congratulate him and ended the letter: "So, the spirit *did* overcome!" Morecambe, the silk, sent him an offer to join his London chambers in the Inner Temple. Jessop argued that a Doctorate at All Souls' should be his next step; this was by far the most prestigious graduate college and it would allow him to stay in Oxford. There was an entrance exam to be sat, but Allan would sail through. He let the decision hang for the moment. He had another task first. He felt as he had done after winning the University mile record: pleased with the job but aware that it only put him at the foot of another ladder. The latest test was not the last, Finals were not actually final. The Wiseman case was the next major hurdle and everything else took second place to that.

He knew it would be difficult. The real world was Wiseman's world, where practice and pragmatism ruled over theory. Out there the rules were more political, more flexible and less rigorous. Justice in practice was a random affair; this case therefore had to be prepared as tightly as possible and he threw himself energetically into it. He combed through everything relevant in the library. He spent hours on the phone to the solicitors in London, to the anaesthetist at Stoke Mandeville who had cautiously offered to sign an affidavit, to a leading Harley Street spinal surgeon who sustained a professional rivalry with Wiseman. There had to be expert witnesses, testimony from junior hospital staff, written evidence and correspondence. It would mean weeks, maybe months.

He told no one about the project on which he'd embarked. He let his mother think he'd dropped the whole idea and was working for the All Souls' exams. He gave Geoffrey as much leeway with Ella as he wanted for his tests. He kept the atmosphere in the house pleasant and relaxed. He joked a good deal; he could see the effect on Dorothy. She took it that she was forgiven and, in return, kept out of his affairs and gave the monkey as much licence as she could bear to.

The summer term drew quickly to its close and the city breathed out again. The students scattered in their various directions and the vacuum was filled with the long, sumptuous afternoons of midsummer. Geoffrey and Melanie stayed up for their researches and for the wedding of John and Linda in early July. This was something Dorothy could not come to terms with. When Allan's hired morning suit was delivered to the flat, she took it into the living room and stood with a puzzled frown on her plumpish, kindly face.

'Surely you can't go,' she said. 'Not now you *know*.'

'But I've accepted,' said Allan brightly. 'It would be rude not to turn up.'

He looked at his mother and saw her relief. Obviously he was over the business of Jock's letter. Oh no, I'm not, he said to himself. I have a secret project, my own holy war. I'm excited, full of private glee. I'm David in a wheelchair. When the day of the wedding comes, I'll be immaculate in my grey tails and polished shoes. I'm the gentleman hangman. I must pay my respects to the victim. I must give him a final looking-over to measure him for the drop. And, what sweet irony, he will look into my eyes and he won't know that he's looking at the image of his own ruin.

Allan looked around the guests in Christ Church cathedral. This was a true slice of life — or a slice of wedding cake perhaps: Wiseman's working-class parents from Leeds formed a fruity underlayer, Linda's retired diplomatic parents made a kind of nutty in-fill, while John and Linda's friends from the theatre and medicine seemed to have the consistency of iced marzipan. Sir Rex Aikman had been at school with the Bishop and had roped the man in to officiate. The audience (Linda's word) packed the pews and spilled out into the aisles. A full house made for a successful show.

Melanie sat at the end of one pew, transformed into a beauty from Tennessee Williams. In his chair in the aisle next to her, Allan watched her with a strange sense of unfamiliarity and yet intimacy. To her left stood Geoffrey, bulging out of his suit and looking at her with his red-flushed head on one side and tender wistfulness in his pale eyes. Allan could almost hear his thoughts: he'd like to grab Melanie by the hand and rush up the aisle and shout, "Us too, Bishop! Geoffrey and Melanie Fish!" Allan coughed softly. Geoffrey looked down, realised the expression he'd been wearing and snorted with laughter. Heads turned.

Ella went off to explore. Allan let her go; she'd come back by herself. The service was long and boring. Towards the end Allan felt his eyes closing gently. There had been hymns, then an address, then the repetition of vows (liturgical jingles, he said to himself, but quite unkeepable) and now man and wife were doing whatever they did in the Vestry. The organ was playing Bach: *Sheep May Safely Graze*.

Gradually the shuffling feet and low whispers began to fade away. The organ music drew him out and upwards. He began to feel the fine, floating sensation. His mind detached itself from his body and rose aloft. He began to imagine. He was up there, above the congregation, high up at the back of the organ. The people were a tiny sea of coloured hats and silver suits, lined in neat rows. Above rose the stone vaulting, quite far above, beautifully carved but not very good for getting a purchase on. There was a small passage way to the organ loft. In it sat the organist, a young man playing with his elbows sticking out. Changing the music. Raising his fingers to hit the first chord.

'Allan, here.'

It was Melanie whispering to him. She stayed sitting while the congregation rose to its feet so that she could hold the hymn book for him. He nodded thanks. The first line of the introduction had finished and everyone was taking a deep breath. Then,

Wham, smash, splash, crash, tinkle, twinkle, trinkle, boom.

A sharp cry from the organ loft, then silence. Was this how Christian soldiers should onward go? All heads turned upwards. The Bishop looked as though he'd taken the wrong turning to Tarsus and met the Devil. There came another cry from aloft. Then, in reverse, boom, trinkle, twinkle, tinkle, crash, splash, smash, *wham.*

Oh God, thought Allan, choking with laughter. Ella's in the organ loft. I knew it! You wilful, clever little rogue, how I love you.

The reception was held in the Deanery, a few doors down the quad from the Cathedral. A Master of Ceremonies had cooped the guests up in the panelled Gothic library and was feeding them out one at a time to the reception line in the dazzling sunshine of the Deanery garden. The atmosphere was full of the sense of relief that comes after an hour on the knees before God and with the prospect of champagne and cake ahead. But Allan held back until the last. Through the open door from the garden floated the burden of azalias and roses on the slow summer breeze. He shut his eyes and inhaled it deeply, concentrating on relaxing. He feared, irrationally, that Linda would somehow read his mind. He nearly turned round to go but the M.C. was bending over him, asking the name. Allan gave both.

'Mr Allan Mann,' intoned the M.C.

Allan didn't move. The M.C. hesitated, glanced down again and, without a trace of expression, added,

'And Miss Ella.'

Sir Rex Aikman was first in the line and with diplomatic courtesy took Ella's paw and shook it. Lady Aikman, a lookalike for the Queen Mother, did the same and asked Allan about his mother. Wiseman senior faltered and his wife giggled nervously; she was a slight, fragile woman and her hand fitted Ella's exactly. The best man wiped his hand on his trousers afterwards as if he might catch rabies. Linda was dressed in white and her fair hair was chastely tied up in a Greek knot. Ella began to growl under her breath but crouched in Allan's lap while Linda bent over him and let a kiss alight on his forehead. It was a warm, tender kiss, an appeal to him, an echo from the past calling for a truce in the future. It was as light as the kisses she used to settle on his eyelids when his eyes were sore from studying too hard. Her scent was the scent she'd always worn and it brought the images careering back from the past: the trip to Paris, their first outdoors lovemaking, sex in the dressing-rooms between acts, dinners after the last shows, the last stolen kisses as he'd climb out of her college in the small hours. He refused to listen to the voice of memory. He was Judas, Judas kissed.

John Wiseman intervened as if to protect his bride from contagion. He clapped a hand on Allan's shoulder. Tanned and sleek, he grinned down at him. 'That's the last kiss you'll get, old chap. Make the most of it.'

Allan looked up into Wiseman's eyes and held them until Wiseman looked away, uncomfortable, and said, 'Allan's the last, darling. Let's circulate. Enjoy yourself, Allan.'

'Good luck to you both,' he replied.

'Thanks, old man,' said Wiseman, already turning away. His tone suggested he didn't want any of Allan's kind of luck. Linda followed, throwing a puzzled, pained frown at Allan. He could see she wanted there to be no bad feeling and that he should simply forgive and forget. It was a look of appeal, as eloquent as her kiss. But in Wiseman's eyes he'd seen what he wanted to find. He was now quite deaf to any pleas.

The garden was bordered by tall stone walls and comprised one of Oxford's finest lawns. (Allan recalled a college scout answering a tourist who'd asked how they got the grass like that. 'Simple,' the man said. 'Just water and roll, water and roll. Do that for five hundred years and there you have it.') He sat on the fringe of the large gathering, not wanting to participate, drinking a lot. Ella tried the champagne too but spat it out. People came up to congratulate him on his First and talk to Ella, expecting her to do tricks. She collected quite an audience when she fed Allan the wedding cake. The afternoon grew hotter, more sluggish and distant. There was so much chatter everywhere, champagne chatter. Allan closed his eyes. The group around him were discussing where John and Linda were spending their first night of marriage together. Apparently it was a cottage in the woods a few miles out of town, before they left for the Indian Ocean. Allan found himself dozing.

Suddenly Linda and John were leaving. Everyone converged on the Deanery front door. Allan didn't see them go off; he was behind, waiting for the crush to pass. A scout told him they'd left in a horse-drawn calèche and they looked a very handsome couple. Allan said nothing. By the time he'd got to the main college gates and found his ambulance, everyone had dispersed. Everyone except Melanie, who had stayed to see him home.

That night was the hottest of the whole year. It had not rained for twenty-two days. Allan lay in bed, unable to sleep. From the open window not the least breath of air came to relieve the oppression. The city sky was orange and, even after midnight, the cars growled and prowled restlessly around the streets. Without turning his head he knew that Ella was out. She loved the night, especially when it was hot. Something deeply primitive called her. He closed his eyes. Two years before, before everything happened, he'd have gone for a burn-up on his bike. Now he'd just have to cope with it as he always did.

He felt his eyeballs revolving backwards slowly and the floating feeling approach. Gradually his mind unstuck itself from his body. He began to rise, first up to the ceiling, then out of doors, swooping down here and there, hovering over the wedding reception, then shooting off on an adventure, somewhere he hadn't been before, somewhere quite dark and jungly and difficult to climb through . . .

A man and a woman are sitting at a table. I can just see their faces, lit by two candles. I recognise them. Last time I saw them, the woman was all in white and the man in a grey suit. They've had a good meal. Two bottles of wine, unfinished plates, a bowl of fruit: a scene from a Caravaggio. There's music, too, coming out through their open window.

It's a pretty cottage with low rough-hewn beams and upholstered wooden furniture. The curtains are light and scarcely move at all. It's airless tonight, hot and close and dry. The man's getting up. He comes round to stand behind the woman. His hands are on her shoulders. He's bending down to kiss the back of her blonde head. His hand slips inside her gown.

171

He's kissing her shoulder now and slipping the gown off her top. Her hands hold the back of his head and she draws him round so that she can kiss him. That kiss. I can feel it on my forehead still.

She says something, coming up for air. He laughs. He takes her by the hand and together they go towards the wooden stairs. He's taking her upstairs. The hands which have murdered me are now to caress the woman I loved. He has killed my body and is now taking hers.

I know what I'd *like* to do. I'd like to get hold of this candle, this one here. I'd like to wait until I can hear the sighings and the heavings from upstairs and I'd like to take it over here where the curtain meets the floor and, quite simply, without any fuss or noise, I'd like to hold the flame until the curtain catches and becomes one huge flame by itself. That's what I'd like to do.

A car's horn coincided with the sound of Dorothy flushing the lavatory. Allan woke. He could feel the sweat around the back of his neck. The pillow was damp and he was panting. A terrible dream.

Ella? Ella! Come back, wherever you are! What are you doing? Am I dreaming? I don't know where you are. Come back. Ella!

He beat his head from side to side on the pillow, trying to shake the dream out of his head. He couldn't breathe. How long did he have to suffer like this? Until morning? Until first light? Until the thunder came to break the spell of heat? Oh God, please help.

Flames! First, small flames at the bottom of the curtain. Then more flames, climbing, taking root in the other curtain. Spreading greedily. Tasting the wooden beams, curling at the bookshelf, biting at the base of the armchair, snatching at the table-cloth, crawling up the log-basket, joining at the foot of the stairs.

And then the noise. Crackling, spitting, splintering, and beneath it all the whooshing sound.

From a distance in the woods you can see the flames coming out now through the bottom windows. And the first fire upstairs. The panes are cracking; there are cries from inside. Wild, frantic cries in the wooded wilderness.

Twenty-eight

Allan slept fitfully. He woke once to the din of a cat-fight and another time to the siren of an ambulance. He was exhausted but afraid to close his eyes and dream. At dawn he fell into a deep sleep. When Dorothy came in he could hardly wake up. At once she saw Ella curled up at the foot of his bed.

'Off!' she shouted and clapped her hands. 'Look at the state of you! Allan, she's worse than a tomcat. You'll really have to stop her going out at nights if she comes back so filthy dirty. I expect she got mixed up in that fight. Did you hear all the catawauling?'

Sleepily he said. 'We can't stop her if she wants to have a scrap. I can't see why she does it, though. Melanie's always saying how gorillas and monkeys are so peace-loving.'

'Peace-loving!' snorted his mother and snapped on a surgical glove. 'I'd like to see anyone get any peace with young madam around. Now let's turn over onto our side, dear.'

She'd heaved him half over when the telephone rang. 'Drat the thing,' she said. 'I'd better get it.'

She left him on his side and hurried to the phone. Ella came out of hiding under the bed and jumped up and began to stroke his hair. He grinned at her. Dorothy was right, the creature was filthy. The black cap-markings on her head looked all smudged and her honey-coloured fur was tangled with burrs and bits of twig. And he smelled the unmistakeable smell of singed fur.

173

From the living room he could hear his mother let out a stifled cry, then lower her voice to a whisper. Minutes passed before she came back into the bedroom.

'Who was that, Mother?' he asked, his face in the pillows.

In a transparently casual tone, she replied, 'Oh, just Geoffrey. He's coming over in the afternoon.'

'Mother darling, something's wrong. Tell me.'

Dorothy hesitated. Ella was swinging above her head on the girder over the bed. She snapped at the monkey. 'Shoo! I told you to go out. I've had just about enough of your pranks. Out!' She clapped her gloved hands and Ella scampered away. Then she went back to the washing of her son's wasted body.

'Mother?' Allan repeated.

'Oh, just an accident. Nothing for you to worry about. Are you working today, or would you like to go round the Parks?'

'Tell me, Mother, and stop pretending!'

Her voice trembled when she spoke. 'It's Linda and Doctor Wiseman. They spent the night in a cottage somewhere in the woods. There was a terrible accident, a fire. I don't know what happened really. Geoffrey said a friend of his at the Radcliffe phoned him. The two of them are there now. Linda's going to be all right, well, just. But Doctor Wiseman, they don't think he'll make it. Oh dear, oh *dear*.'

No. Dear God, no. Not that. Not that way.

Allan buried his face deep into the pillows and howled. What was going on in his head? Was he going mad? Was it the tablets? How could he have dreamed of a cottage fire and now it had happened? How could he have *seen* it happening?

Had he started the fire himself, because he hated John and Linda? When he lost the physical strength from his body, had it somehow been transferred to his mind? Could he make things happen by imagining them? If Wiseman died, had he killed him? If Linda was disfigured, had he maimed her? Was it him?

Or Ella, was it Ella? Ella, dirty, filthy, scratched, torn, covered with thorns and burrs. And singed. It couldn't be Ella; monkeys hate fire. All animals hate fire. Only man uses it.

It could be.

'Get her!'

Dorothy had been shaking Allan, worried, alarmed. 'Are you all right, my love? I'm sure they'll get better. You mustn't be upset. They'll do all they can.'

174

'Get her, Mother. Lock her in the broom cupboard.'

His mother rolled him onto his back. 'Why, she's not all *that* dirty. I'll have her cleaned up in a jiffy.'

'Mother! Get Ella and lock her up!'

She finally obeyed. Allan could hear the whelp and the scuffling as she grabbed the monkey and bundled her into the dark cupboard among the brooms and the hoover and the dusters smelling of polish. He called out from the bed, 'And make sure the door's properly locked!'

When she'd finished getting him up, he went straight to the broom cupboard. Inside he could hear Ella whimpering. He leaned forward in his chair and took the pain-pack control in his mouth. He puffed hard and went on puffing, giving the monkey one jolt in her back after another until he grew tired, tired of her screams, tired of hearing her crashing against the door and tired of wishing that by punishing her he could undo the work of the night.

His face ached from the contortions and his eyes were scorched with tears when he finally pulled away and went into the kitchen. There he said, 'Mother, please would you phone the Radcliffe and see if they're allowing visitors.'

That morning the weather broke. At eleven o'clock the heavens opened. By midday the streets were overflowing onto the pavements and in parts of the city the telephone lines were down. Allan and his mother arrived at the hospital drenched.

Outside the intensive care unit they met Linda's parents, Lady Aikman shrunken and wrinkled, Sir Rex ashen and bowed. They had just received news of John Wiseman: he had not survived an emergency operation. Allan could read the shock in Linda's mother's face. He knew what it was like, the exact sequence of disbelief and numbness, of anger and sorrow. He'd been through it before: not for a child of his, but for himself. This was not the *real* world for her. Reality was the buttonholes still fresh on the dressing table at home, the small boxes of wedding cake to be posted to friends abroad, the Order of Service still in her handbag. What had turned reality into this nightmare?

He was allowed to see Linda for a minute. She lay on a pneumatic cushion behind a muslin curtain, for she was burned all over and the burns couldn't be covered. Allan was scarcely able to speak. She drifted in and out of consciousness and a nurse was constantly beside her. After a while she opened an eye and murmured,

'Allan, it's you. John . . . is he . . . is he going to be all right?'

Allan's throat wouldn't let the words pass. But he nodded. The nurse said, soothingly, 'He'll be fine. And so will you.'

Linda seemed to smile, relieved. Then she said, drowsily, 'It's me. I'm bad luck. First you, and now John. The two men in my life.'

He could still say nothing. The nurse made a sign that he should leave now. Linda managed a few more words. They weren't lucid, but he thought she said, 'Odd *you* coming to see *me* in hospital, it's a funny way round.'

He wheeled up close to her. He tried to bring out some words but they only emerged as a broken croak.

'Fight, Linda. *Fight.*'

She seemed to hear but then lost consciousness.

The storm had blown itself to a drizzle when Allan and his mother left the hospital. She was about to phone for an ambulance to take them home when he stopped her.

'Wait a moment. There's a store round the corner that'll be open. It sells everything. Leave me here and go and buy a collar and a lead. And we'll need a big roll of chicken wire and some nails.'

Dorothy looked surprised. 'For Ella?'

'For Ella.'

The rest of that afternoon and most of the evening were spent turning the flat into a prison.

They started first on his bedroom. It wasn't easy. Dorothy worked under his instructions and complained of being all fingers and thumbs, 'or what's left of them'. She tore her skin on the sharp edges of the chicken wire and she regularly hammered her thumbs. In the bathroom the lavatory seat cracked under her weight. In her own bedroom the curtain-rail came down.

'Allan, *why* don't we get a man in to do it tomorrow?' she pleaded at one point.

He was firm. 'No. It's got to be done tonight.'

When it was all finished, he went on a tour of inspection. Every window in the flat was covered with heavy wire netting, firmly nailed into the frames. The windows could be opened through the netting but no monkey could escape.

'I don't think we need worry about burglars now, do you?' he said with a smile. 'How about a drink?'

He could see his mother was happy, despite the torn fingers and laddered stockings. She couldn't see why Allan should want to punish Ella so severely — the creature had been out often before and got just as dirty — but he had his own reasons for things. She simply sensed the balance of power tilt in her favour. She poured the sherry with something close to triumph.

'I think Ella can come out now,' he said at last.

But when Dorothy opened the cupboard, the monkey refused to move. She sat huddled in a foetal ball, sucking her thumb. It was nearly midnight before hunger drove her out. She went first to fetch her Thing, then took it on a round of the house. She tested the windows, one by one. Then she seemed to understand. She was a prisoner in her own home.

'Mother, fetch the collar and lead,' said Allan.

He made the clicking sound and Ella came up to him. The Skinnerian behavioural conditioning worked. She sat obediently at the foot of his chair while his mother cautiously slipped the collar round her neck, did it up, latched the lead on and finally locked the lead around the table-leg. At first Ella prowled in circles like a goat around a stake, but then she became restless and pulled at it, then she began to fight, to panic, to hurl herself about so violently he was afraid she'd break her neck. She started to howl. The howl rose to a shriek and the shriek to a screech. He yelled at the top of his voice,

'Ella, *stop that!*'

She turned and he caught her eye. Each stared at the other. Gradually the monkey quietened down but she would not take her eyes away. Nor would he, until she was crouching and huddled up and subdued. Then he released her. And he turned away so that she should not see his tears.

Twenty-nine

Geoffrey left the hospital in a daze and walked slowly towards Allan's flat. He felt numbed; the sight of Linda through the gauze curtain of the Intensive Care unit had deeply shocked him. He struggled to digest what had happened but put it to one side in his mind to consider the events of that morning in the labs.

Professor Burbage had descended in his majesty and had paid him a visit. 'Geoff,' he said, using a diminutive Geoffrey detested, 'we may have something in all these shenanigans after all.'

Damn right, he thought. The results *are* bloody good. He'd scaled down the tests with Ella during Allan's exams and afterwards because the six monkeys in the lab were now well advanced on the drug. They weren't doing so spectacularly, but even so their performance on the key learning and recall parameters was well over average, and improving daily. He was glad not to have to rely on Ella and on Allan's goodwill any more. When it came to scientifically presentable results, the six in the lab were productive enough. And he still had his informal, unofficial human experiment going with Allan. He could now afford to sit back and wait on that front.

Geoffrey recalled the meeting that morning, how Burbage had put his head round the door and said, 'Let's talk turkey, Geoff,' and how he'd made sure the door was firmly shut before broaching the subject. He'd sat casually on the lab bench, stroking Geoffrey's report. They talked turkey. The Professor wanted a deal. The work was so promising, he's hinted, that it put Roach's in the shade and could be the basis for deciding who should fill the vacant Chair. There could be extra funds for the research and Burbage himself would take a very personal interest. Roach would be kept out of the picture. Next, thought Geoffrey, Burbage would propose the findings were published under their joint names. Already he'd baulked mildly at Geoffrey's choice of name for the new drug compound: *Piscalin*. Dr Fish was writing his name into history.

It was a grand reversal, but he wasn't to be hoodwinked. Burbage had made no clear promises, no hostages to fortune. If something went wrong, he'd drop it and Geoffrey with it. If it went right, Geoffrey would have to contest the success with his boss. Still, it was better than before. So, when he arrived at Allan's flat, it was not to do tests on Ella but to take his friend out for a walk in the Parks. Allan wanted to stay in. But Geoffrey insisted; the air and open spaces would do him good.

He wheeled Allan around the paths and under the trees in the great university parks. He kept up a constant chatter. Occasionally he passed someone he knew and they'd stop and exchange gossip.

'Dorothy tells me you're punishing Ella very hard,' he said. This had worried him; he wanted all his options open. 'Conditioning is more effective than discipline, Allan. Especially if you punish after the event. There's an optimum time lapse between a stimulus and a reward — or a punishment — and that's a matter of seconds. If you punish her today for something she did yesterday, she won't make the connection.'

'She's been a bad girl, that's all,' said Allan flatly.

'Take my advice,' he went on, 'use the pain-pack. That's what it's for. Give her a shock the moment she does wrong. Keeping her in the flat is okay, even if it means chicken wire everywhere, but I'd take her off the lead. For her it'll be like going back to her cage in the labs. She's tasted freedom. You can't take that away without losing goodwill.'

Allan said nothing. A large red kite suddenly crashed to the ground in front of the wheelchair. A little girl in pigtails ran up. She snatched it up quickly as if afraid he would get up and pounce on her. From a safe distance she kept staring at him. They went on in silence.

Then he said, suddenly, 'Do they know what caused the fire? A cigarette or something? The woods were as dry as tinder.'

'They're treating it as arson.'

'Oh?' Allan sounded casual.

'It's a mystery. They say the fire started inside, at the curtains. I'd say it was a burglar dropping a fag. An arsonist would have used petrol, probably. Anyway, it beats me how they can tell anything at all from a pile of ashes. It's a tragedy all round.'

'Yes, a tragedy.' Allan fell silent again.

A woman with a pram crossed in the opposite direction. Geoffrey exchanged glances with her, each walking their charge, one young and the other older but both incapable.

'Tell me,' Allan began again. 'Could a fire be started by telepathy?'

'You mean by telekinesis?' said Geoffrey. 'There are a lot of reported cases of that kind of phenomenon, but never with enough evidence to be conclusive. Not to convince a sceptic like me anyway. It's hard to test paranormal events. They're often called *shy*; they don't like performing under laboratory conditions. But there are plenty of accounts. Jung, for example, is full of them. He tells a story about how his wife went on and on at him to give up smoking. He put his pipe away in a cabinet and vowed never to touch it again. They had a row. He said *dammit* and went to the cabinet. Just as he reached for the pipe, it exploded. Spontaneously. Into a thousand pieces.'

'Caught fire?'

'No, just fragmented. But fire is possible too.' He paused and looked about him. The grass and trees were suddenly green again after the rainfall. He went on, 'PK, psychokinesis I mean, is generally associated with frustration. You find it a lot among young people who are sexually frustrated. It seems to give them a particularly concentrated power. But half the people who claim PK powers are as mad as meat-axes.'

'How about cripples? A cripple's a pretty frustrated person. Physically, sexually, emotionally. Are there cases of cripples doing these things? Knocking vases off mantlepieces, shattering windows, stopping trains, that kind of thing?'

'And starting fires?' A gong was sounding in Geoffrey's mind. He felt his hand sweating on the chair-handles. In a mild, offhand tone he said, 'Why's all this? Are you having any . . .

strange experiences? What's on your mind?'

Allan said nothing for a moment. Then, 'Can we stop here for a moment?'

Geoffrey wheeled the chair onto the grass and sat down on his raincoat. In the distance a cricket match was in progress and the Parks were full of strollers and joggers, lovers and loners. But Geoffrey saw none of that. He folded his hands over his knees and looked hard at Allan. He noticed, as always, how transparent the sun made his friend's skin. His eyes were sunk in their hollows and his head looked more out of proportion than usual. A brilliant brain, thought Geoffrey, reduced to a tadpole in a bath-chair.

'I came across a letter in Mother's things,' Allan said. Without meeting Geoffrey's eye he told him about Wiseman and the operation, the untested experimental technique which failed, the false assessment of the risks told to his parents. Geoffrey listened to the bald recital of facts, strangely unsurprised. Somehow it made sense. He'd always thought Wiseman a charlatan and that Allan's parents had some quarrel about the man which they kept covered up. But he could also sense where Allan's line of thought was going. He had to put it to the test. He tried a diversionary angle.

'Look, Allan, it's certainly possible that hatred and anger of this kind could create the preconditions for PK to occur. That's to say, frustration is a necessary condition, but it's far from a sufficient one. Otherwise you'd have all the patients in Stoke Mandeville raising fire by thought-power. I don't know what you want to achieve by dabbling in all this. If you mean to solve the riddle of Wiseman's death and launch your legal career by claiming it was a paranormal event, you'll have your evidence laughed out of court. But if you're thinking what I *think* you're thinking,' and he looked hard into his friend's eyes, 'then you're out of your fucking tree.'

Allan looked away. 'But the tablets I once took? Ella's tablets?'

The tablets you're still taking, corrected Geoffrey to himself. But still he pushed in the opposite direction. 'Look, mate. I've got six Ellas on a similar drug. Six bright monkeys who're bloody great through the mazes. But not six telekinetic monkeys. They haven't set fire to the print-outs. They haven't melted the bars of their cages. Or not yet.' He forced his face into a mask of a grin,

181

but inside he was cold, watching for every clue. 'If my six can't, I don't think Ella can, I don't think *you* can. *Piscalin* is a memory drug, for heaven's sake, not something to turn you into Uri Geller. Listen, if you're feeling off I can get you something. I'll fix you something from the lab chemist.'

'No thanks.'

'Or is it something else you haven't told me?' Geoffrey carried on gently. Allan didn't respond. He went on carefully, 'Look, if you're really interested in that telepathy crap, I'll get you some articles to read. You'll soon see what I mean. Okay?'

'Thanks. If you would.'

Geoffrey frowned. He was still nowhere nearer getting at the root of it. But he knew Allan; to force the issue would only make him back off. He'd have to wait and watch. Dorothy had been talking of taking him off on holiday, to a nursing home by the sea. He'd have to suggest it was not such a good idea. Not now, not yet. Not while there was this thing troubling him. This thing: *what thing?*

He changed tack. 'How's the work anyway?'

'The what?' Allan was miles away.

'Your All Souls' entrance. I suppose it's any day now.'

'Oh, that. Yes, that's right. Any day now.' Allan looked down at him on the ground. 'I'd like to go home now, please.'

'Sure.'

As Geoffrey wheeled his friend back home, certain memory-traces began to form links in his brain. He recalled the night he'd taken three tablets of *Piscalin* and known, without seeing, that the monkey Nixon was at his feed-hopper. And then this business of the afternoon on the punt and how Allan had known that John and Linda were up in Oxford. It required looking into and he'd start just as soon as he'd taken Allan home.

It was a simple experiment to make a simple point. Back in his lab, Geoffrey took down two bottles of placebos, pills with no active contents. He took six blue pills and six red ones. On one of the red pills he painted a coating of quinnine, transparent but bitter to the taste. He took his catching-pole and hooked Nixon out of his cage and brought him into the experiment room, partitioned off at the end of the lab. He put one blue pill and the coated red pill in front of him. The monkey picked up the red pill, put it in its mouth and spat it out violently. Then he did the same with the blue pill, but chewed it; it was sweet. Geoffrey made Nixon taste the red pill another two times, to make sure he'd learned. Then he left the room with Nixon shut inside.

One by one he took the other five monkeys into his office, also separated by a door from the main lab area. He placed red and blue pills in front of each, the blue ones at a distance so that the creatures would have to stretch for them. In every case they ate the blue pills and refused the red. What Nixon had learned, they now knew.

Geoffrey put the monkeys back in their cages and went slowly to the library. His hand was shaking and he stopped several times in the corridor to think.

Allan was terrorised by uncertainty. He was the mouse hypnotised into paralysis by the snake. He didn't dare let himself fall into his daydreams again. He had a large Scotch before bed, sometimes with a sleeping pill. He avoided his bedroom during the day, knowing the temptation he always felt in front of the window to close his eyes, gently drift away, disconnect from his body, float upwards, and to see, to move, to run, to climb, to race . . .

Geoffrey brought along a stack of periodicals and books as he'd promised: Freud on the *Interpretation of Dreams*, Michel Jouvet on *States of Sleep*, the works of Kuella and Oswald, Chalmers and Strumwasser. Was this the state he called daydreaming? *Was* it dreaming at all? Jouvet had identified two separate kinds of sleep: slow-wave and paradoxical. In slow-wave sleep, the head often rested lightly on the chair-back, while in paradoxical sleep the muscles relaxed and the head slumped forward and the eyes flickered rapidly. How could he tell with himself? Dreaming happened most often in paradoxical sleep, but also with the other kind. So had he simply been dreaming in slow-wave sleep? But was it dreaming? Freud and Jung wrote a great deal about the interpretation of symbols in dreams; but his dream about the cottage fire was no collection of symbols, it was an actual vision of something that was happening. Then he sought an answer to the question, what is the *function* of dreaming? No one could answer that clearly, except by analogy and metaphor. The neurobiologists called it the result of random inputs triggering memory

183

sequences at a time when normal waking control mechanisms were off duty. Lacking a filter, sequences otherwise blocked could occur, perhaps triggered off by some cortical cell firing at random. And so on. Nothing seemed to fit. His 'dream' had none of the chance leaps and inconsequential links that characterised the dreams he read about. It began to look as if *daydreaming* was the wrong term. Perhaps a euphemism.

The accounts of paranormal events were equally confusing. Telepathy was discussed in terms of special ESP cards and the odds of such-and-such an event occuring against probability. Psychokinesis was people separating egg whites from yolks through a tank of water. Telekinesis was about influencing the fall of dice between Leningrad and Murmansk. Then the more way-out fringe: psychotronics and thought as a weapon of war, auto-hypnosis and dematerialisation into the fourth dimension. In fact, of everything he read, Allan found the Madame Blavatsky type of accounts of clairvoyance far closer to what he recognised as his own experience. But then, one knew what to think of those old witches' tales.

It was a long search, and frustrating because fruitless. It only served to make him more uncertain and more anxious. And more afraid of his daydreams. That was why he was being so hard on Ella. He didn't directly blame her: if she'd been the instrument, he'd been the mind. But he was afraid of his love for her, his need of her. He had to keep her away, at a distance, out of reach. And so he punished her.

More accurately, he merely allowed Dorothy to have her way with the monkey without interference. Ella, the lover, was demoted to housemaid. Dorothy, the servant, was promoted to mistress of the house. She laid down a new regime. Ella now took her food on the floor; she slept in the kitchen; she wasn't allowed in Allan's room while he was working; she couldn't put a foot outside the house and, inside, games and high-jinks were strictly forbidden. The pain-pack came back into use. She was banished to the corner of the room for an hour at a time. In exceptional cases she spent the night in the broom cupboard. One morning Dorothy found she'd messed there and rubbed her nose in it, like a puppy. Thus, inch by inch, often with more than a trace of vindictiveness, his mother won back the ground she'd lost over the past months.

He couldn't bear it, but he forced himself to go through with it. For a while he denied himself the tablets, but took them again when he felt something between him and Ella going fuzzier and weaker. And he began to realise what he dreaded most of all: without Ella, his whole life began to slow down and lose its purpose. He ignored the All Souls' application forms. He tried to read light novels. He went for long excursions into the Parks on his own. He even tried to talk about it to his mother, but was too afraid to reveal his mind. In the end he fell to drinking Scotch in the mid-afternoon and watching television through until close-down. Dorothy, the District Nurse, Geoffrey, were all worried. There seemed nothing they could do.

Thirty

Geoffrey wanted another angle on the problem, and he wanted it to come from outside the Department. He thought at once of Melanie. She was an expert on human interactions with gorillas and maybe she could apply it to monkeys. Her approach was always diametrically opposite to his own and besides, though he would not admit it rationally, he also sought a *woman's instinct*. Over dinner two days later he said to her, 'I think you ought to take a look at Allan. I'd like your opinion. I think he may need help.' The following morning Allan received a call from Melanie inviting him to lunch. With Ella.

Ella's small wrinkly pink face had grown into a pool of perplexity and hurt. She'd spend much of the day whimpering and hugging her Thing, morose and thoughtful. She'd sit on her perch on the bookshelf at the times she was allowed into the living room, watching and trying to puzzle it all out. Or else she'd sit on the window-sill in Allan's bedroom and stare, as he used to, out at the burgeoning green trees and the open Parks beyond. She cried a good deal, though quietly and to herself. Sometimes she tried to play again. She'd hide Allan's mouth-stick, she'd dance on her hind legs like a tiny bullfighter, she'd swing round and round on the girder above his bed — all the things that used to make him laugh. When that didn't work, she cried in the corner.

Dorothy scared her. She gave her the pain-pack frequently, often for a reason of her own invention, rather than for failing in a

186

task the monkey had been trained to do. When she approached, Ella cringed and arched her back against the pain. Her fair coat grew dull, she slept little and fitfully and she fidgeted more than ever. One night she completely unravelled one of Dorothy's jerseys. The following day she was fitted with a pair of pink baby's gloves and made to wear them every night. She bit Dorothy, but her gums didn't hurt. She alternated between careering around screaming frantically and sitting huddled and whimpering to herself. Allan felt he couldn't bear it any more. He tried not even to look at her. And he tried to avoid thinking of the problem. It was like trying to catch an eel in the dark with bare hands.

And then came Melanie's invitation to lunch. He'd assumed it would be another of her usual parties, but they were alone. When she opened the door he realised again how beautiful she was; how interesting and lovely her face with its precise, neat mouth and nose, its dark liquid eyes full of intelligence and humour. And her hair, dark and wavy and now longer, her wide-boned shoulders that made her body hang so elegantly, her slender legs and her rounded breasts. She wore a short-sleeved blouse, a pearl choker, tight jeans and red Italian sandals. She bent forward and kissed him on the cheek. Her scent was faint as a distant echo in the memory; it lingered in his mind long after it had faded from his skin.

She walked before him into the main double room. The French windows onto the garden were wide open and rich summer smells and sounds wafted in. She took Ella's collar off and at once the monkey spread-eagled herself against her front.

'I'll give her the pack if she's a nuisance,' said Allan.

'Don't you dare! She's just after affection.' Melanie tickled Ella behind the ear. 'What'll you have? Wine or sherry?'

'White wine, if it's open,' he said. He watched her walking to the kitchen, then looked away. This was bad, this was dangerous, this was playing with the fire of feelings. He mustn't think of her like *that*.

He cast his eye around the room. Instinctively he felt at home there. Her life was like her house: open, expansive, generous. His flat had become closed and oppressive. He looked at the kelims and the Arabic coffee-pots, the fretted tables and the camel rugs.

'I love the way you've done the place,' he said.

'Thanks,' she called from the kitchen. There was a pop of a cork. 'I guess I was lucky with the builders.' She came in. 'Here. I hope it's cold enough. Let's go into the garden, shall we?'

She sat down in a white wrought-iron garden chair. The table between them was laid. Allan made the clicking noise and Ella hopped up and held the beaker of wine to his lips.

'Cheers,' said Melanie and shook her dark hair. Then she looked at him with a serious expression. 'Geoffrey tells me you're punishing Ella a lot these days. You know, you shouldn't need to punish an animal. It shows you don't understand it.'

'Geoffrey says it shows poor conditioning,' he said and looked out at the garden. It was long, narrow, bordered by aged creosote fencing, soused by the sun and overlooked a tiny tributary of the river, bordered by tall chestnuts.

'Oh, Geoffrey would say that,' she replied with a small laugh, half scornful, half kindly. 'He and I don't see things the same way. I say that taking a monkey out of its habitat and putting it in a cage is totally artificial.'

'He'd say it was the only way to learn about its behaviour scientifically.'

'It isn't. Don't talk to me about behaviourists. They treat all forms of life simply as a series of stimuli and responses. It's not only misguided, it's degrading too. No wonder they're all fascists.'

'Geoffrey a fascist?' asked Allan with a laugh.

'Geoffrey's too unpoliticised; a typical armchair liberal. But look at the others, Roach, Burbage and the rest. Give them half a chance and they'd round up all their 'anti-social elements' and lobotomise the lot of them into model citizens. Don't be fooled. Why do you think Experimental Medicine is the only Science faculty that has received in *increase* in its grant, not a cut? It's all aimed ultimately at social control.'

'Come on, Melanie. Geoffrey's only playing with monkeys and their learning patterns. We're a long way from *1984*.'

'Are we?' She stroked Ella's head unconsciously and Allan noticed how slim-boned her hands were. The monkey sat quietly at her side. 'Geoffrey's too well-meaning to see it. He thinks everyone else is well-meaning like him, that they play the game according to the rules. This is the real world, Allan, not a school

188

rugby match. Anyway, if you don't believe me, read Delgado's book, *Physical Control of the Mind*. Behaviour control is already with us. Back home in the States they're implanting radio-controlled electrodes in the brains of prisoners and mental patients. They're regularly doing amygdalectomies on "un-cooperative" patients. True, Geoffrey's not actually cutting up brains. But psychochemistry is just as bad. Look how they deal with dissenters in the Soviet Union. Read Medvedev's account of what they did to him. They've invented a diagnosis, "schizophrenia without symptoms". I ask you! They forcibly feed them anti-depressants like Tofranil and tranquillisers like chlorpromazine. Look at the West too. Don't even go to the prisons and mental homes. Go to the classrooms. Every day a quarter of a million American kids are given amphetamines to reduce "hyper-activity". They've invented another illness and called it "minimal brain dysfunction". All that means is the kids can't, or don't, adjust to the system. Pump them full of drugs and, if that doesn't work, get out the knife. You wouldn't believe the number of leucotomies performed every year on children diagnosed, basically, as unmanageable. I'm not mentioning the billions of pills half the population of the West is encouraged to prescribe for itself — a nice form of political self-control. I won't mention the use of neurochemistry in warfare. It's systematically anti-human. Geoffrey, of course, can't see it.' She paused, then smiled. 'I'm sorry. I go on about it. I feel very strongly.'

Allan smiled too. He liked Melanie's ferocity and was surprised he hadn't seen that side of her before. He said, 'I can see you feel strongly. But I don't somehow think that Ella's learning pills are going to make anyone start writing two plus two equals five.'

She laughed, then became serious again. 'Of course, not in the limited sense. Ella serves a function with you and everything done to improve her learning improves her usefulness, I grant that. I was speaking of wider principles. Shall we eat now? I'm starving.'

She got up and brought a tray into the garden, loaded with cold chicken and salami and salads already cut to the size he needed. As she served him she said, 'I'm not against developing drugs to help mankind, of course not, although I deplore the fact that a thousand animals of various kinds — monkeys, cats, dogs, rats

189

— will be made to suffer if Geoffrey's drug is going to be made safe for human consumption. But then it becomes political, whatever he thinks. A new wonder learning drug! Does the Red Cross send it to the Third World where it would really do some good? Or is it used in police cells in Northern Ireland and mental hospitals in — I don't know — Alabama for social conditioning? We'll have to see. I'd stake my bet right now, though.'

With his mouth half-full, Allan said, 'Whatever your wider principles are, Ella's an absolute boon to me. She's not a bad advertisement for Geoffrey's drug either.'

'She's remarkable,' Melanie agreed. 'More wine?'

'Thanks.' He added quietly, 'This is wonderful, Melanie. Thank you.'

She looked up. Allan thought she was blushing. Turning away slightly, she said, 'It's just a light snack. I did want to see you; it's been so long since we talked together. We always seem to meet when there's lots of other people around.'

He nodded. He wondered if he could tell her the real worries in his heart. What would she say? Would she echo Geoffrey and say he was *out of his tree*? He couldn't, he decided. Everything was too ill-formed. What lay at the root of his fears was that somebody might do something that took Ella away from him. If he carried on treating her hard and refusing to allow himself the daydreams, maybe it would all sort itself out.

Ella had finished the plate and was wiping his mouth with a napkin. He laughed and pulled back. 'No, no, darling. Stop it! It tickles! God, it's agony when your lips tickle. I'll have to teach her to scratch me somehow.'

'She's very fond of you,' said Melanie.

'Sure. We're mates. Except when she's a bad girl.'

'Even then,' she said and poured him more wine.

'How can you tell especially?'

'For one thing, she's showing what's known as reciprocal altruism. She's doing the feeding and cleaning without receiving a banana pellet or some other reward. And without expecting one, though Geoffrey wouldn't agree there. Anyway. The principle is basically you-scratch-my-back-and-I'll-scratch-yours. You find it in man, of course, and in very few of the higher primates. A gorilla, for example, may want to displace a rival but he can't do it alone. He'll get a friend along to help. The friend gets no reward, indeed he may be damaged in the fight. But later he can come along and demand a similar favour in return; he'll call in the debt. It's a very advanced piece of social behaviour, evolutionarily speaking.'

'I'm sure,' said Allan. 'Ella gives me a lot, but I give her things in return: a home, safety, food.' She gives me more, he was thinking. Far more. She gives me the forbidden daydreams. She lets me out of my dead body and takes me running and flying and scampering everywhere with her. That's what she gives me, or gave me.

'Yes. But the kind of behaviour I referred to isn't found in monkeys. You see, it needs consciousness.'

'Ella's conscious! Look at her. She's a live little devil!'

'No, no,' Melanie laughed. 'I mean *self*-consciousness. Awareness of herself as a separate identity. Reciprocal altruism can only work, for example, if the second gorilla can be sure the first one won't cheat him and renege on the deal later. He could find that out maybe by simply observing its behaviour, but more likely by direct empathy. But empathy holds a danger. It's hard for us to understand: you know you're Allan and I know I'm Melanie. A cat doesn't, though; a dog doesn't. Monkeys don't. They don't see themselves as different entities from the world around. They can perceive differences between other objects, of course, but they don't see themselves as other and distinct from them. They merge with the world, if you like. It's a very high order of evolution when you find self-consciousness.'

'But Ella's brilliant!' exclaimed Allan. 'I won't have her maligned. She's *super*human!'

Melanie laughed. 'I'll show you then.'

She went inside and a moment later came out carrying a large Maltese mirror and a packet of self-adhesive tags. She took her chair over to the shade and propped the mirror on it. She picked Ella up and deftly stuck a small white circular label right in the middle of the black markings on her forehead. She waited to make sure Ella didn't dislodge it and said, 'Okay? She doesn't know she's got the patch on her head, right? Now watch.'

She put the monkey down in the chair in front of the mirror.

'That's not fair,' cried Allan. 'She doesn't know about mirrors. She scared herself once and ever since she's avoided them.'

'Look anyway.'

191

He looked. Instead of sparring and dancing, Ella stood very still. She stared into the mirror. She moved her head closer. She pulled back and began to chatter. She cocked her head on one side, then the other, then peered closely again.

'She'll think it's another monkey,' Melanie whispered.

But Ella lifted up one paw, then the other and, quite deftly, picked the white spot off her forehead. She hadn't thought she was seeing another monkey; she knew the reflection was her. She knew she didn't have a white spot on her forehead. And instead of picking the spot off her image, she'd correctly reached straight for her own forehead. She knew what she looked like.

Melanie drew in her breath sharply and squatted down beside the mirror at once. 'Wait a minute!' she breathed. 'That's not possible. You can't do that! What's Geoffrey been teaching you?'

Allan laughed triumphantly. 'Well done Ella! Geoffrey's never taken a mirror anywhere near her. She's brilliant! What did I tell you?'

Melanie put the mirror slowly against the fence and brought her chair back to the table. She sat down and spoke in a low, careful voice. 'That's generally considered a definitive test of consciousness of self. A major leap in evolution. It can't be right, not with a Capuchin. I don't understand.'

Allan had gone quiet too. A slight breeze blew on his forehead. He looked out towards the trees as if the answer lay buried among the green canopies of the chestnuts. After a long pause he said, 'This business of reciprocal altruism. Maybe it's possible with Ella. Between us, I mean. I get something from her and she gets something from me.' He listened to the breeze ruffling the trees. An idea began to fit into place. 'And Ella does things for altruistic reasons. For me.'

The cottage blaze, he was thinking. Did Ella do it *for him*?

Melanie stood up and stacked the plates absent-mindedly. She went into the kitchen; he could hear the sound of the coffee being ground. He looked at Ella, who had hopped up onto her chair and was picking the crumbs off the table.

You did it for me, he thought. You did it because you felt it was what I wanted. And look how I have repaid you.

Melanie came back with the coffee. As she poured it out she said, 'I'd really like to put Ella in front of some Zener cards. They're simple cards designed to test awareness of symbols. I

192

don't suppose it'll show anything. My gorillas tend to eat them.'
She smiled. 'Milk or cream?'

'Milk, just a drop. Thanks. What would symbol cards show?'

'Well, one of the chief characteristics of man, the highest
primate of all, is his ability to make abstractions. Abstracting is
the ability to see reality in terms of tokens and symbols. It's one of
the few characteristics that's unique to man'.

'Oh? What else is unique to man?'

'Only man uses tools. I'm excluding cases like birds which use
stones to break eggs. No, tools and fire. Only man uses fire.'

'Fire?' Allan gave a start.

'Animals won't go near a naked flame,' she said. Then, 'I've
got some Zener cards in the Department. Can I come over one
afternoon?'

'Whenever you like,' he said. Her dark hair was shot through
with the sun. 'I'd love to see you anytime.'

One key measure of scientific validity was repetition. Geoffrey
repeated a lab test using a Y-maze one hundred times with
various monkeys on *Piscalin*. It worked best with Nixon who'd
been given the extra dose. The results went way off the scale of
probability. At the end of two days' work, Geoffrey tore up the
print-outs and went out for a walk. He didn't believe it, he simply
did not believe the results. There was an error in the methodolo-
gy, a short-circuit, a feedback loop. He went through every step
in his mind; the method was crude but structurally faultless.

At the time Allan was dozing in Melanie's garden after lunch,
Geoffrey returned to his lab to start again. Simplest of all, he ran
the very first test, but reversed the red and the blue pills. The red
ones were now the sweet ones and the monkeys went for them
every time.

The afternoon was slow and sultry. Melanie was working
indoors on an article for the *Journal of Zoology* and the synopsis for
a feature in the *National Geographical Magazine*. Allan had gone to
the foot of the garden and sat in the shade of a tree. Through a
break in the fence he could see the spreading fields beyond the
small stream. Ella was curled on his lap, chewing a tassel she'd
found. He looked down at her and she looked up. The hurt and
perlexity still shone from her bright, dark eyes.

Forgive me, Ella. If you did it, it was done for me. You wanted to punish them for me. You loved me and I refused you. You fought for me and I turned against you.

I'll pull down the netting at home, you can come and go as you please. You can run around the house and scamper into the garden and play as often as you like. You'll sleep on my bed again. Mother won't use the pack on you any more. It will be like it was. I promise.

Ella?

Forgive me?

She cocked one ear and a frown passed fleetingly over her pink forehead. She began to chatter softly. She looked at Allan and away. Then quite suddenly she reached up on her hind legs and pressed her face under his chin and kept it there. A tear fell down his cheek. He closed his eyes; he knew what was coming next. Ella soon grew restless. She slipped her head away and, a while later, hopped down onto the grass. He kept his eyes closed. He could feel it coming over him like a hypnotic hand. One moment he was locked inside himself, the next he was out, free, floating, riding above the grass.

Melanie is at the table, reading with glasses. From time to time she jots down a note, without looking up. The carpets are thick and soft and they go in one piece all the way up the stairs. The first floor: strange, unknown territory. There's Melanie's bedroom, Moroccan rugs on a low, wide bed and a smell of powder and scent. On the bed lies a kanga, bleached by the sun and soft to the touch. Nearby stands a camel-saddle chair and, beyond a dressing table with ornaments and photo-frames, is the window. The view is fantastic, over the chestnuts and to the fields beyond. Red-leaved creeper grows thick down the back wall, right to the ground. The stems are thick and pass directly by the kitchen window on the ground floor. There's the remains of the chicken on the kitchen table. It looks very tempting. The window's shut, but that's no trouble to fix.

A cat! A cat with purple-black fur and green slit-eyes! Melanie must have locked it in the kitchen on purpose. The row, the howling, the screeching it makes! It's dashing everywhere, onto the fridge, over to the sink, upsetting the racks on the draining-board, then leaping to the table and sending a glass crashing to the floor. But the noise of broken glass has terrified it.

It's seen the open window and in a single black streak is up, out and away.

'Hey, stop it, you two!'

Melanie's yell brought Allan round. He turned in his chair. From the bottom of the garden he could see her face at the kitchen window, calling the cat. He heard a swishing and cracking in the tree above him. He craned his head back. It was Ella, swinging down from branch to branch until she was low enough to drop onto his lap. There she stood on her hind legs and beat her bony little chest with her fists until Allan thought he'd fall out of his chair laughing.

Thirty-one

Allan did not reckon on his mother's reaction when he told her that the *status quo ante* was to be restored. He'd tried often enough to put himself in her place and understand what she must be going through. He'd try to be sympathetic, but so much of her manner was well-meaning but infuriating. He didn't realise what a turning-point Ella's regime and incarceration had been in Dorothy's life.

Previously she'd concentrated simply on coping with the household. She'd go without things she wanted so as to put money by for Allan. Whatever private grief she felt for her husband and her son, she kept it to herself. She kept the bedroom door locked when she was out, hiding the altar to Jock's memory she'd made of her dressing table. But the day Ella began her punishment, Dorothy changed. She bore her cross more gladly. She took a new interest in her appearance. She sold Jock's golf clubs and bought a smart dress; she went to the hairdressers; she put on perfume before going to work and she went on a slimming course. She stayed late at the office because the personnel manager, a Mr Daventry, offered her a lift home. They'd have a drink and Dorothy would say when she got back, 'Such a nice man, Mr Daventry. He's so interested in how you're getting along. I'd like to invite him over to meet you.' She was at home when Allan returned from Melanie's that day and had a cup of tea ready for him. He told her his decision about Ella.

'I'm not taking the netting down,' she said firmly. 'I know it's

196

unsightly, but it keeps young madam out of mischief.'

'Mother darling, Ella's done her term,' he said. 'She's had her punishment. Geoffrey says we'll lose her goodwill if we carry on.'

'Geoffrey says,' Dorothy snorted. 'I say if she needs a beating she'll have one.'

'She's to go back to sleeping in my room.'

'I won't hear of it!'

'And take her meals properly, like one of us.'

'She's *not* one of us!' his mother cried. 'We were getting everything back to normal and the creature in its proper place and now you want to upset it all again. Really, Allan, I don't know what's come over you.'

They were in the living room. In the background *The Archers* was on the radio. Allan wanted to ask her to turn it off, but controlled himself. Instead, he asked his mother to get him a Scotch.

'Lovey, do you think you ought to? Isn't it rather early? Jock never drank before seven. It's not as if you're celebrating anything.'

'We are celebrating!' cried Allan. 'We're celebrating Ella's release. She's forgiven.'

'Well, not by me she isn't.'

'Don't be so hard-hearted, Mother. She went out and got filthy once too often, that's all. I used to get filthy as a child and you didn't lock me up all day indoors.'

'That's different.'

'Why is it different? Anyway, how about the Scotch? If I ask Ella she'll only spill it.'

'Oh, very well,' said Dorothy. She went to the cabinet and poured him a drink. He called, 'Top it up, Mother. I'm not an infant.'

She held the glass while he drained it, with a look of distaste on her face. There was more she wanted to say. She stood so that her back was turned to Ella and spoke in a low voice.

'I've been thinking,' she began. 'I may be silly at times but I can think for myself, you know. That night Ella came in all filthy dirty. Well, it's not like you to hurt her like you did, not for something like that. And then the telephone call. Linda and John and the cottage burning down. And when I come to clean Ella up, she's all charcoally and full of cinders and ashes. Well, you may not like it but I have my own ideas.'

He felt himself turning white.

'Yes, Allan. I'm serious. I'm worried.'

His eyes were drying in their sockets. In a hurt tone, he said, 'Give the poor thing a break, please. She's only a monkey. We've punished her enough.'

Ella sat on her perch all the while and watched. Dorothy turned to her son again. 'I saw how you looked when I told you about the fire. Of course you were upset, but there was more than that. Then you took it out on Ella. I'm sorry. You may think it's nothing, but I've a good idea that that monkey had something to do with the fire. She's evil, that one.'

'That's absurd. She couldn't have. Besides, monkeys hate fire.'

'Not Ella,' said Dorothy. 'You should see her playing with the spills in the kitchen.'

He said nothing. His throat had closed up. She went on, more to herself.

'Anyway, whatever you say, I'm going to speak to Geoffrey about it tomorrow. He'll know what to do.'

There was nothing more to say; her mind was fixed. She prepared supper and no more was mentioned about it. She put Allan to bed before ten, for she wanted an early night and there was some film on television he wanted to watch. He could watch it in bed. All evening long he racked his brains. He had to find a strategy to stop her. Damn her interfering! He had until morning to come up with something.

In her bedroom, Dorothy lit a cigarette. This was the only room in the flat where she smoked. She allowed herself one before bed; it calmed her nerves. She undressed quickly in the half-dark and in the corner furthest from the mirror. She flannelled her face in the mirror over the basin and wondered if she'd noticed that tiny, burst blood vessel before. She pulled on her dressing gown quickly and slipped out to the kitchen for a glass of milk. The sound of the television filled the flat; Allan was wrapped in a cowboy movie. Back in her room, she got into bed, drank the milk and began to re-read a chapter of Georgette Heyer. She was too sleepy. She shut the book and turned out the light. In a short while her breathing had found the slow rhythm of sleep.

In another short while a fair hairy arm stretched out tentatively from under the bed. It was followed by a pink-faced, dark-capped head, then a skinny body, skinny back legs and a long tail. Ella sat on the bedside rug. The moon sent a cold gleam of light across the blankets and onto the door. She moved closer to the bed, standing on her hind legs. A few inches away, Dorothy began to snore.

On the bedside table lay the book, the cigarettes, the door key, the ash-tray and the matches. Ella took the matches and crouched low, listening to Dorothy's breathing.

She struck a match and held it to the bottom of the coverlet. It went out. With a second match the flame caught and spread fast and greedily. She dropped the matches and turned for the door, but then rose on her hind legs and snatched the door key off the table.

Allan was watching yet another assault by the Indians. Their war-cries grew louder. They seemed to come from all around him — from the corridor, from his mother's room. They became screams. Choking, coughing, suffocating screams.

'Mother!'

He yelled in a frenzy for Ella. She didn't come. He jabbed his head forwards to the Possum controls and snapped the television off. He could now hear Dorothy's yells quite clearly.

'Help! Fire! Someone help! The door's locked. I can't get out. Help!'

He heard furniture crashing and more coughing, long, desperate, hacking coughs. He could now smell the acrid smoke of burning plastic. He yelled, 'The window! Throw something through the window!'

From inside came the frantic cry, 'I can't! The netting!'

He grabbed the Possum control that linked to the phone. He made mistakes, puffing and sucking wrong. Finally he got through to the Fire Brigade. And then he lay back, helpless, beating his head into senselessness on the pillows, crying and shouting himself mad as the smoke in his room grew thicker and the cries from the corridor grew thinner and thinner until there was nothing more but the crackling of the fire and the first heavy blows of the firemen's axes on the front door.

Thirty-two

He could see them bending over him, shutting off the daylight. He knew the feeling well. Sedatives. He was pumped full of sedatives.

'It's too tragic. First his father, now his mother . . .'

Oh Christ. What a bloody mess.

'. . . she smoked, of course. One before bed, like a nightcap. That must have done it. So dangerous, smoking in bed. And then to lock her door! The firemen had to break it down . . .'

Wait. Hold it right there. They'd got it all wrong. His mother couldn't lock her door from inside. They'd had the inside part blanked off so that Ella couldn't get into the room and lock herself in as she'd done before. They had to have a man to break the lock and get her out. After that, it could only be locked from the outside, never from the inside. So Mother couldn't be dead.

'. . . the funeral arrangements as soon as possible . . . no need to involve Allan . . .'

They thought he couldn't hear them. Funeral arrangements! But nobody was dead!

'*Someone help! The door's locked!*' His mother's voice. And suddenly he remembered.

'. . . really feel we must send the monkey back while Allan recovers from all this . . .'

No!

'. . . he's coming round . . . pulse, nurse? . . . Easy now, lad, it'll be all right . . .'

No! You're not going to get her! She's mine. She stays here. What more do you want? You've got my body. Isn't that *enough*? Take my brain. Help yourselves. Take out this bit or that bit but most of all the bits that make me love Ella so madly, that make me need my daydreams, that make me wonder so much, wonder for all these terrible hours on end, wonder if something's wrong, if it's Ella, or it's me, or it's Ella and me together, if she reads my mind, if she knows what I want, if she takes my vengeance into her own hands, if she strikes where I would strike, if she kills what I would kill . . . but I would not kill, I could not kill, not *kill*, not *that* . . .

Geoffrey saved Ella. Later, Allan accused him of wanting only to save his project. But he gave his opinion that the monkey was safe and even necessary to Allan in recovering from his mother's death. Melanie went along to the coroner's court with him. The fire officer reported how they'd found the door locked and had to kick it down, and how the fire itself was consistent with a typical smoking accident. A verdict of misadventure was recorded.

The stench in the flat lasted for weeks, searing Allan's mind with the memories of his mother's death. The pain was like a thick grey blanket round his head. But by a ferocious application of will-power he refused to think about the manner of her dying.

Geoffrey organised some friends to clear up the wreckage and the mess, take down the wire netting and board up Dorothy's room until the builders could come. The District Nurse dropped by every day and appointed a contract nurse to do the shopping and the other chores Dorothy had taken charge of. Everyone was sympathetic to Allan's wish to be left alone; within the space of a week the gap left by Dorothy seemed almost to have closed over and the household to have returned to normal.

That was how it appeared from the outside. The reality was rather different.

The first major act of Ella's reign was the abolition of the pain-pack. Seven days after her accession Allan was in his chair in the living room, about to drift off for the second time that morning into his daydreams. Ella decided it was time to do the housework. She fetched a feather duster from the broom cupboard, hopped up onto the table, found some reggae music

201

on the radio and turned the volume up to maximum. Allan's ear-drums were splitting.

'Ella, turn that filthy row off!' he yelled.

She ignored him, dusting the table and then the window-sills as she'd been taught. She bobbed up and down on her hind legs to the beat.

'*Tssss!*' he warned. 'I'll count to three. One . . . two . . .'

On the count of three he leaned forward and puffed the tube controlling the pain-pack. She didn't wince or stop what she was doing. He puffed again. She didn't even turn round.

'The bloody thing's bust!' he exclaimed.

Then Ella looked up. She sauntered to the table and picked up an object from behind the typewriter. It was the pain-pack fuse. At that moment Allan began to understand. A bloodless coup had taken place; a new régime was in charge.

'Put the bloody thing back!' he stormed, driving himself towards the table. He could feel his veins tightening against his collar.

She let him come as close as he could, and then with a deft movement flicked the feather duster right in his face. It made him sneeze. He shouted at her, reversed his chair and drove into the corner of the room — what used to be Ella's corner — and sat there, fuming in silence.

When, later that morning, the contract nurse asked what shopping he'd like done, he said that Geoffrey had prescribed for Ella a diet of very ripe bananas and nothing else. At lunch Ella understood the deception. She ate the food prepared for Allan and began force-feeding him the banana until he spat it out at her. He cursed and swore and promised her he'd report her to the District Nurse when she came by to put him to bed. But he didn't.

The war lasted just three days. Tactically and strategically, Ella was superior. She'd make him plead for his food, holding the spoon just out of reach like Tantalus's grapes. For a while she withheld the tablets. When he shouted at her, as he did for hours at a time, she'd simply put on the radio and the tape cassette full blast, simultaneously. Towards the end of hostilities, she came into his bedroom when he was in bed, jumped up onto the covers and shook a box of matches in her hand until he woke up. Then she swung down onto the floor and, for a moment, there was silence.

'Ella, what are you doing there?' he asked plaintively.

For a reply, she struck a match. In the dark it flared brightly, throwing a shadow from the girder above the bed onto the ceiling like a gallows. What could he smell? Singeing drapes? The match died.

'Ella, stop that for Christ's sake!'

The next pause lasted perhaps two minutes. Allan was praying, muttering, weeping in fury and frustration, waiting for the next match to set his coverlet on fire. She had proved to him what he did not want to know.

Ssstch! The second match flared. Ella held it up this time, so that he could see it, then let it drop. She struck a third and a fourth. Each one she let drop. He shut his eyes. She had made her point.

She reserved the clinching weapon until last. For an entire day she prevented him going into his daydreams. He would be on the verge of floating off when she'd jump up and tweak his ear sharply. She wouldn't let him shut his eyes for more than a moment before disturbing him. And once, deliberately, she went into the broom cupboard where it was dark and shut the door.

'Please, Ella darling, please,' he pleaded. 'Let me go away with you. Not into this dark. Please.'

After twenty-four hours Allan was beginning to go cold turkey. When the District Nurse came in, she asked with concern if everything was all right. He was running a temperature.

'Have you been sitting in draughts?' she asked. 'Is Ella looking after you properly? Behaving herself? Everything all right?'

Allan nodded. In a small voice he said, 'Yes. Everything's all right.'

That night Ella prepared a love feast for Allan.

First, in the afternoon, she went on an escapade. It was a warm, restlessly cloudy day. For once she slipped over the wall into the neighbour's garden on the right and landed on a rockery thick with herbs of every kind: thyme already in flower, sage gone to seed, mint dusty with the pollen from overhanging wild roses. She looked round; there was nobody to see. In the centre of the rockery, as if on a plateau, grew a marjoram plant so thick and so perfectly formed that it might have been moulded in a vast basin. She stroked the small, soft green leaves with her hands and brushed her arm through the undergrowth. To the side grew a low, close-cropped lavender plant, with bees that flew away when she reached forward to smell its purple flowers. She stretched her whole body over the lavender and allowed herself to sink into its young shoots. She rolled onto her back and rubbed her shoulders and her thighs so that the rich scent rose in the warm air and her coat was perfumed by the aroma. Lying there she looked up; above her trailed a honeysuckle and she reached to draw a tendril to her lips. Above still passed the clouds in shifting grey layers.

Slowly she got to her feet and strolled away down the path to the foot of the garden where brightly-painted gnomes stood guard over a goldfish pond. The fish fled to the green murk at the sight of her, but she lay down on her belly very close to the grass roots and waited for them to rise again. A mosquito crash-landed on the surface and flailed helplessly for a moment until a fish, bigger and whiter than the others, swooped up from nowhere and snatched the fly down. It was gone in a silken flash and left only widening rings on the water's surface that spread in perfect circles until they lapped against the pond's edge.

A gnome was looking at her fixedly. She returned the stare, cocked her head from side to side, muttered a little and reached out and gave it a small tug. It fell face first into the pond with a splash that wetted her. She walked off, smelling the wet patch on her arm that gave off an enriched odour of animal fur and lavender. Next she explored the garden shed, a rusty old lawn-roller, a discarded watering-can among the nettles, lichen growing in the frost-cracks of the garden wall. Then she swung herself up onto the top of the wall and ran along it to a tall plane tree. She shinned up it, arm over arm, sometimes using her tail as a fifth hand, sometimes loping along a straight branch and dropping to another below just for the fun of it. She'd climb for a while, then hang by one hand and let go. Down she'd fall for a second, then catch herself by the other hand and swing fast from branch to branch to regain height. It was three-dimensional walking, walking through space.

This tree was taller than all the others around and gave a view that stretched from the city, beyond the Parks, to the distant foot-hills of the Cotswolds behind. She was the highest object she could see, as high as the college spires in the distance and with nothing between her and the whole vast ceiling of sky. The clouds in the furthest distance had parted to reveal a chink of brilliant blue. Below, in the Parks, matchstick-sized punts moved slowly on the brown ribbon of the Cherwell and small figures, no bigger than specks, strolled on the lattice of paths. A gust of wind rippled the far chestnut trees, turning their foliage a paler hue and descending to stir the open grass into eddies of silver. She could see it approaching long before she felt the branches of her tree rocking beneath her, making her tighten her grip.

She only came home when she thought Allan had enjoyed his treat enough.

She prepared the meal carefully that evening. Every few minutes she came in to check that Allan was awake and not dreaming. She'd made it clear that supper was to be a surprise. He sat in his chair, quiet and obedient.

'Is it ready yet?' he called finally.

By way of answer she hurried in and, from the arm of the chair, reached for the matches on the mantelpiece. She held them up for him to see and then walked, on hind legs, and with great dignity, out of the room. Oh no, dear God, not again, he begged.

'Ella darling, put them back. Please. Please?'

He wheeled himself out of the room after her, but when he reached the kitchen he understood. The lights were out. On either side of the table were two lit candles. The table was laid for two. In his bowl was cold meat cut into cubes, mixed in with tinned fruit salad and covered in what looked more like a chocolate sauce than gravy. Ella stood on a stool with a look of triumph on her face.

She fed him from her own spoon and the two of them stayed there quietly together, long after they'd finished eating and until the candles finally died.

Thirty-three

'Allan! *Allan!*'

Fingers were snapping in front of his eyes. A hand shook his jaw. He knew that scent; it was Melanie's. He opened his eyes fractionally and saw her outline against the window, with the low-slanting late-afternoon sun behind. Her dark hair was fringed by the light and her eyes were full of concern. Go away, Melanie, he thought. He didn't want to have to choose between staying where he was and coming back to her. He had been enjoying the cricket.

'Are you okay? Allan?'

That American lilt, altogether too lovely. That slim womanly body. Please go away.

'I rang and rang. The doorbell must be broken. I knew you must be in, so I came round the back. I saw you through the bedroom window here and got in by the back door. You shouldn't leave the key under a flowerpot; it's asking for trouble.'

The doorbell: Ella had disconnected it. She didn't want visitors. Nor did he.

'I was just dozing,' he said, blinking and smiling weakly.

'Dozing?' said Melanie. She looked at him intently, then went and sat on the ledge by the open window. Any minute Ella would return. 'I've never seen anyone dozing like that.'

'Oh? Like what?'

'With your eyes open and your eyeballs rolled backwards. Your eyelids were fluttering and you were chattering like my apes do.'

He swallowed. Caught redhanded in a daydream. 'Would you believe, I was just daydreaming. Imagining I was at the cricket in the Parks. We were 198 for six when Peters was out, caught off Roxburgh. One of the most brilliant catches I've seen. Were you there?' This was safe ground. Americans and cricket never went together.

'Sad to say, no,' she said, choosing her words carefully. 'Where's Ella?'

'She wanted one of the bails as a souvenir. You should see her collection, it's very impressive. Thimbles, buttons, cotton-reels, keys . . .'

Melanie smiled sympathetically but he sensed he'd put a foot wrong. What had he said? Talk, he told himself. Keep talking. 'What brings you here? I hope it's not to do those Zener card things. Can we do that another day? Thanks for telling me about the doorbell; I'll get it fixed. How about a glass of wine, or a cup of tea?'

'No, thanks, I just came to see you. To see how you were. And to find out what's happening about All Souls.'

'Dr Fry's fixed me up with an *aegrotat*,' he said quickly. 'With all that's been going on recently I think I deserve a sick-pass.'

She ran a hand through her dark wavy hair. 'Dr Fry didn't give you any such thing. I met her in the street yesterday. In fact, she's very worried about you. She says you haven't even filled in the All Souls' exam application form. And you've been avoiding her. You've not set foot in the library for weeks. She told me you were throwing away your future.'

Allan raised an eyebrow and said, 'Oh I see. That's why you've come. Not because you want to see me but to spy on me for Fry. Well, I don't need anyone or anything. I've got Ella; she's all I want. I wish people would just leave me alone.'

Melanie got up and came and knelt on one knee in front of his chair. Her pale-skinned, oval face looked up at him earnestly. He wanted to look away. He didn't want to face questions, or to have the answers forced out of him. Not by Melanie, of all people. Ella would be back soon. Suddenly he didn't want the two of them to meet.

'Allan, listen to me.' She spoke slowly, seriously. 'I'm trained professionally to observe animal behaviour. You know that. I've been watching Ella and you for a while now. Not spying, just seeing what I'm trained to see. And I'm worried. I believe you're getting too attached to the monkey. It's not good. You're over-dependent on her. Your work is going to pot, you've neglected your friends and your social life, you've cut yourself off totally from the outside world, you're in the process of cutting yourself off from the human race . . .'

'Melanie, stop it!'

But she went on, more urgently. 'And for what? For this state you call daydreaming. I call it a self-induced trance. I've been speaking with the Contract Nurse. I've also had a word with the District Nurse. You're going into these 'dreams' *all the time!* You imagine yourself capering around the countryside with Ella. It's fine as entertainment once in a while, if that's what it is. But it's becoming the most important thing in your life, something you're sacrificing everything else for. That's wrong. It's escapism.'

'So I'm escaping. If you really knew what real life is like for me, you'd understand,' he answered sullenly.

'Allan Mann, am I hearing right? Is this the brilliant boy with the Congratulatory First, whingeing in self-pity like this? Pull yourself together!'

Allan began to shout. 'You don't understand! You think that just because you had polio as a child it gives you a right to tell me what to do and feel. You can't know what it's like for me. I can't handle life without Ella.'

'Stop it at once!' Melanie commanded. 'If this is true, I'll tell Geoffrey he's got to take her away. She's letting you destroy yourself; you'll end up a mental cripple too!'

'Go away!' shouted Allan, pulling back. 'Leave me alone. I didn't ask you to come and interfere. I want to be alone with Ella. Ella, not you!'

He shut his eyes and rolled his eyeballs upwards until he could feel the first hint of the floating feeling. Then Melanie slapped his face hard. He opened his eyes immediately, wild with fury and shock.

Melanie cried, 'Come back! You're not to go off there! You belong here, with people, not in some dream world with a monkey. I won't let you ruin yourself!'

Their faces were very close. Allan was filled with impossible feelings, all his desire for Melanie on one side and all his urgent need for Ella on the other. Then he looked down. In a voice close to despair he said, 'I'm sorry, Melanie. Maybe you're right. But it won't work: I can't live without Ella. Who else could give me a fraction of all that she does?'

Melanie put her hand on the side of his face and drew his head round so that he was looking into her eyes.

'*I* could, Allan. I could give you everything a person could. I've always loved you, right from the start. I thought I'd feel differently when you had the accident. But I didn't. I'll give you the love you need, a human's love. I'm not asking you to give Ella up completely, but just not to live your life through her. Have her as a pet, a companion, but for God's sake not as a crutch. You can come and live with me. My house is big enough. I'll look after you. You need somebody, you need proper love. Say you will. Allan?'

His eyes were filling with tears. He looked deep into Melanie's. Of course he loved her; he knew it with complete certainty. As he was about to speak a small movement caught his attention. It was Ella, sitting on the window-sill, behind Melanie. She, too, had her eyes fastened on him and was waiting for his reply. He dropped his eyes.

'No, Melanie, I can't. It wouldn't be fair on you.'

Melanie was about to say something, but stopped. As she got up, Ella hopped down into the room and walked over to Allan's chair on her hind legs. She jumped up and placed a small wooden object on his chest. It was the bail of the cricket stumps.

Melanie stared for a long time at the bail before speaking. She smoothed her skirt down and said, 'Well, I said what I came to say. At least think about it.'

'I'll see you to the door,' said Allan. He could feel his voice trembling.

Melanie led the way in silence. As they passed the kitchen, she went in and poured herself a glass of water from the sink. As she drank it she looked around the room and her eyes came to rest on the table. It was laid for two. There were two candle-sticks, their candles burnt out, and a box of matches.

'Well, it seems you haven't quite left the human race,' she said with a small laugh. 'A little supper for two?'

He could feel the hurt in her voice. Did she imagine he'd got a girlfriend? He heard himself saying, despite himself, 'Oh, that was Ella and me. Last night.'

Melanie put the glass down and said in a careful voice, 'A candlelit supper? I suppose Ella lit the candles?'

Allan merely laughed. But from the look on Melanie's face which she carried to the front door, he knew she wasn't satisfied.

Of course! Melanie shook her head as she let out the clutch and drove off. That's why the monkey was behaving so oddly: she was on heat. And the business of the cricket-bails was a typical joke of Allan's. Monkeys always hoarded things when on heat. Anyway, it was good he was happy, even if it had to be Ella who made him so.

He sat before the open window. The warm midnight air stirred his shirt and caressed his lanky dark hair; the moon cast a pool of light at his feet which lit the posts and girder of his bed with its reflected pallor. But he was not there to see any of this. He was out.

A tree stirred above, and he jumped. Two bats darted noiselessly into the open, then were blotted out against the dark form of a building. Something fell nearby, perhaps a chestnut, perhaps a fledgeling. In the longer grass there was movement, slithering and stopping, then darting close past. A dark form, long and low, maybe with legs, maybe without, delving into the deeper grass with only the waving tops to show where it was going. The building was very tall and somehow familiar. The glass windows, quite dark, were watching. A hundred eyes, just watching. The breeze grew chill.

There was something inside that building, something calling, attracting as the building repelled. And the eyes continued watching, seeing.

He moved a few steps closer. A door dimly marked 'Fire Exit' was open a few inches. He knew he would go inside. The call seemed to be coming directly through that opening. He moved another few paces towards the door until he was below the five storeys of window-sills and the eyes could not see him.

But the dark was not proper dark. It was a blurry greyish darkness, perforated by neon sparks and sudden streaks of light as if he'd walked into a field of meteorites. And then the zoom.

He felt his eyelids fluttering and his mind zipping back along its elastic to where he sat in his chair, facing the bright moonlit garden. And then the zoom back, back to the door at the base of the black rearing building and the strange lights like interference on a television screen, the black-and-crimson zig-zags alternating with the blurriness of a camera going out of focus. The blur itself began to dissolve into fade-out.

No, Ella, please not this, Ella darling, please, he heard himself stuttering. Keep me there, keep me with you, don't stop it, don't cut me off.

Ella chose to take the overhead piping in the low corridor and swung arm over arm in the semi-darkness until she came to a wire-glass door. She pushed it open and, up several stairs, she found herself in the main entrance hall of the Department building. She listened; there was not a soul about. The basement throbbed quietly and an electric clock above her flipped over a numeral and made her start. There was a smell of laboratory chemicals and disinfectant, and it grew stronger the higher she went up the stairs. She climbed up on the inner side of the bannisters, to avoid the dim floor-level lighting. At every landing she paused and listened.

She had trouble with one of the doors on the fourth floor, for the handle was slippery, but she managed it. She was getting closer, and she knew it. She arrived at the last door, but this was the one with three locks. She could sense the excitement inside. But she knew the locks: they were impassable. She let out a low moan. From within she was answered by a louder cry. The heat and weight in her stomach was unbearable.

She retraced her steps to the landing. A window was open and she could see that above it ran a ledge around the building. She swung herself quickly through the window, reached up to the narrow ledge and went hand over hand along the dark concrete until she came to the lab. The corresponding window there, too, was open. She climbed in and dropped to the floor.

There he was, in his cage with the other five. She knew how to work the catches and she had him free in a moment. He was on top of her at once, growling and sinking his teeth into the nape of her neck. But she broke away and dashed for the window. He followed. She led the way back along the ledge. He hesitated for a

211

moment before the open window, then looked out at the full moon, took a breath and howled a long, wild, primal mating call and raced after her. In the window, down the bannisters, across the hallway, through the fire door, down the low corridor, through the rear door and out into the living night.

Thirty-four

Nixon glowered at Geoffrey from his cage on the floor by Professor Burbage's desk. His ears were torn, his wrinkly face scratched and his fair-haired coat matted with blood and dirt. As Burbage spoke to the uniformed commissionaire, Nixon broke wind.

'Thank you, Hoskins. I'll take it from here.'

Hoskins, the Commissionaire, wiped his head and put back his blue cap. Still breathing heavily, he cast Geoffrey a sour look and left the room. In a flat voice Burbage told Geoffrey what had happened: the early morning jogger in the Parks who'd phoned the Police, the call he'd received while shaving, Hoskins' near-heart-attack while recapturing the monkey. Burbage massaged his face as he spoke.

'I'm not going to speak about lab security,' he went on. 'I'm not going to mention how embarrassing and careless and incompetent and negligent I consider this whole affair. We'll come to that later.'

'I can't imagine how it happened,' said Geoffrey. Who the hell had let Nixon out? Roach? Dimly he planned to dust the cage for finger-prints and switch cups with Roach during the morning coffee-break . . .

'Today of all days,' Burbage continued. 'When Pollard's coming.'

'No harm's done. The animal's back. The work on *Piscalin* won't be affected.'

'The work on B-287, to which you refer as *Piscalin*, is the subject of Pollard's visit.'

'Fine,' said Geoffrey easily. He flexed his broad shoulders and stuffed his hands in his pockets. 'It'll all blow over. He won't find the place picketed with the anti-viv mob. I don't see what all the fuss is about.'

'The anti-viv mob? Do you think I'm worried about *them*?' Burbage got up and came round the table to Geoffrey's side. Whoops, thought Geoffrey. He put his hands on his hips to match Burbage's pose. *Posture echo* this was called. It was supposed to put the other at his ease. It didn't.

'It's about time you grew up, Fish,' said the Professor. White spots had appeared on his cheeks. 'This little escapade could cost the Department half its funding. Bang goes B-287 and the Experimental Medicine chair with it.'

'But the Grants Committee have just voted . . .'

'Forget the Grants Committee, Geoffrey. Who do you think is funding your work? Not the MRC, not Wellcome, not Nuffield, you know that. And not the Grants Committee. They're all cutting back, slashing projects, freezing posts. No, my boy, you'd better wise up. Over eighty percent of your budget comes directly — well, not exactly *directly* — from certain Government Ministries. I'll spare your sensibilities and we won't go into the mechanics. Let's just say that certain Government bodies are taking a special interest in B-287.'

'Why didn't I know about this before?' Geoffrey demanded. Which Ministries? Defence? 'I presume you mean the MOD. So we're going to have monkeys guiding missiles? Kamikaze Capuchins? Who's this man Pollard, anyway?'

'Don't be facetious, Geoffrey. Dr Pollard is coming to look over our work, that's all. He's interested in the potential social applications of B-287. In our hospitals, institutes, prisons. I'm relying on you to play the game and give him everything he wants.'

'I see,' said Geoffrey. He felt his colour rising and his speech growing more punctuated. It should have been obvious. A drug to improve learning, to speed up the adoption of stimulus-response patterns . . . to re-educate criminals, to re-direct social misfits, to re-programme psychopaths, to brain-wash entire sectors of society . . . In a taut voice he said, 'I'm not sure I approve of this. I've always taken our function as pure research. You said so yourself.'

'That's right, that's right,' said the Professor more eagerly. He sat back on the table. 'Our function here *is* pure research. We leave the application to others. What they do with our work is not our concern. Of course what we do has an end-use. Why do you think we're here at all? To play with rats and monkeys like kindergarten kids? To raise the IQ of the world's lower primates? Of course everything has an ultimate objective in improving human life and society. But that isn't our job. Leave the application to others.'

'Yes, but we must have regard to *how* our work will be used.'

'Geoffrey,' said Burbage in the patient tone of one addressing a child, 'Do me a favour. Don't start giving me the old Hiroshima argument, I'm not interested. You're either with us or you're against us. If you're not happy, then go. If you want to stay, then by God keep your personal views to yourself and make damn sure Pollard gets what he came for. Now get on with it.'

Burbage returned to his desk and made the pretence of going through papers. Geoffrey stood without making a move until Burbage looked up and caught him staring at his beard. He cleared his throat.

'Get this bloody animal out of here too,' he said. 'And take the back stairs.'

Roach had an alibi. He'd been all night in London, taken the early train back and, to prove it, was red-eyed and hung-over. He was shaving with an electric razor when Geoffrey put his head round his lab door. So it wasn't him.

His technician, of course, knew nothing. A good Union man, he'd knocked off at five to five. He'd checked all cage doors as a routine before leaving. Geoffrey was perplexed. For a start, there was no one else with a set of keys. And Nixon couldn't have let himself out; the cages were unopenable from the inside. While he pondered the mystery he gave the monkey a thorough check-up. Respiration normal; heartbeat perhaps low; blood pressure slightly high. Superficial cuts and bruises, which Geoffrey anointed with iodine. But the genitals: the foreskin was stretched and slack and the testicles were unusually small and withdrawn into the body. *That*'s what he'd been doing. Oh God, thought

Geoffrey, there'll be a complaint from the Oxford Dog Lovers' Association.

But Pollard was already in the building. Geoffrey quickly tidied up his office and checked the cages once again. He put together a folder of all the Piscalin results to date, complete with computer print-outs and graphs. When Pollard arrived upstairs, escorted by Burbage, Geoffrey exchanged his file for the man's card. It read *Dr Maurice Pollard, Senior Research Officer, Special Projects, Home Office.* He interrogated Geoffrey for an hour on the data: whether the drug had any known side-effects, how widely it had been tested, whether trials had been run on other animals, how much had been publicised, what visitors he'd had from what organisations and on what dates. There was a seventh monkey, was there not, asked Pollard. Ella was no longer being given Piscalin, Geoffrey lied. The other man frowned and made a note. Then, in a sweetly tactful voice, he began to give instructions. This was valuable work, he said, of national significance. It merited a security classification. Thenceforth the project was to be run on a confidential basis. Results to be kept in the Department safe. A Home Office courier to come once a fortnight to collect copies. No other copies to be made. A shredding machine to be installed. Burbage, Geoffrey, Roach and the two technicians to be the only personnel cleared to work on the project. Geoffrey to have one week in which to collect all key material, to destroy all working papers and to hand over the dossier to Burbage for safe-keeping. Finally Pollard said, 'I'll be down in a fortnight to check the security arrangements, if that is convenient. Let us try and avoid a repetition of last night's little incident, shall we?'

After he'd left, Geoffrey went for a walk in the Parks to clear his mind and calm down. He was fuming. This was his work, his idea, his discovery. It had to be published; that was how academic reputations were made. He didn't want to work for the Government. This was Oxford University, not Porton Down. Science was public property. No jumped-up prick from Whitehall was going to tell *him* what to do with his work. Bugger the lot of them.

It had rained in the early morning and a crop of mushrooms had sprung up under the trees. Geoffrey walked through them, kicking off their heads. He swiped the nettles with a stick and slashed the foliage of the trees. *Bugger the lot of them.* He was at the top end of the Parks by the time he'd calmed down, at the gate that led round the corner to Allan's flat. He'd look in on him. At least Ella had slipped the security net.

When he rang the doorbell there was no answer. He went to the window, cupped his hand over the glass and peered in. Allan was in his chair at the far end of the living room, his back to the front window. Ella wasn't to be seen. He rapped on the window. Allan didn't stir. Geoffrey became alarmed. Then he remembered he had a key and let himself in. It was mid-afternoon but the flat was dark and half-curtained.

'Oh, it's you, Geoffrey.' Allan's tone was unwelcoming. He blinked himself awake. 'What are you doing here?'

'What's all this?' Geoffrey asked, looking about him. 'Sleeping in the afternoon?'

'I'm tired.'

Silence fell. The air was not and still. He leaned against the mantlepiece and looked intently at Allan.

'Where's Ella?'

'In the bedroom, sleeping it off. Don't disturb her.'

There was another pause. Geoffrey said, 'Mind if I put the kettle on? I'm parched.' But instead of going straight to the kitchen he put his head round the bedroom door. Ella was curled up at the foot of the bed. She didn't even register his presence, but what he saw made his pulse leap. Her ears were torn. All over her back and flanks were bites and scratch marks. Her fine coat was matted with blood and burrs and thorns. And in the room was the faint, sweetish, musky smell that told him she was on heat.

In the kitchen he made the tea, deep in thought and conflict. He brought two cups back into the living room. Holding Allan's to his lips he asked his question gently.

'How did she get in that state, Allan?'

'What does it look like? Fucking.'

'Rubbish,' he said carefully. 'There's not a zoo for miles. And I don't somehow think she'd fancy the alsatian next door.'

'Another monkey, fool. One of yours. Don't try and trick me.'

'How could it be one of mine? The labs are locked at night.'

'Don't come that with me, Geoffrey. You've been to the labs this morning? Then you'll know one of yours was missing. Now you see Ella in this state. I mean, credit me with half a brain.'

'Yes,' he said and dropped his eyes. 'One of mine was missing, as it happens. He's back now, though. But how did you know?'

'I guessed. Ella went out on the tiles and got laid. Anyone can see that. What else should I think? Cats, dogs, ducks, birds? So I guessed right, that's all.'

He held Allan's cup an inch away from his lips so that he was forced to hear what he said. 'You didn't guess, Allan. You *knew*.'

Allan glowered. 'Did you watch the cricket? Roxburgh was terrific. Took four wickets.'

He put his own cup down and lowered himself into a chair facing Allan. He crossed his hands over his stomach and smiled. 'I've got all day,' he said. 'All week. I'm staying here until you face up to this. I want to know exactly how you knew. Exactly.'

'I guessed, like I said,' responded Allan. 'Maybe I imagined it. I don't know. Can't remember.'

'Can't remember? Very well. Then I'd say this was schizophrenic amnesia, a well-recognised syndrome. One side of your personality does something the other doesn't approve of and so represses it. You call it forgetting. You haven't forgotten, Allan. If you really believe you have, I think I'd better give my friend in the Warneford Hospital a call. You need treatment. I can see they'll take you in right away.'

'Just you try. Don't threaten me, Geoffrey. As I told you, I just guessed, that's all there is to it. Everyone's entitled to a lucky guess once in a while.'

Once in a while Allan just guessed that Linda and John were up in Oxford on the afternoon of the punting party. Once in a while he'd himself imagined the monkey Nixon was at his feed dispenser. Once in a while, like a hundred in a hundred, the monkeys got the blue and red pills right. So this *was* it. How could he get Allan to confirm it with his own mouth? He found his hand beginning to shake. He went over to the drinks cabinet and said, 'Mind if I have a whisky?' He held the bottle towards Allan. Allan nodded and he poured two glasses.

The silence stretched between them. Allan glared at him, but from time to time dropped his eyes and appeared to be wrestling with some internal problem.

At last Allan said hesitantly, 'I . . . I do feel very close to Ella. It's almost as if we're one at times. I often wonder . . .'

'Yes?' Geoffrey coaxed gently.

'Well, I wonder if I can make her do things. I mean, if she does things, is it because she wants to please me? Or because I make her? *Will* her?'

Play it very carefully, Geoffrey said to himself. Be disingenuous. In a tone of sympathetic concern he said, 'I think that's natural empathy. You spend a great deal of time with Ella. Naturally you feel close. To suggest it's more is anthropomorphising. You're going to tell me Ella's becoming human next. That's confusing empathy with humanity. You can't be wishing your feelings onto her, if that's what you mean.'

'Ah.' Allan looked relieved. Then his face closed up again.

Geoffrey realised he'd played it wrong and the man was clamming up. He walked to the table and perched against it. He swilled the whisky around his glass and said, 'Mind you, they've done some interesting experiments recently. There's a chap called Osis. He can direct cats through mazes simply by using telepathy. And, of course, there's the familiar experience they call psi-trailing. You know, you take a dog a hundred miles away from its owner, let it go and it can find its master again. And I don't mean simply going home.'

He looked up at Allan, but his face registered nothing. Suddenly the hairs on the back of his neck rose. This was what Pollard was interested in! He had spotted something in the *Piscalin* results which Geoffrey had missed. Allan knew what it was, but was too afraid to admit it. Goddam it, what *was* going on? Could it really be *that*? Allan held the key to it. Allan could speak; the monkeys couldn't. Take Ella somewhere else and then run tests on Allan.

'I've raised this before,' he began, 'but I think the time has come for some in-depth tests. If I might, I'd like to suggest I took Ella . . .'

'Ella's staying right here. Get any ideas like that out of your head.' Allan's voice was quiet and cold.

'I'm thinking there might be dangers . . .'

'Look, drop it. You're welcome to sit here all afternoon but I've said all there is to say. Why don't you just call it a day, Geoffrey? I've been rambling on and we're both tired. Why not go home, eh?'

'I need you to tell me how you *knew*,' Geoffrey persisted. He knew it was hopeless; Allan was so damned stubborn.

Allan looked him firmly in the eye and said, 'I guessed, just as I said. Now, if you don't mind, I'm going to my bedroom. Okay? Will you see yourself out?'

What the hell, thought Geoffrey. There was only one scientific way of finding out. Reason was law; logic ruled. In the beginning was the word, the logos. Damn Allan and his monkey. In the labs there were six others, all on the drug, all showing the signs. He'd start there. Scientifically.

'I'll see you soon, Allan,' he said and saw himself out.

Ella my darling, my loved one, force of my limbs, power of my lungs, breath of my body, elastic of my sinews, you who are in my leaping and in my moving, Ella, listen to me.

We must take care. Be vigilant. They are waiting for us to drop our guard.

Melanie noticed the candles. She will refuse to believe it, but her subconscious knows that you're not afraid of fire.

And Geoffrey. Geoffrey's under pressure, anyone can see that. He's worried; he's worked out where you were last night. He guessed how I knew you'd been with that other monkey. He threatened to separate us; can't have that. But Geoffrey's a scientist, he'll rationalise, he'll find an explanation: schizophrenia, juvenile dementia, hallucination. He won't rock the boat; his career's on the line.

Words. Words and empty sounds. I hear my words but I don't recognise them. They come out like strangers I haven't been introduced to. I talked to Geoffrey so clearly, so distinctly, but now I've forgotten what it was all about. I remember the feeling of speaking distinctly, but the words . . . the words have flown like a flock of birds, taking their meaning with them. I don't remember any of them. Vague sounds remain, strange sounds wheeling in my mind, but nothing distinct, nothing to pin down with any certainty. Fires. Deaths. Life. I had a life once, long ago. I'm on my second. Or third. Cats have nine. Monkeys? Oh, a dozen at least. We have one together. One life, one body. We're one. Come closer, little Ella. Nestle into me and we'll go back to sleep together.

Thirty-five

Geoffrey took a plastic tray to the coffee machine in the corridor and slotted four cups of the brown liquid into the tray holes. It was going to be a long night. An aperitif of caffeine to be followed in three hours by a kicker: Drinamyl or Preludin or whatever he felt like at the time. He'd need a steady hand, an alert mind and a lot of patience. It was a long time since he'd done a 2-DG brain analysis.

He'd given his technician the afternoon off. Roach had gone home early to recover from his London orgy. Burbage's car was not in its allotted space. By six o'clock he had prepared the apparatus in the experiment room, the partitioned area of Roach's lab where the vivisections and the autopsies were performed. It was a low room with a large central light-pool and a small operating table. The smell was different from the other labs, the animal house, his own monkey cages. He shivered inside his white lab coat and swallowed. This was Roach's kind of work.

Nixon sat in one of the smaller portable cages. He was recovering from the first anaesthetic, an injection of methohexitone strong enough to allow Geoffrey to implant the catheter in one of his femoral veins. The drip was connected to a feed bottle, hanging from a hook outside the cage, and through it a solution of [14 C]-2-deoxyglucose, or 2-DG, was slowly feeding into the monkey. The idea was simple. Glucose is the only substrate the brain can use for energy. This is not brought directly to it by the

221

blood, as it is with any other organ of the body, but through the blood-brain barrier which passes the glucose nourishment into the cerebro-spinal fluid surrounding the brain. Now, the more active a particular region of the brain is, the more glucose it consumes. By injecting a modified type of glucose mixed with a radioactive label, Geoffrey could find out exactly which parts of the monkey's brain were working and to what degree. The heavy-water radioactive marker was necessary so that he could later measure the exact amount of glucose taken in by the particular cellular region. If Nixon was like Ella, then he might just find out what the hell really was going on.

The catheterisation took about an hour, during which time Geoffrey made Nixon perform some basic behavioural tasks. The monkey's learning capacity still amazed him. He would never get used to the results of Piscalin. Then he checked that the perfusion set-up was properly fixed. Disconnecting the 2-DG feed, he introduced a large dose of sodium pentobarbital into the vein. An overdose. In a moment Nixon slumped forward, heavily anaesthetised. Geoffrey left the catheter in place and sat the monkey on his buttocks in the perfusion frame. This closed round the base of his head, below his jaws, so that his whole head was firmly positioned for Geoffrey to work on. He took a somewhat larger syringe and filled it with formalin. This he carefully fed into the carotid artery in the monkey's neck so that it was pumped around his body by the animal's own circulation. Formalin was a fixing agent. Geoffrey wanted no unnecessary degeneration of the brain tissue. He judged it right, so that Nixon's heart did the pumping until all the blood above the neck was properly replaced with formalin. A brief moment later, his heart stopped.

A mile away, Ella howled into the night.

Geoffrey took a deep breath. He hated this moment, the particular feel of a knife through skin. He angled the overhead light better, picked up a scalpel and made a single long incision from the bridge of the nose round to the back of the neck. The skin peeled back easily, like a tangerine's. With a small electric saw he cut through the bone in a perfect circle just above the line of the eyes. The skull came off like a cap. With a few quick cuts he severed the spinal column and, working his fingers gradually under the brain, began lifting it free, cutting the connective tissues and muscles as he went. In fifteen minutes the brain was out.

Next, he weighed it. That was his first surprise. But he recorded the figure and went on. As he was about to immerse the organ in the liquid nitrogen for the freezing process, he gave it a quick visual inspection. He frowned. With a magnifying glass he peered into its surface. There was something odd about this brain. Abnormal surface markings, and distinctly more gyra, more folds, especially in the frontal lobes. Geoffrey peeled the main sections of the brain apart. His pulse was speeding up.

The cryostat froze the segments to allow him to slice them into very thin sections, no thicker than twenty microns, perhaps not much thicker than individual cells. This was a slow, laborious task. Each wafer had to be arranged in correct order and then placed on an X-ray film plate. Here, slowly, over time, the carbon-14 radioactive marker in the glucose would activate the silver grains in the film and give Geoffrey an indication of glucose intensity, and thereby the activity of the brain by region. This could take days, but he'd speeded up the process by taking a chance and increasing the tritium content in the 2-DG. He needed the results fast.

During the long silent hours after midnight Geoffrey laboured away. Some sections he put aside; he performed standard histological tests on these, including the basic Golgi staining process. Under a light microscope he saw his first concrete results and stepped back so sharply that he knocked a tray of X-ray plates to the floor. It was then that he decided he needed a break and some more coffee. Later he went back to work and examined one slide after another under the microscope. He was no histologist but he could read a Golgi stain.

It was shortly after eight in the morning when Geoffrey had the first real evidence he was after. He sat back and scratched his head. Outside he could hear the street coming to life. Within the hour his technician would arrive, then Roach, then Burbage. He took the full set of X-rays to his own office and locked himself in. There he sat, rubbing his sleepy eyes, as one by one the trays of plates told their story. By mid-morning he had his third wind and was running a computer count on some of the plates. The computer built up an accurate count of the silver grains affected by the radioactive label and plotted these as a matrix showing the varying intensities of glucose take-up. The results confirmed what Geoffrey had suspected by visual inspection. And they hit him smack between the eyes.

The X-ray plates showed a cross-section of the monkey's frontal lobes. Where the glucose had been taken up, the grains had turned black. The resulting picture was like a Milky Way in negative: a thick band of minute dark grains scattered in a regular ribbon at a particular depth in the cortex. It was easy to see where. Extraordinary, phenomenal activity had been taking place in the third and fourth cortical layers, close to the bottom of the cortical sheath where the grey matter becomes white. Under the light microscope, Geoffrey could see the single short-axon stellate cells in these layers. These appeared to have multiplied out of all proportion and every one of them seemed to have been in a state of high activity.

Beritoff had shown that the function of the short-axon stellate cells in the third and fourth cortical layers was concerned with image-forming, conceptualising and idea-generating. Here was a major morphological change in the animal's brain, a change in its brain structure. Structure is function: that was a cardinal principle of biochemistry. Change the structure and you change the function.

Geoffrey's hands were shaking when he took down a book giving an account of Beritoff's work. He read aloud, 'The predominance of neurons with short axons constitute the main difference between the cerebral cortex of man and of animals, and these account for the greater complexity and structural perfection of the human brain.'

It was at this point that he got up, locked the plates and the slides carefully away, stretched his aching body and went for a very long walk.

Geoffrey's walk lasted two and a half days. He kept away from the labs. He phoned his technician once to tell him to get rid of Nixon's corpse. Roach could have the eyes, but the rest was to be incinerated and the cabinet containing the plates must remain locked. Geoffrey drove far out of Oxford, north or west or wherever it was. He had to distance himself, to think on his own,

224

to work it out. He found a small country pub with a room to let. It might have been Wales, or Warwickshire. It was certainly wet; he got soaked on two occasions. He forgot to eat. He lost track of time. He slept an hour here and there, not taking a bath or shaving, prowling the country lanes at night, combing the fields by day. His mind wouldn't rest. For all his efforts to tame it and channel it along strictly reasoned paths, it kept returning to one thing, one word. Evolution.

Geoffrey was not a neo-Darwinian. Of course, chance mutation as an evolutionary force worked: there were enough studies on the melanisation of white moths in black industrial settings to prove that. But it was not the *only* force, and probably a very unimportant one. He was convinced that evolution was not solely a matter of gene mutation. As he strode over the wet dales, he held debates with himself, often aloud. 'What about the desert wasp,' he yelled to the dripping oaks, 'which copulates with a cactus flower?' The cactus has developed a flower that perfectly mimics the rear end of a female desert wasp: colour, shape, scent — God knows, the feel of it too. In spending its days in glorious fucking, the male wasp is also pollinating the cactus. Can anyone really believe this has developed over millions of years merely by chance genetic mutations, so that the ones where the furry bits aren't quite right or the scent's wrong get passed over and die out? And the only ones to survive are those which by incredible chance happen to have got the whole thing right? The strain would become extinct if everything was left to trial and error.'

And later, stopping at a country pub for a beer, sitting outside on a bench: 'What about the violent breaks in morphology you see in fossil strata? What's happened to the missing ones? Got washed away, lost, eaten up, what? No! Huge morphological changes in living organisms can happen in a matter of maybe a couple of generations, maybe even less. And that's without the prodding of a psychochemical.'

On the way home, in the car, he kept muttering, Is this God? *L'âme vitale*? Or, put another way, the imbalance of one electrical field with another? You can stop a plant limb regenerating in the normal way by forming an inhibiting electrical field around the broken end. Why shouldn't the reverse be true? Even of brain cells, which today are considered to be non-regenerating? Nixon's brain had quantifiably altered in its morphology. Its surface had grown very wrinkly, as folded as a psychozoon, a thinking creature, a creature like man. Its brain weight had increased by twenty-five percent to over eight ounces. The stellate-cell count showed at least one order of magnitude increase. We have a change in structure here. Change the structure, change the function . . .

The Broca area, which people call the "speech centre", was also highly enlarged. Did that mean the monkey was on the point of developing language, a vocabulary way beyond the thirty-two speech elements found in chimpanzees, a vocabulary based on making symbols and abstractions and images? Image-forming in general, and speech in particular, were uniquely human abilities. Through images, conscious thought was possible. Through thought, a personal reality could be constructed. Through that, conscious action could be taken. Conscious action: the province of humans.

What did that do to the old proposition that animals are reactive and only man is active? What was the line now between man and animal? Was it, as Korsakoff suggested, a threshold gap, a dialectic leap, a gulf between two entities different in *kind*? Or was it a gap merely to do with positions on a single spectrum, a gulf between two entities different only in *degree*? If the former, then was Piscalin creating the conditions necessary to hoist the animal up the step onto the level of the human?

And what about the goings-on in Allan's head, his *knowing* what Ella was doing? Was Ella growing into a small human-being? Or Allan into a big monkey? Or both together into something different still? Or was it nothing like that at all?

The answer, as Geoffrey saw it, came when, returning finally to Oxford, he went round to Melanie's house and asked if she'd give him something to eat. He looked appalling: unshaven, unslept, raw-faced, smelly, his raincoat torn and damp, his face red and blotchy. The moment Melanie saw him she put out her hand and pulled him indoors.

'Where *have* you been?' she exclaimed. 'You look like a tramp. I've been desperate to get hold of you; I've been ringing every hour. They're worried at the labs. You'd better call them up.'

'They can get stuffed,' said Geoffrey and slumped down onto a pile of Moroccan cushions on the floor. He knew he'd never get up again. He'd lay his head there and die. Die in Melanie's sweet company. She poured him a large whisky, ran him a bath, hauled him upstairs, threw a shirt at him (one of his own, he noted without pain) and soon, through the scent of the foam bubbles, he could smell the aroma of garlic and spices coming up from the kitchen. No, he'd drown there. Open a vein and just ebb away. He felt his eyes closing. His hand holding the glass relaxed and bathwater lapped into the drink. No, on second thoughts, he wouldn't die there. Not with a bubbly whisky in his hand. With a great effort he washed himself and got out.

He had meant to tell Melanie everything but in the event he found he didn't, or couldn't. In truth, he was afraid it would sound incredible. As it was, she had a lot on her mind. She served the chilli con carne before she spoke. He looked at her with fresh eyes: so slim, such breasts, such a positive face, such lovely dark hair, such a blend of the practical, the political and the poetic. He'd been lucky.

'I was walking past Allan's house the other day,' she was saying. He found himself listening to her light American accent rather than the words. Her voice had the same cool, smooth quality as the yoghurt on the chilli. 'Outside, there's a skip where the builders have thrown out the bits from his mother's room. In the skip I saw her bedroom door.'

'His mother's bedroom door,' echoed Geoffrey in the same tone. 'Melanie, this chilli is wonderful. You always knew how to get to my heart, and beyond.'

'You're not listening. I remembered about the door; how they had the keyhole blocked from the inside when Ella was always locking herself in.'

'Melanie, do we have to talk about Allan's mother's bedroom door? I've had a hell of a few days.'

'We have to talk about the door,' she said and put down her fork. 'I didn't want to tell anyone until I'd discussed it with you first. You've a right to be consulted first, it's your project. I think you'd better listen, Geoffrey.'

Geoffrey listened. His weariness left him as he followed Melanie's argument. She'd been very thorough. She'd even been back to the coroner's court and looked at a transcript of the fire officer's evidence. *He'd kicked in the door because it was locked.* She then made Geoffrey think back to the days after Linda and John's accident. *Accident*, she repeated with heavy innuendo.

227

'Geoffrey, primates are peace-loving. They don't kill, except under extreme provocation. Ella is responsible for two deaths. I leave the conclusion to you.'

He felt an unpleasant sweat breaking out over him. Suddenly the food looked nauseating, redundant. He pushed his plate away. Without looking up at Melanie, he quoted,

'The devil is nothing else than the personification of the repressed instinctual life.' He paused. 'Melanie, we're in danger of reversing civilisation.'

She looked puzzled. He got up, stiffly, drank down his glass of wine, pulled his tie up and swing his jacket over his shoulders.

'What are you going to do?' she asked.

'Finish the business.'

Thirty-six

The night was restless. Squalls of light rain combed the dark streets. Geoffrey's car radio forecast storms. He drove badly. He forgot his headlights until he'd almost arrived. Twice he nearly hit an oncoming car but drove on still more forcefully, leaving the horns complaining in the distance behind him. He parked round the corner, not in the Department's car park. Some lights were still burning, but not Burbage's. Nor Roach's. Good.

It had to be done. He refused to go through the arguments again. After days of wild fantasy alternating with cold rational thought, Melanie's evidence had tipped the balance. What had to be done had to be done.

He took the lift. The building seemed deserted. He walked slowly along the corridor and locked the door of his lab from the inside. He took a piece of tape and covered the peep-hole in the outer door. Then he went straight to his office, took off his raincoat and put on his white lab coat and elbow-length rubber-gloves. From the top drawer in his desk he took the key to the drugs cabinet. It was then that he noticed another key was missing — the key to the cabinet containing the X-ray plates and computer count sheets. He took off his gloves and rummaged around in the drawer. He found it, but not in its right place. He went straight to the cabinet and unlocked it. Someone had been there; the plates were tidy but not exactly as he'd left them. He went quickly through them. Nothing had been removed, but they'd been looked at and carefully replaced. Geoffrey stormed over to the telephone and called his technician at home.

'We couldn't contact you, Geoffrey,' said the technician. 'Professor Burbage insisted I gave him the key. There was nothing I could do. Is anything wrong?'

Geoffrey replaced the phone without replying. Perhaps it didn't matter. They wouldn't be able to recreate Piscalin, not now.

From the drugs cabinet he took a full bottle of sodium pentobarbital. One syringe would be enough. He replaced his gloves and mask. The first monkey to go was Roosevelt. He was easily caught; the needle sank into a fold in the skin above his shoulder. The monkey went limp. Then the second, the third, the fourth and the fifth and last. It was a quick, painless death. He laid them on the table in the centre like a bag after a day's shooting. From a cupboard he took out a heavy opaque polythene waste bag and dropped the corpses into it. He tied it with tapes and went into his office.

First the phials of Piscalin. Then the cultures and enzymes from which the compound had been formulated. All needles, swabs, syringes, test-tubes, dishes, oxydising agents and any staining fluids bearing traces of the drug. Next, the paperwork. The reports and test results which he'd already collected in a large box following Pollard's orders. The computer print-outs, including the carbons. His working notes. Pads and clip-boards and files. The computer programme itself, which he erased from the memory along with all data kept on central computer files under his user-code. Finally, he wiped off the scribbles on the board beside his desk, emptied the contents of all the drawers and made sure that the incubator and the cryostat were empty. He cleaned the surfaces of the desks, the shelves, the lab bench and racks. He even threw away the sticky coffee mugs and about thirty plastic cups glued to various surfaces around the room. His desk was clear. The room was tidy. The lab empty. There was not a trace of the work he'd been doing.

He took the six large sacks of waste down to the incinerator in the basement. He had to make three journeys, and it took half an hour to feed them in so that he could be sure all evidence was thoroughly destroyed. Then he returned to his lab.

On his desk he'd retained two articles: the syringe and a small green bottle of a quick-acting poison. He took off his white coat and put his old raincoat back on again. The syringe and the drug went into the pocket. He looked around the office; it was pristine. Before finally leaving he pulled down his Garbo poster and tore it up. He went for his technician's centre-fold pin-up and did the same. Then he turned off the lights.

As he closed the outer door into the corridor and locked it, he paused. With a quick movement he pulled his name card out of its metal slot in the door and crumpled it up in his pocket. Then he turned sharply on his heel and made for the exit. The next step was going to be more tricky. And more unpleasant.

The District Nurse had been and gone. That night, as on several occasions in the past weeks, she'd allowed Allan to stay up in his chair. He said he slept better that way. It was all the same to her; so long as he was clean, fed and warm and the battery charged up, she'd done her job. The moment she left that evening, Ella leaped up onto Allan's chest and began to play. He felt like a child after lights-out. In the living room the atmosphere was charged with excitement and restlessness. Outside the wind scurried through the trees, hissing and moaning. Indoors the gas fire was on low, for the night was chilly with the first hints of autumn.

'Let's go away, my love,' he said as she sat in his lap, fiddling and grooming herself and playing with a pom-pom from one of Dorothy's slippers she'd chewed off months before. 'We'll go away for a year and a day.'

But Ella was too restless. She dropped the pom-pom and took a flying leap onto the table. She played with a biro for a while until she got bored. The curtain sash caught her eye and she made a playful lunge at it, but shortly gave even that up. She began to prowl around the room as if looking for something. Every now and then she'd rub her back against the leg of a chair or the table and let out a soft purring growl. She walked in an odd, stilted manner as if her stomach was heavy with some burden. Allan understood.

'Darling, you've been out the past three nights and you can't get into the labs. So stay in with me and we'll have a quiet evening together.'

Ella looked at him, then went over to the window-sill. The catch was just above her head. She gave a plaintive, urgent moan.

'For goodness' sake stop it. Just for once stay in. Come on, we'll have a drink. Get me a whisky, will you.'

The monkey hesitated, reached up to the latch, then withdrew her hand and hopped down to the floor. She sat watching him, her head cocked on one side. He repeated, 'Whisky. From the cabinet. No water. Straight.'

This time, when she obeyed, she didn't spill the bottle of Haig as she unscrewed the cap in both hands and tilted it carefully to pour a glass. She brought the glass and put it to his lips. She'd filled it full.

'Have a sip yourself, you young lush,' he said. 'Monkey's ruin. Go on, try it.'

Ella looked uncertainly at the drink. She sniffed it and recoiled. Finally she put her pink lips to it. The moment the whisky touched her mouth she sprang back, spilling it on his jersey and screeching as if she'd been poisoned. She took the glass and hid it behind the armchair by the skirting board. It was not good; she wasn't going to let Allan have it either.

He yawned and said, 'I'm tired, my love. You've worn me out, going out on the town every night. Tonight you're staying in. We'll have an evening together, just the two of us. No one will disturb us.'

Ella continued her restless prowling but there was nothing Allan could do. She moved under the table and beneath the chairs like a small ghost, occasionally collecting something she'd dropped or rearranging her possessions. She went out of the room and he could hear her in the bedroom, then the bathroom and the kitchen, finally the hall. She was turning off lights.

'There's no need to do that,' he called.

But he could hear the switches being snapped off one by one. Then she came back into the living room. He called her softly to come to his lap, but instead she went over to the table and climbed up. She reached for the telephone and put the receiver to her ear.

'What are you up to now?' He began to smile. 'Calling up your friends in the lab?'

She kept her back to him and didn't respond. She looked into the earpiece for a moment, then put the receiver back down on the table, not on the cradle. He could hear the purring of the dialling tone from where he sat. She swung herself to the floor and for a moment was lost in the shadows. Then there was a click and the standard lamp went out. She'd turned it off at the wall. Another snap and the reading light on the table went out. There was only the centre light still on. Ella went over to the door, turned and climbed back onto the table top. She hopped back down carrying his mouth-stick. On her hind legs and stretching as far as she could, she just reached the light switch. The room was in darkness.

Ella went silently around the room. He could hear her path by the soft brushing of her coat against the chairs and the slight rustle as she picked up the electric cables to the Possum and the lamps and appeared to be feeling them. Then after a while she climbed back onto the rear window-sill and sat in profile against the yellowish night sky outside, no longer staring out but looking directly at him.

How sweet of her, he thought. She wants me all to herself.

Thirty-seven

Geoffrey tried the doorbell; it didn't even ring. He called through the letter-box; Allan didn't respond. He tried his key in the front door; it was chained. He went round the back and the kitchen door was locked. The house was in total darkness. But the window in Allan's bedroom was slightly ajar. Geoffrey was a big man and the window was small. He almost got stuck. Inside, he tripped over a small table and sent something crashing to the floor. He groped his way to the light switch and blinded himself as it came on.

'Who's there?' Allan called from the living room.

'It's me. Geoffrey.'

He put on a cheerful, bluff voice; it came out strangely thick. He walked down the corridor in the shaft of light from the bedroom. Occasional beams from car headlights lit the walls and ceilings for a brief second, then died. As he fumbled for the living room doorknob, Ella darted out and past him. Not now, he told himself; not yet. He groped for the main switch and flooded the living room with light. Allan was sitting in the centre, blinking angrily.

'Just came to see how you were getting on,' said Geoffrey. He could hear the false note jarring.

'Breaking in like a burglar to see how I was getting on?' Allan raised an eyebrow and looked sourly at him. Geoffrey felt his hand shaking, betraying him, and he thrust it into his raincoat pocket. It touched the syringe.

'Well, you know, I was just passing. The doorbell doesn't work. I called and you didn't answer; I thought something might be wrong. Well, here I am. How about a drink?'

'Just passing?' echoed Allan. 'Help yourself.'

Geoffrey took a large slug of whisky. He said, 'We ought to have a chat, Allan. I really wanted to say I'm sorry for barging in like that the other day. Well, I suppose I'm doing it again tonight. Things have been a bit strained between us. I felt it would be good to talk.'

'You do pick your moments, Geoffrey. And you've upset Ella. I do appreciate what you're saying, but honestly I prefer being left alone with her. Now you're here, at least take your coat off and sit down.'

'No, I'll keep it on,' Geoffrey said. He shifted in his shoes. He couldn't take his coat off: he didn't trust Ella's prying little fingers. 'Is there any ice in the fridge?'

'Of course. Go ahead.'

From the doorway, Geoffrey asked simply, 'Why's Ella upset?'

'Oh, I don't think she was expecting visitors.'

Ella was in the kitchen, skulking under the table. Geoffrey went to the fridge and got out the ice, making a noise as he did so. Then he went and stood under the fluorescent light. Ella had crept out and climbed onto the top of the fridge. He looked behind him in case Allan had wheeled up. No. He was alone with the monkey. He took the syringe and bottle out of his pocket, turned the bottle upside down and carefully filled the needle to its fullest. He put the bottle down and turned for Ella.

'Ella, come here, there's a good girl,' he intoned.

She backed away. But this time he was quicker. He shot out his left hand and grabbed her by the neck. He brought the needle quickly round into position and bunched up some flesh at the nape. Then came the shout from the living room.

'Geoffrey! What in Christ's name? Geoffrey!'

Allan yelled at the top of his voice. Ella flicked her head away and let out a terrible shriek. She squirmed violently and slipped free. *Shit!* Geoffrey swore. He went after her, carrying the needle ahead of him. She went berserk. She tore into the living room and leaped up onto the table and from there onto her shelf, scowling and spitting. Geoffrey tried to hide his syringe but as he turned he saw Allan sitting with his eyes rolled back and the lids fluttering rapidly. Just as Melanie had said.

He went for Ella. A vase smashed to the floor. Two reading-stands fell like ninepins. Geoffrey kicked the whisky glass under the armchair; it shattered against the skirting board. Ella was screeching. Allan's eyes were on her and he was yelling. The monkey made a dash for it. She bolted for the door and Geoffrey rushed after her. He caught her hiding in the broom cupboard. With a single quick thrust he slammed the door tight shut and locked it. Ella threw herself frantically at the door from the inside. But she was now his prisoner.

'Get out!' Allan was almost screaming now. 'Get out of my house. Murderer! Get out!'

Geoffrey got him by the shoulders and shook him as hard as he could until he thought his eyeballs would fall out. He was shouting at the top of his lungs too. 'Listen, you fucking stupid cripple, that's what happens with you and Ella, isn't it! That's how you knew everything. You *saw* it. That's what the drug's done. *That's* Piscalin.'

'Fuck Piscalin. You're insane. See a doctor. Get out. I don't ever want to see you again.'

'I get it. You think it only goes *one way*. You sit there getting nice little television pictures from her. But that's only half the story, you idiot. *She* gets things from *you*! That's what counts.'

'You're mad. I'm telling you, you're mad.'

'Look,' Geoffrey spat out and pulled away. 'I operated on the monkey Ella let out. I opened up its brain. And I found a massive change in its structure, in the areas which control thinking. Areas which are taken as being uniquely human.'

'Bully for you,' Allan said sourly. 'So Ella's a little human being. I could have told you that.'

'She begun to feel and react like a human. She's at home with fire, for instance. But whose feelings does she have? Her own? Someone else's? *Yours?*'

'What are you getting at?' croaked Allan.

'I've been speaking to Melanie. There have been two fires and two deaths. Not accidental deaths, Allan, I know you know that. Who is responsible? Monkeys hate fire. Monkeys don't kill of their own accord. Ella's fundamentally innocent. She doesn't know the difference between good and bad. She doesn't have a human value system. But you do, I do, we humans do. That's

236

what stopped you going out and killing Wiseman yourself, for instance. That's *morality*, Allan, and it's a product of civilisation. But what's being repressed when you do the civilised thing? I'll tell you. You're repressing your primal aggressive instincts, your primitive urge to kill in revenge, the darker side of your psyche. And that has now found an outlet, an agent. Ella.'

'You're sick!' cried Allan. 'I'm the killer, is that what you're saying? What about Mother?'

'Yes, what about your mother, then? *Think*, Allan. Be honest. If it weren't for civilisation, would you be sitting there? You'd have been eliminated the moment you had the accident. Now you have a career ahead of you. That's what evolution's done for us. Civilisation. And now a single drug could reverse all that.'

'Screw my career. I want Ella!' Allan shouted. Flecks of spit landed on Geoffrey's face even at the distance.

'Do what you want. I've already destroyed everything in my lab. My monkeys, my research, everything. Every trace of the drug. Every slice of brain tissue. If a single cell of the tissue remains, they'll be able to recreate Piscalin. Now there's only Ella left. Ella's brain. I've come for it. I'm sorry, but I'm going to have it.'

'You're not! I forbid you!'

Allan stormed forward in his chair. Geoffrey stopped and looked about him. In the corner was a broom the contract nurse hadn't put back. He threw it through the spokes of Allan's chair, immobilising him. 'I'm sorry,' he repeated as Allan streamed abuse on him. He went to the door, his hands hanging by his sides, ready for murder.

At that very second the lights throughout the house snapped off. The fridge in the kitchen shuddered to a stop. Geoffrey swore. Of course, the house fuses, in the broom cupboard. Ella!

I'll get the little bitch, he swore. He retrieved the syringe from where he'd laid it on the table and held it up to the moonlight; it was still full. Allan was yelling himself hoarse. Geoffrey closed his mind and went to his business.

He groped his way forward, holding the needle ahead of him. He found the cupboard and carefully unlocked it. Getting to his knees, he slowly opened the door a crack. The smell of polish and dusters met him, but there was no movement from inside. Ella was lying in wait, in hiding. Just a little jab, Geoffrey prayed;

237

that's all it needs. Just so she'll go limp and I'll finish it off later with a proper overdose. His hands trembled. He listened for a sound; there was a rustle, hard to pinpoint. Then, suddenly, without any warning, he got it in the eye, a stick or a rod, something with a very sharp point, jabbed hard into his eye, his left eye right by the nose. Pain tore through him and he cried out. His hands shot to his face, and the syringe fell to the floor. He leaned back, rocking on his knees, trying to get to his feet, clutching his ragged and bleeding eye. Then came the prick, the needle-prick in his thigh. Deep, stabbing, grinding on the bone. He shot backwards and grabbed the needle by the shaft and wrenched it out like a poisoned arrow. He pulled himself up, staggered to the hallway, to the living room, to the phone.

'The bitch! She's got me!'

He was sobbing. Then he felt the first wave. It lapped around his legs, it crept coldly upwards, it spread gently from below as though he were being gradually lowered into a cold pool.

'Allan, help me! Get the phone. The hospital! There's an antidote in the labs!'

'I can't move!' cried Allan.

But Geoffrey found the phone and began to dial. Then the line went abruptly dead. In the shadows by the skirting board he could see Ella. In her paws she held the loose end of the telephone wire, pulled out at the socket. He moaned. The water lapped higher now, up to his waist, blurring his mind. He had to fight. He had to get out. He stumbled to the front door, couldn't work the chain free. Crashed back into the living room. Picked up a chair. Suddenly felt a huge burst of strength. Hurled the chair through the window and the glass shattered. There were fragments everywhere. Heard his own mind shouting, Strain, strain towards the night air and the escape lying out there, impossibly far out there. He wanted to shout. He wanted to yell, *help!* He wanted to scream. He tried to scream but nothing came out. A dry whisper, that was all. His throat was frozen over. Speech blocked. Discoordinated. Total sensory dysfunction. So this was how it was. Was that how he'd expected it to be? Like that, yes, but not quite *that*. He tried to move, tried to articulate, but his hands and feet elongated way out of his reach, way out of his control, and he was sprawling like a whale on the table top, spreading out to hold onto the sides but sliding backwards, giving in to the waves now lapping all over him and to the gloved hands which had already worked their way behind his eyeballs and were lifting at the roots of his brain, gently raising it, cutting off the connective tissues and muscles and lifting the whole organ up, up and out . . .

Ella! What have you done! Oh my God. Is he dead? I didn't will that! You did it, by yourself. He was my best friend. What are you doing there behind my chair? You're fiddling with my fuse-box. Put it back!

Listen, it's all right. You're innocent. Geoffrey himself said so. You picked it all up from me, from my subconscious. You didn't mean evil; you don't know good and bad. You did it all for me. You're still my love, my limbs, my eyes. Put the fuse back, please. Get me a drink. I'm so thirsty. Please, Ella. What are you playing with? Take it away! No!

Had she meant to do it to him too? Or was she merely play-acting, holding the syringe over his lap like a dart, ready to drop it point-first? Allan dared not think. He'd willed her to take it away, ransacking his mental powers for the force he'd used for winning races but which now had to be cranked into action like a rusty old machine. Yet she'd obeyed, finally. Or had she merely changed her mind?

The rain was squalling in through the shattered window. Letters and papers had been swept off the table top and the pages of a newspaper lay flung to the furthest corner. A single sheet had settled like a shroud on Geoffrey's lifeless body in the shadows at the foot of the table. The lampshade in the centre swung crazily back and forth and one segment of the fire was blown out. It was very cold. Allan sat with his head crouched into his chest, wincing each time the wind blew round his neck. He was spent, spent in anger, spent in energy. There was nothing he could do except try and survive the night. He tried humming tunes to himself but he grew afraid of the sound he made. He didn't want to attract Ella's attention more than necessary.

Ella was a moving shadow among shadows. At times he'd glimpse her silhouette against the window for a brief moment, then she'd let out a small whimper and leap onto his lap and nestle her head very close under his chin. Her soft paws would reach out to his cheeks and she'd lie in the embrace for a minute or two, muttering in the intimate, tender way he recognised. But she'd seem to remember something and her mood would change. She'd rear back and look at him coldly, then part her lips into a broken grimace and disappear into the shadows again. There he'd hear the slithering of electric cables and other sounds he couldn't place but which terrorised him. She avoided Geoffrey's body as if it was not there at all.

Allan had withdrawn into himself so far that he didn't hear the clatter of heels coming up the path and onto the front porch. But he heard Melanie's exclamation, 'Oh my Lord!' She had seen the broken window. Then her shouts, 'Allan! Allan!' What should he do? Hide? Hide like a tortoise with head in jersey? Then Melanie called, 'Geoffrey? Geoffrey? Why aren't there any lights on? *Geoffrey!*' Of course, she'd seen Geoffrey's car. What should he say? Call out and tell her he'd gone to the pub? The pubs were closed. Gone home on foot because the car wouldn't start? Gone to get a man to fix the window? Anything to get her away. This was no place for her.

She was looking in through the broken window. There was a flash of lightning. She called again and hammered on a pane. *Go away!* Where was Ella? Would somebody please take him away from all this?

Melanie was climbing in. She'd opened the window through the broken glass. The wind poured in behind her, wild and wet and terrible. Suddenly he saw Ella, lurking in the shadows. He had to tell Melanie, warn her. Then Melanie was pushing past the table, stumbling over something on her way towards the light switch. No light. She came over to him. He wanted to run away.

'Allan, what's happened? Are you okay? Where are the lights. Why's the window broken? Where's Geoffrey? He left my place in a mad state. I thought he'd do something crazy. I called and called, then I went to the labs. Burbage was there; he said Geoffrey had gone berserk. He went off to Geoffrey's flat, but I guess he'll be along here soon. I tried calling you but your phone's out of order. So where *is* Geoffrey? *What's going on?*'

He looked at her with her dark hair wet and straggly, her eyes glistening and wild, her skin smelling of rain and the city. She didn't belong there in that nightmare.

'Melanie, go home. Geoffrey's not here. Please go.'

'Don't be idiotic! Where is he and what's all this mess about?'

Allan refused to answer. She made an angry noise and demanded to be told where the candles were. In the kitchen drawer, he said. She fumbled past Ella in the corridor and cried out. Ella was darting to and fro, jittery and wild. Melanie brought in a handful of candles and lit a twist of paper in the gas fire. The paper went out. She drew the curtains against the wind and managed to get three candles alight. Two she set up on the mantlepiece; the third she carried with her.

'Where are the main fuses?'

'In the broom cupboard,' said Allan. 'But please, Melanie. Just do as I ask. Go home. For your own sake.'

'Be quiet,' she said sternly. As she went to the door, in the light of her candle, she saw the body. She drew in her breath sharply, dropped to the floor and felt the pulse. She pulled back the eyelids and felt the neck arteries. The body was lifeless. She turned to Allan.

'Ella,' he said simply.

At that moment Ella darted out from the shadows beneath an armchair. She held a stick-like object in her hands, wielding it like a lance. Melanie made a grab for her as she passed, missed and went after her. She barked her ankles on the brass fire-rail and shinned herself on a fallen book-stand. She cried out in pain, but the monkey was too quick for her.

'Don't!' cried Allan. 'You won't catch her like that, it's hopeless. Leave it, Melanie. And go, go away!'

Melanie came round the other side of the armchair, following Ella's shadow. As she passed the front of the chair, the monkey darted out once again. She jabbed her stick between Melanie's legs, and Melanie came crashing to the floor with a cry. There was a sharp crack as her head hit the fire-rail. Then silence.

'Melanie? *Melanie?*'

Allan craned forwards. Her candle was on the floor, out. In the feeble dancing light from the two on the mantlepiece, he could see her head. It lay in a tangle of dark wet hair, at an odd angle with the rest of her body. A thin wet trickle began to creep from the base of her neck.

What followed took place as if choreographed for slow motion. Ella came into the light, carrying a spill. She put it carefully into the flame of the gas fire. It flared, lighting the whole scene brightly. She took the spill over to Melanie's body and held it against her thin raincoat, at the hem. There was a slight hiss and the spill went out. The coat was too wet. Ella went back to the fire, paused for a moment with her head cocked on one side, then made up her mind. Allan understood.

'Melanie!' he yelled. 'Wake up! Get up!'

Her hand stirred, but nothing more. Allan redoubled his shouts. She *had* to come round! But by now Ella was back beside the body. She held the syringe in her hands, with the needle point directly above Melanie's neck, a pale stretch of soft flesh exposed and ready. Oh God, he sobbed: no pain-pack, no wheelchair, no arms, no legs, no hands. I'll sing. I'll shout.

He shouted. But Ella was already beginning a war dance and ignored him. She jigged up and down around Melanie's head. All the time she held the needle of the syringe pointing downwards. It was still half full, as he could see in the flickering light of the candles. Her shadow leaped back and forth, doubling her movement until he could scarcely follow what she was doing. But he could see the trial jabbing motions she made as she looked for the right spot on the neck, measuring the distance but stopping just short of the skin each time. Another jab and in the needle would go, barely a drop of blood squirting out but the plunger driven home and Melanie there, writhing her life out at his feet like a fish on a landing-hook.

'Tclick! Tclick!'

Ella ignored the signal. He repeated it; she wouldn't look up. She bent over Melanie's body and stroked the neck with her hand, just as the nurses did when seeking a spot to give Allan an injection. He made the clicking sound again. She half turned.

The darker side of your psyche. Geoffrey's words reverberated through his mind. How could he stop her if she was an extension of him? Not by getting into a daydream, for she had the power there, she'd even blocked him off that night at the labs. Not by threatening her, for what did he have to threaten her with? He was divided against himself. How had he controlled the pain of the torn muscle that day he broke the mile record? With will-power, power of the mind, the only thing left to him.

'Ella?' he whispered.

She turned and looked up. Their eyes met. He held hers.

Hold her there. Fix her so she can't look away. Hold her in a

242

vice, never blinking, never deflecting for a second. She won't drop hers first. Pin her, freeze her, make your eyes claws reaching out from their sockets to fasten onto hers. Hold firm.

Now muster the force, dig it out from the recesses of the mind, wheel it in, bring it to bear on the two glistening dark eyes. *Will* her to put the syringe down, there, into that little box over there with its lid ready open, the box that used to imprison the pains and agonies. She is an extension of me; therefore I can control her, as I control myself. If I cannot, then she is the master and I am part of her, I am her extension, without independence.

Ella began to back away, still holding Allan's unflinching eye. She clutched the syringe to her chest. Melanie was stirring. Ella stopped, half turned her body towards the woman but couldn't tear her gaze off his. For a moment he felt something like a flow of energy in the reverse direction, a wave of force from Ella pushing his own back on himself. Harder, he sobbed to himself, push harder! His parched eyes seared with pain, his neck muscles locked tight in a shuddering spasm, his brain felt it had turned to vapour and was being beamed through his eyes upon the small upright creature before him. Melanie's feet were moving, he could hear. So could Ella, for again she repulsed his force with a sudden effort and the frontier began to inch back towards him. Then he gave it everything he had, and more still. He began to *know* he'd won, just as during the mile race when he'd placed the pain beyond the finishing-line. To survive as himself he had to win, and to win he had to know it was already done. And he pushed. The frontier between their wills moved steadily back towards Ella and locked itself behind her eyes.

Scarcely moving his lips, speaking in a precise, taut voice, he said to Melanie, 'Move. Move slowly. Gradually. Move away.'

Melanie moaned. She must have opened her eyes and understood. She obeyed, every movement smooth and unhurried as she slid away out of the direct line of the syringe. Ella's lips were peeled back and she was chattering soundlessly. She'd begun to tremble and sway, but she stayed rooted to the ground. Allan winched his grip tighter. His brain was a volcano; a blow-torch was playing on his eyeballs. At the edge of his vision he saw Melanie reaching for an object.

'Do it *now*!' he hissed.

It was the typewriter. Melanie swung it high and brought it

down with both hands upon the monkey's head. The syringe skidded away across the floor and Ella disappeared in a crushed heap under the machine.

Melanie stood back, a hand to her mouth. The wind outside gusted violently, ripped the curtain open and blew out the candles.

'Oh my God,' Melanie whispered. 'I've killed her.'

'Get the body!' he croaked harsly. 'Get the thing and destroy the brain. You must get rid of it. Cut it out. Burn it. Anything. There mustn't be a single piece of the brain left. Do it quickly!'

She straightened, her face bloodless in the moonlight, then bent down and moved the typewriter aside. She took Ella by the tail and went to the door, leaving a smeared trail of blood on the floor. She left the room with a kind of serenity, sleep-walking. He heard the thump as she dropped the body into the sink. Then the same steady, measured steps back down the corridor to the broom cupboard. The flare of a match and, a moment later, the snap of a master switch. The house was swamped with light. Allan shut his eyes; they felt scored with acid. He kept them shut, but not tight enough to prevent the tears springing through the lids. Nor could he hold down the choking sobs that burst to the surface as he tried to close his mind to everything and to close his ears to the terrible sounds now coming from the kitchen, the hideous grinding and chewing and rasping sounds as the waste-disposal unit in the sink bit and clawed into the skin and bone.

It was only when the greedy screech of the waste unit had finally stopped that Allan became aware of the hammering on the front door. There were two men's voices, shouting. They kicked at the door, then launched their shoulders at it. The lock burst. Three hefty kicks snapped the chain. They tumbled into the hallway. The first was Professor Burbage, the other a man Allan recognised as Geoffrey's technician.

'Where is it?' demanded Burbage, bursting into the living room. 'Where's the monkey?' His short raincoat was soaking and his face was red and violent.

'I phoned the Professor after Geoffrey called me,' the technician was saying. 'We had to find him, you see. Where is he?'

'Use your eyes, idiot,' snarled Burbage. He'd found Geoffrey. He didn't need to take a pulse. 'Get an ambulance over here. Right, where's the monkey?'

'It was an accident,' said Allan.

'The coroner will decide that,' said the Professor curtly. 'I'm only interested in the monkey right now. Well, where is it?'

He followed Allan's eye to the doorway behind him. There was his answer. Melanie was standing there, her hair dishevelled, her eyes wide and the beginnings of a mad grin on her lips. Very slowly she raised her hands. She was bloodied up to the elbows. Burbage drew in a sharp breath and stepped back. Then he ran forwards and raced down the corridor.

From the kitchen he yelled to the technician, 'Get the car started!'

In a moment he was back with Ella's decapitated body in a polythene kitchen bag. He knocked Melanie aside and made for the front door. His cheeks were purple with fury.

'God help you bastards,' he spat and stormed out of the house. The car roared away into the night.

Thirty-eight

It was good at Melanie's. It felt like coming out of a long, dark tunnel into the bright sunlight. It should always have been like this.

Builders had been in to fix up Allan's special bed and to adapt the bathroom; they'd now gone, leaving only the faint smell of paint and putty behind. The downstairs double room had become his bedroom and study, one part divided from the other by a large screen fretted with arabesques. His books shared the shelves with Melanie's and his stands stood over by the window. He had come home.

During the day when Melanie was out, he would sit with the French windows onto the garden slightly open so that he could smell the damp humus and the shrinking autumn sap. From the doorway he could look out at the yellowing chestnuts and the red creeper growing over the fence at the foot of the garden, with the shouts of the first rugby matches coming faintly from the distance. And he'd smile to himself. Sometimes just the thought of Melanie, a mental image of her wrestling over a béchamel sauce or of one of those long silences when they'd look at each other and forget what they'd been saying, often merely the sound of her name quietly whispered would bring tears to his eyes. One afternoon, watching the stream of students over Magdalen Bridge in the distance, a new generation with new enthusiasms, he found himself aching with sheer happiness.

The old stones of the city were yielding their second harvest and Allan shared the feeling of revival. He'd begun to work again seriously. Dr Fry had accepted his thesis outline; All Souls had allowed him to sit the exam late and had accepted him. During the first few days of term he went to the Sports Ground for the first time since his accident to open a new block of changing-rooms. His old trainer had shown him where they'd put up a small plaque to his mile record. And he'd begun teaching at the Faculty. With the tuition fees and several grants, he felt relatively well off.

He allowed the past months to melt into a haze in his memory, trying neither to retrieve them nor suppress them. His life with Melanie had grown so all-embracing that the past seemed to belong to another man. Yet at times he missed Geoffrey, his closest friend. There had been an inquest and a verdict of accidental death was recorded. Allan had been outraged. Professor Burbage had come round afterwards to bind him to silence. He pleaded with him to let sleeping dogs lie; those were his actual words. They'd had a shouting match and Burbage had left in a black fury, but Allan took it no further. Dragging everything into the open wouldn't bring his friend back. But he never told Melanie about Burbage's visit or the special reasons for his interest in Geoffrey's work; she wouldn't have let it rest there. She'd formed her own rationale for having had to kill Ella, and he let her think what she wanted.

He concentrated on the present, on his immediate life with Melanie. He felt *right*, as if something he'd struggled with for a lifetime had suddenly slotted into place. They went to the theatre, they invited friends for dinner, they planned a trip abroad for Christmas. Once or twice, when a mood of depression would creep over him, he'd wonder if he hadn't capitulated in some way, rejoining a world which treated him foremost as a cripple. Was that compromise or was it facing up to reality? It didn't much matter what label was used; perhaps it was merely a way of rationalising the pain he still felt when looking at Melanie and wishing for her sake he were whole.

But she gave him the strength to fight off the black moods and to believe in his own future. Her love was so obvious, so incontestable, that it left no room for doubts of any kind. Throughout the days, lecturing or studying, he'd yearn for the evenings when they'd talk and kiss and tease. Often they'd laugh themselves to a standstill. And sometimes at night she'd come and join him; she wasn't put off by his body nor shy of her own lying beside his. As a lover she was skilful, tender and open. She was the first complete woman he'd known, and she made him begin to feel a complete man.

And yet he missed Ella too: her company, her tricks and games, her endless inventiveness and mischief. Often a memory would come to mind, never of the last weeks, some incident from the time when their life together was a honeymoon. Once he even went and sat before the French windows, just in case something would happen, just to remember what it was like. He let himself slide into his dreams and, for a brief flash, he thought he was getting it back. He saw a reddish blur, dark and indistinct, a formless moving reddish blur, and his heart leapt. For several days he tried it again, but gave up; he could never get a proper picture, only the reddish-brown moving shapes. It must have merely been the light coming in through his eyelids.

But as time passed, his new life absorbed his heart and mind. It was ordered and contented, safe and secure. He was in love and a great sense of ease grew over him. He belonged there, with Melanie, living this life in this house in this city. He couldn't remember a time when he'd been so profoundly happy.

Professor Roach peered in through the perspex isolation screen at the tiny new-born monkey. It was sucking on its mother's teat and its eyes were not yet opened. It was minute and almost bald but perfectly formed. It looked like any other monkey born in the labs; but it wasn't. And the female which had given birth to it a few hours earlier was not its real mother.

Roach watched for several minutes and then went over to a bank of instruments which gave readings of the mother's physical state. They weren't taking chances on this one. His eye flicked over the heart-rate, the blood pressure, the chemical analysis of blood that was constantly being monitored. An almost perfect birth. A triumph of micro-surgery, implanting an embryo in a host mother's womb. Thank God they'd caught it in time, before it died, starved of blood oxygen. It had been very close.

The baby monkey was a female. Professor Roach closed the partition door carefully and checked the alarm monitor was correctly on. Then, treble locking the outer door, he went downstairs to his superior's office. Burbage had been present at the birth and wanted to be kept informed of progress hourly. The two men had much to talk about. For the real work was now beginning.